Savage SAINT

VICIOUS EMPIRE: FOUR

LUNA KAYNE

Savage Saint by Luna Kayne

Copyright © 2022 by Luna Kayne

This book is fiction. Any similarity between the characters and situations within its pages and places or persons, living or dead, is unintentional and coincidental.

Book cover design: Pretty Little Design Co.

Cover model photographer: Wander Aguiar

Cover model: Clayton Wells

Editor: Caroline Knecht

First Printing, 2022

ISBN (eBook) 978-1-989366-36-3

ISBN (paperback) 978-1-989366-37-0

Luna Kayne, Kayne Publishing

Savage Saint is the fourth and final book in the Vicious Empire series. It is NOT recommended that the books in this series be read as standalones as there is an ongoing story that began in the first book, **CRUEL SAINT**, and will continue through the four books in this series.

The phoenix didn't just rise from the ashes. She was first the fire.

— LUNA KAYNE

PROLOGUE: LENNOX

TWENTY YEARS AGO

"What do you think is gonna happen?" Dagen trails behind me by a few feet, not stopping to wait for an invitation when I enter my room.

He doesn't need one. None of my brothers do.

He walks to my bed, kicking his legs up and landing on the mattress with a bounce.

"How should I know?" I shrug, trying to play it cool in front of my younger brother.

Inside, I'm pretty excited.

Dad has been talking about my sixteenth birthday with his guys for years. *Wait until you turn sixteen*, they would say with smug arrogance, like they all knew something I didn't.

My father is the head of an empire. He's been telling me for as long as I can remember that someday, my brothers and I will run everything.

Every time I asked to go out with Dad and the guys, he would tell me it was grown-up stuff. He'd tell me that it would make Mom mad, that he promised her he wouldn't teach me anything about our business until I was a man.

Apparently, being sixteen meant you were a man, because today, I'm finally invited along.

Being the oldest means I get to do everything first, and it means Dad takes the most interest in me. I'm not going to lie, it's a pretty damn good feeling.

Mom keeps telling me that I can choose to be my own man, and that's what I'm going to do. I'm just going to learn from the best man I know.

Dagen has been following me around all day since Dad told me he was taking me out tonight on special business.

"Maybe you'll get to see some tits." Dagen cups his hands, holding them in front of his chest, and I roll my eyes.

We know what kind of businesses our father owns. It's a badge of honor around all of our friends at school.

"Fuck, Dag. If you want to see some tits, just ask Jackie out. She's shown hers off to half the high school."

Rolling into a seated position, he cocks his head to the side at that little bit of information, and a soft knock at my open door catches our attention.

I already know who it is before looking.

Our mother is the gentlest person I know.

She looks between us, then decides to focus on my brother. "Dagen, go tell Cole you're calling dibs on the shower."

"But I already had a shower." He lifts a hand above his head, then smells his armpit as if to make sure he doesn't need another.

"I know you did, but Cole doesn't, and he's refusing to get ready for bed. If you tell him you're taking a shower, then he'll miraculously decide that getting ready for bed is a great idea just to start a fight. You know how he is. Scrappy little shit." She manages to say it with all the love in the world.

I know my brother wants to stick around in the hopes that

he'll find out more information about tonight, but my mother isn't having it.

"Please. I want to speak to your brother—alone." Her eyes flit across the room to me.

"Ugh. Fine." Dagen stands and drags his feet as he crosses the space between us before he turns to me. "I'm staying up. I want to hear all about it, okay?"

"Sure." I smile and nod toward the door, silently telling him to listen to Mom, and he does.

I unbutton my shirt and exchange it for a T-shirt and sweater as Dagen leaves, and Mom closes the door behind him before turning to me.

She's been looking at me differently for the past few months, and I haven't quite figured out if it's a good thing or not yet. Sometimes I think I recognize pride in her eyes. Other times, it looks a little like apprehension.

"Your brothers look up to you, Lennox." She reaches out for my hand, tangling her fingers in mine, and tugs me toward the bed to sit with her.

I shrug it off and pull my hand away. As soon as I do it, I feel bad.

"You're growing so fast." She whispers the words to herself as her eyes turn glassy.

"Is everything okay?" An inkling of concern settles in for the first time. "Should I be worried about something?"

"No. You know me. I just love my boys so much. I don't know where your father is taking you, but I'm sure you'll have a great birthday with him. You know he owns those clubs. Just—protect yourself and be safe, and I want you to know you always have a choice."

"Ugh, Mom." I scrunch up my face. Now is not the time for a sex talk with my mother. I try to brush it off, but she pulls me into a hug.

An attempted conversation about sex followed by hugging my mother on my bed better be the low point of my evening because I don't feel like cringing my way through my sixteenth birthday.

"Oh, right. Your father is downstairs waiting. I just wanted to tell you I love you and wish you a happy birthday before you go. Ryder is just falling asleep, so I should check on him."

We stand together, and she looks like she wants to hug me again before she thinks better of it. Dad always chastises her about how she coddles us, and I think she's starting to become aware of it as we grow.

When she leaves, I take off down the hall and practically slide down the wooden staircase before straightening my clothes and stopping outside of my father's office. One of the first things we've all learned is to always knock when Dad is in the office, even if the door is open.

"Ah, son, there you are. You remember Paulie?" He stands from behind his desk, and the man with him rises as well. "Here." He hands me my own glass filled with the whiskey he normally drinks. "Drink up before we head out."

I've had liquor before.

My father let me have a sip here and there at his parties, but I've never gotten my own glass. When I look at my dad, there's a knowing smile on his face when he nods for me to drink it.

It burns going down. It always does, but I try to limit my coughing in front of Dad and his guy.

"Get the car." Dad dismisses Paulie then turns to his desk, grabbing his keys and phone.

I'm not sure if I should ask, but curiosity is making me crazy.

"So, where are we going?"

Normally my father doesn't like questions. We boys ask a

lot of them, but since I'm growing up, I need to take more initiative if I want to show my old man I can help him run things.

"We're going to take care of some business, son." He takes my empty cup from me and sets it on the shelf beside him.

My stomach turns, and I'm not sure if it's the whiskey or the anticipation of the unknown.

I follow him out of the office and to the front door.

My father doesn't look back, but I steal a glance over my shoulder and catch Cole wrapped in an oversized bath towel at the top of the stairs.

When I wave, he straightens and tips his chin, trying to nod like he's one of the men our dad usually has around. It looks funny coming from a nine-year-old.

Paulie is in the driver's seat, and a second guy is waiting for him by the car.

This time, my dad doesn't introduce me.

When the car pulls out of the driveway, I want to ask where we're going again, but I learned a long time ago that if my dad doesn't answer a question the first time, he won't answer it no matter how many additional times you ask.

He's in a good mood now, and I don't want to risk fucking up my birthday by making him mad before we've even left our property.

My silence is matched by everyone else in the car as we drive through Seattle. Our family owns most of the area around the docks, so it isn't a shock when we stop at a row of warehouses along the wharf.

A horn blares from somewhere on the water, drawing my attention away from the buildings in front of us. It's gotten too dark to see anything other than the odd light bobbing on the watery horizon.

My father doesn't call me to join him. Instead, he makes his way across the pavement toward a door left ajar in front of us. It's expected that Sebastian Saint's sons always keep up with him, and I turn on my heels and jog until I match his pace, only a few steps behind his group.

I'm the last into the building, and as each man enters they step to the side until I'm the only one left standing at the entrance.

The scene in front of me steals my breath.

"Gentlemen, thank you for your patience." My father speaks to the gagged men kneeling on the floor in front of us as though they had a choice, when anyone can easily see they don't. "This is an important night for my son." He motions to me, and the three who are still alive look over at me with panic in their eyes.

It looks like they started out as a row of five. Two from their group—one on each end—are lying facedown and unmoving in pools of blood.

My stomach lurches again, but this time I know what's causing it.

As my father walks among the men, saying something about disrespect, I take a step backward toward the door, but Paulie is quick to wrap his fingers around my arm and steady me before my father glances over.

Paulie shakes his head once in warning and returns his attention to the men kneeling before us.

I know Paulie didn't stop me from running to protect me, but I'm thankful all the same that he did. My father doesn't take disobedience well, and he will most certainly make an example out of me if I embarrass him now.

Regardless of our name, we are no saints.

I know my father is using the docks for illegal activity, and he has a host of bars, strip clubs, and even the odd sex club under his belt. Our family business has always walked a fine line. He used to tell me there is legal and illegal, but, if you invest in the best lawyers, there is also the gray area.

I thought he was talking about money laundering.

The gunshot blasts through the warehouse. Its sound is visceral, as though the bullet has ripped through my own skin. Only when I look at one of the three men as his limp body bounces off the pavement do I realize I've just witnessed my father taking the life of another man.

When I look over at him, the man I thought my father was is nowhere to be found.

This man in front of me is invigorated, his lips twisted into a sneer. There's no remorse, no regret.

He simply strolls over to stand behind the next man and pauses as if the guy's fear is breathing new life into my father's body.

Each of them is gagged, and only muffled grunts fill the room.

The thick scent of rust and urine fills my nose, and I swallow the urge to vomit the drink I had earlier in front of everyone.

He meets my eyes as though I'm as much of his prey as these guys kneeling in front of him are, and my blood runs cold.

"Come here, son."

As I approach my father, I hold his stare and clench my teeth to keep the stoic expression on my face. Fear courses through my veins, and I worry if I look at these men, I'll show weakness in front of my father and his guys.

Is this what my father meant all of those times he spoke about me growing up and becoming a man?

The memory of Cole nodding at me from the top of the stairs hits me and settles into the pit of my stomach like bile. Dagen was elated earlier when he was trying to guess what my surprise would be. A wave of nausea hits me, but I widen my stance to steady myself on my feet.

"These men stole from our family, and we're going to send a message that no one fucks with the Saints." His voice rises with his words until he's yelling and red in the face.

Spinning on his heels, he turns away from me for a few seconds. When he turns back, he's restrained himself as much as he's going to.

Unlike the two men left kneeling, I'm fairly positive I'm walking out of here tonight, and I'm terrified.

There's no getting out of this.

I can't ask to wait in the car like a little boy.

I thought growing up was some sort of stupid rite of passage. Dagen thinks it means I get to see tits. None of my brothers know what's in store for them.

This isn't who we are.

This isn't who I am.

You always have a choice. My mother's voice surrounds me like the blanket I wish I was wrapped up in.

As if testing her theory in real time, a nudge at my arm pulls me out of my thoughts.

I look down to where my father tapped me, only to see his arm extended with the butt end of his gun held out toward me.

"Take it, son." He doesn't bother to meet my eyes. He has every confidence the apple of his eye is just like him—all rotten inside.

"What did they do?" I regret the question as soon as it leaves my lips.

When my father does look at me, I catch the familiar tick in his jaw. Apparently, clenching our teeth to hide our emotions runs in the family.

"They disrespected us. That's all you need to know." He speaks to me in a slow and even tone.

It's a warning to shut the fuck up and do as I'm told.

One of the guys on his knees starts shaking his head violently, as though he wishes to deny the claim, and my father kicks him in between his shoulder blades, sending him falling forward. Since his hands are zip-tied behind his back, he isn't able to brace against the fall, and his forehead cracks against the cement.

My father grabs my hand, shoving the butt of the gun into my palm, then aims it toward the one who is still on his knees before taking a small step back and nodding for me to follow in his footsteps.

When my hand starts to shake, I lower the gun.

"Dad, I can't." My voice is just above a whisper, so his men don't hear.

"LEAVE US!" he roars, tipping his chin at Paulie.

I stand in place, frozen like a statue as his men file out through the door we came in through.

Instead of leaving, Paulie shuts the door and stands in front of it.

Silence hangs around me like a noose slowly wrapping itself around my neck. A cold chill runs the length of my spine, and my limbs have gone numb.

My father takes an angry step toward me, lifting my hand and pointing the gun at the back of the man's head once more.

"You can, and you will."

I cringe in disgust at him and at myself. The esteem my father held in his eyes when he handed me my drink earlier is nowhere to be found.

"I don't want to do this. I can't just shoot him." Without the rest of his men in the room with us, I raise my voice just enough to plead with him.

When I try to lower the gun this time, my father glares

daggers at me, challenging me to follow through. I back down a little and keep it trained on the guy's back.

"I knew I shouldn't have waited," he mutters to himself. "Your mother always coddled you boys. She made you soft."

I blink rapidly, trying to keep my tears from showing. "It's not that. Dad, I—"

"I've heard enough. Sixteen is too old to start learning what is expected of you."

His words make me feel like I'm five years old, but I don't care. I'll endure any verbal abuse he wants to sling at me as long as I don't have to kill a man.

"I knew I should have started sooner. But I have more sons. I'll find the right age."

"Wh-what do you mean?"

"My sons will be deserving of my legacy." He tilts his head, a sneer creeping across his face. "If you won't kill him, I'll have Paulie drive home and pick up Dagen. Maybe I should have started with you when you were thirteen. We'll find out soon enough." He stands to his full height, giving his threat the space it needs to sink in. Then he keeps on going. "Or maybe I should have started when you were nine." My mind flashes to Cole, how the oversized towel practically covered him completely as he stood at the top of the stairs.

Cole and Ryder still believe in Santa Claus.

My heart fractures.

"You—can't."

That was the wrong thing to say.

The gun feels heavy in my hand. My shoulder aches just keeping it raised as my father leans over, getting in my face.

"No one tells me what I can and can't do, boy."

In the two seconds it takes my father to stand up straight, I make the decision to choose for myself, and I choose my brothers.

I can't let this be their fate.

Just as my father is about to nod at Paulie to go get Dagen, I check out of my head.

I push down my morality along with the whiskey that is threatening to come back up.

Then I raise the gun to the back of the man's head, and I pull the trigger.

1

SLOANE

It seems like every time we get close to an answer, two more questions pop up and knock us back.

What started out as Ryder, Cole, and I trying to find out who killed Grayson is now a group effort that includes Dagen, Amara, Harlow, and now Lennox.

I'm reminded how far we still have to go every day when I look at Henry.

His father, Grayson, was taken from us before he was born, and I won't rest until I know the truth.

We were so close to recovering the microfiche that would tell us who Elia Lucciano's son is, and it would have solved everything.

And now Ryder has asked for patience while he and Cole head up to Canada to help Lennox get Dagen across the border.

That was three days ago, and patience is the only thing I have left—that and anger, but I've been pushing my pain down. It doesn't serve me to have so much rage until I know who to direct it at.

Instead, I've focused my attention on spending time with Henry.

Cole dropped Harlow off when he picked up Ryder, and it has been nice to catch up with her on different terms than before.

Amara has a bit of a workaholic streak in her, but even she has been on cloud nine since she has an excuse to stay home from work and play with her nephew.

It kills me that we can't all come clean yet.

Not only is Amara missing out on officially being an aunt, but she has to hide her marriage with Ryder. She handles it well though, always smiling when people ask me about my upcoming wedding to her secret real-life husband.

It's ridiculous, really, but at least we laugh about it behind closed doors.

I hate all of the lies, but at the same time I wonder what will happen when the truth comes out.

I'm not engaged to Ryder, and Henry isn't his son—he's Grayson's.

Neither Henry nor I will have any connection to the Saints once this is all over. Outside of being Ryder's friend, I really am no one to the family. The realization hurts because I still think of Ryder, Cole, and Dagen as brothers. Ryder is my best friend, and now Amara is too.

In my heart, I know why I'm holding on to all of them, but I won't allow myself to admit it. I worked too hard to move past the worst moment of my life and grow from it, and in the end, my path led me to Grayson and now Henry, and I wouldn't change anything.

But there are moments that I slip into the sadness and regret over what happened with Lennox. There are few places where I feel like I fit in, where I don't go through the motions, where I feel like I am myself.

I'm close with my parents, so I always have a place there, but outside of them, my place was with Grayson and now Henry. Before them, it was with Lennox, but I don't dwell on him anymore.

We aren't meant to have everything we want in life.

My phone vibrates on the little table beside me, pulling me from my thoughts, and I check the call display.

"Hi, Mom." I keep my voice low, so Henry doesn't wake up early.

"Hi, Peanut. Where are you?" My father's short tone catches me off guard.

He's not a fan of technology and is rarely the one who calls.

"Dad? Hi. Is Mom okay?"

He must sense the worry in my voice because he answers quickly. "Oh, yes. She's fine. We—um, we need to see you—and Henry. Can you come over here—right away?"

The large clock hanging on the wall tells me I've been daydreaming for longer than I thought I was, and Henry only has five to ten minutes left before he'll start to stir.

"Well, I—" I glance around the open room, hoping to find a good excuse to explain why I'm under a sort of house arrest that won't worry my parents. We've all gone to great lengths to keep the people around us in the dark when it comes to what we've been up to. My parents would just demand that I move home with them so they could watch over me. "I'm not sure if this is a good time."

There's a long silence on the phone.

"Sloane, honey, your mother and I need to see you and Henry right now. This can't wait."

"Dad, you're worrying me. Is everything all right? Where's Mom?"

I stand and turn in a circle, trying to get my bearings, when movement out the sliding glass door catches my attention.

Amara and Harlow have their arms linked together, and they're making their way slowly across the yard and down the slight slope from the main house. Harlow points toward the garden as Amara lifts a hand to her forehead, blocking out the sun. Then she says something in return, and they both laugh.

"Your mother is here. We need to see you. Can you both come over—alone?"

Every time my dad speaks, it sounds more and more curious.

"Henry's just waking up from a nap. We'll be there in twenty minutes."

There's a pointed pause before he tells me they'll be waiting and hangs up.

I'm staring at my phone when Amara slides the door open and quietly pokes her head into the room. "Is he still out?" she whispers with a smile.

"Uh, yeah."

"What's wrong?" Her eyes lower to my phone. Then she hurries into the room with Harlow right behind her, shutting the door behind them. "Did you hear from them? Are they okay?"

"No."

Amara gasps, covering her mouth with her hand, and I quickly recover. "I mean, no. I haven't heard from them. That was my dad. They need to see me right away. They need my help with something. I have to go."

Harlow and Amara look at each other, then at me. We all know what we were told when Cole and Ryder left. We were to stay put.

"Sloane, you—"

I raise my hand, cutting Amara off. "I know what they said, but I think my parents might be in trouble. My dad wouldn't say what it was on the phone, but they need to see me right now. Do you think you can cover for me?"

I don't bother to tell them they were also specific that I bring Henry and come alone. It would raise too many red flags, and Amara is fiercely loyal to the people she cares about.

Amara worries her lower lip between her teeth as she considers my request, and I try to offer her more to consider.

"It's twenty minutes there; I can make it in fifteen. I'll find out what they need, and I'll be back before Yuri does another check-in. I just need you to hang out here and cover for me if anyone comes by. Just tell them I'm lying down for a few minutes—too much sun."

I walk between them to the door, grabbing my purse off the table and hooking it over my neck, crossing the strap diagonally across my chest and lowering it to sit at my hip.

"You want us to watch Henry?" Harlow asks, and I'm happy that she sounds like she's on board and willing to cover for me.

Amara still looks unsure.

"No. I'll take him along for the drive. He's been missing his grandparents." I try to make my answer sound casual.

Just as I'm about to ask Amara for her answer, Henry calls for me from the room he uses when we stay out here.

I hurry in to lift him up, and his sleepy smile greets me.

Amara follows me into the room and gushes all over her nephew, which makes him squeal with laughter. Then she turns her attention on me.

"Fine. But why don't you take Yuri with you? I'm sure he'll be happy to drive you."

"It sounds like my parents really need to talk to me, and I don't want to ask only to be turned down. I don't know how strict Ryder's rules are, and I don't want to lose my chance, you know?"

Amara is already nodding at my answer. She knows firsthand how stubborn her husband can be.

It isn't the first time we've been kept out of the loop by Ryder and his brothers, and if they've given the order that no one leaves, then I will have tipped my hand, and they'll be on high alert.

Harlow joins us in the bedroom. "How are you going to get past the guys at the front?"

"My car is sitting in the lot right outside of the gates. I just need a distraction."

Amara's smile turns devious. "Well now, this just sounds like fun. It serves those boys right for making us sit around here all day. They have to know we were bound to get up to no good." She winks at me, and I smile to cover my deception. "Just there and back, right?"

"Right." In my heart, my answer feels like a lie, and I hate it.

I should probably tell Amara I'm more worried than I'm letting on, but I need to get home.

What's one more lie in the sea of deception that we've all been floating in for years?

When I have Amara and Harlow on my side, there is nothing I can't accomplish. Henry and I were able to get off the grounds and to my car in just over five minutes.

I can't help but smile to myself when I think about the worry on Harlow and Amara's faces when they talked about the possibility of getting caught. Since their relationships with Ryder and Cole are different than mine is, I imagine they would get in a different kind of trouble, whereas I would most likely be verbally chastised and made to promise that it wouldn't happen again.

When I open the front door to my parents' house, they aren't there to greet us, and their absence is yet another red flag.

"Mom? Dad?"

Footsteps from the back of the house draw my attention toward the kitchen. "There you are, Peanut. I was, um, just making lunch for you."

I flip the face of my phone up to confirm that it is way past lunchtime.

"I'm not hungry, Dad. Where's Mom?"

Her own, softer footfalls on the steps coming from the second floor answer my question.

"Hi, sweetheart." She closes the distance between us, dropping an old suitcase in the middle of the room and reaching out for Henry. His little arms stretch toward his grandma, and she takes him over to the area with his toys before returning to join my father and me.

"Can we all sit?" When she looks from my father to me, I catch a better look at her face. Her eyes are red and puffy, and she looks older than she did just last week when I saw her.

"Mom?" Everyone startles at my tone, and I correct myself so I don't worry Henry. "You're scaring me."

"Please, Peanut, sit." Even my father sounds exhausted.

I sit on the couch, and just before my father joins us, he looks over at Henry and says, "I want you to pick out your five favorite toys, buddy. But look at them all real close. Put the ones you like the most in a pile, okay?"

When Henry smiles and nods back at him, my father joins us.

I've never in my life heard my parents beat around the bush. We've always had an open line of communication between us, but now it feels as though a wall has built itself up between us overnight.

"What's going on?"

I look between my mother and father to try to decide which one to push for information when my mother's chin trembles, and her eyes rim with tears. She breaks, burying her face in her hands as she sobs quietly. My father moves from his place in the chair to her side on the couch and hugs her to him, comforting her with hushes before talking to me.

"You have to know—everything we did was to protect you. We made a promise, and we love you."

"What did you do?" I glance first at Henry, playing quietly on his own, then around the room. Then I remember the suitcase my mother carried down the stairs. "Are you going somewhere?"

"We don't have much time." At first, I think my father's words are for me, but when I look at him, his attention is on my mom.

She sniffles, then nods and hands me a folded piece of paper. Its stiffness makes me think it's old, but it looks well preserved, as though it has been hidden away and never looked at.

Until now.

Carefully unfolding the paper, I scan its contents. I know it isn't an official birth certificate. The one I have for both myself and Henry are very different than what I have in my hands.

"I don't understand. What am I looking at?"

"It's called a certificate of live birth. They are issued by the hospital at the time of birth, before the actual certificate is sent." Since my mother is a nurse, she explains the hospital procedures to me with authority.

"But this isn't mine. That's not my last name." Even as I say the words, a sense of familiarity sends chills up my spine.

It's my mother's maiden name.

I zero in on the listed mother's name, saying my version of it out loud. "Auntie Selina?"

My mother sobs some more. "We wanted to tell you so many times, but it wasn't safe."

"Why wasn't it safe?" I mutter the question to myself as my eyes return to the piece of paper I'm holding gingerly between my fingers.

I have my answer as I scan further down the page to the father's listed name and my world shatters.

"I'm Elia Lucciano's heir?"

2

LENNOX

I should have insisted Cole sit in the passenger seat for the drive back to Seattle.

Between Ryder telling Cole what to do from the driver's seat and Cole pushing every button Ryder has left from his spot in the back, I'm ready to get out and walk across the damn border by myself.

We drove like that for a solid thirty minutes before I realized we'd all retreated into our coping mechanisms.

The four of us handle crises differently, and we're in the middle of one after another at the moment.

Dagen has a healthy sense of humor and sarcasm. He's always looking for silver linings, and he has a way of lightening dire situations.

And he's a dad to a little girl. I chuckle at the thought. I can't wait to see how he holds up when she takes an interest in dating. That guy is going to have a mental break one day, and I have a feeling it's probably a four-year-old with pigtails who's going to push him over the edge.

Cole challenges the world around him when everything

starts closing in and things aren't going to his plan. He fights back and lashes out, like he's doing with Ryder right now. I won't be surprised if Ryder tries to kick his ass before this road trip is over.

I'm the furthest removed from Ryder in age, but as I sit here and watch him deal, I'm quickly realizing we're the most alike. We both crave order and control, except we handle it differently.

Ryder just takes it back. He reacts swiftly, which is both a blessing and a curse because sometimes it's done without proper thought and preparation.

I get quiet.

I plan and I orchestrate.

I compartmentalize what is happening externally until I've removed my emotions from the equation, and then I retaliate accordingly.

The one thing I have in common with my brothers is that we are relentless in our execution. Whether we plan our attack or come up swinging, we are all vicious in our own way.

I'm quickly coming to realize that being this different from each other is what's going to pull us through this mess.

This is why our father preferred that we compete against each other instead of working together. When we are on our own, we are easy to analyze and manipulate. Our father can foresee our next move, and he uses us like puppets. But when we combine our strengths and weaknesses, we open ourselves up to additional choices. Our path forward becomes obscure, even to us, and there are too many variables.

As we inch closer to the border crossing, I feel a pang of apprehension in my gut. I'm second-guessing leaving Dagen and Nyla behind. In my mind, I know they're safe. No one knows where they are, and Cole just heard from his tech guy that the hit on them has been canceled, but I can't help feeling like this calm means a storm is on the way.

I've also been dreading spending time with Ryder and Cole without Dagen.

I've been using Dagen as a buffer between myself and my two youngest brothers for a long time.

When I shattered the innocent lens I viewed the world through, I vowed that my brothers would keep theirs intact for as long as they could, so I put myself in between our father and the three of them whenever I could.

At the same time, I kept my distance.

I'm not proud of the man I had to become.

Our father urged us to compete against each other, and his respect and admiration were always the ultimate prizes.

I vowed to use that against him.

He was never home for his boys, and I inserted myself into his role whenever I could. A tarnished light still shines brighter than no light at all.

I used his absence to wedge myself between him and my younger brothers. I did whatever he asked of me. I made sure he never had a reason to look beyond me when he needed someone to dirty their hands and darken their soul in the name of our family business.

Piece by piece, I tore away at my own humanity so they could hold on to as much of theirs as they could.

I was willing to sacrifice everything. There was never anything I wanted for myself—until the night Sloane walked into our nightclub six years ago.

Everything about her was forbidden: she was my youngest brother's friend, there was a ten-year age gap between us, and, even though her half-assed forged ID said she was twenty-one, she was still three months away from legally being allowed into the club. But then again, so were my brother Ryder and his best friend Grayson.

By then, my father was full-on grooming me to take over Eros, and, at the time, it was attached to the nightclub. It was popular with the younger crowd, who loved to dance and get drunk on watered-down sugary cocktails.

My father was a sick old man—he still is. He preferred to either spend his time in the sex dungeons at Eros or gawking at the college girls as they bounced around on the dance floor. Working and managing his businesses no longer interested him, and I gladly filled his void again.

I remember when I first laid eyes on Sloane. I was called up to an issue at the front door of our nightclub. It was winter, and fat snowflakes were falling but quickly melting once they hit the pavement. Ryder didn't bother to show fake ID—he knew I'd be called to the front as soon as he showed his face.

When I arrived, Ryder and Grayson were standing shoulder to shoulder, looking for entry. They had someone behind them who I couldn't see, but it didn't matter.

I was about to send them packing when they parted and she turned around, and my heart grew full in my chest.

The moment she met my gaze, her eyes rounded. She tried to cover her reaction by humbly lowering her gaze to the ground between us, but I had already felt her pull, and I knew I wasn't going to let her leave.

She wore her guilt in her expression as she played with a stray strand of hair, anxiously twirling it just below her collarbone.

She knew what they were doing was wrong, and when she looked at me again, it was with an unspoken plea in her eyes that acknowledged the power I held to allow her entry or deny her request.

She hit all of my buttons and checked off every item on the list I didn't even know I had.

Reaching my hand out to the bouncer, I took the fake IDs that she and Grayson handed over, quickly crumpling Grayson's and shoving it into my pocket.

I always liked that kid, and I was determined to keep him on the same narrow path I wanted for my brothers. He groaned but quieted when I raised an eyebrow and glared at him, daring him to back up his objection.

I remember holding up her ID and asking her if that was her real name, to which she only responded, "It's Sloane."

I kept her ID as well. If she was going anywhere while she was underage, it would only be here, where I could watch over her. I still have it in a drawer of things I never look at anymore.

***

"Lennox. Your passport." Ryder smacks my arm, pulling me from my memory and back into the passenger's seat of the car.

Guilt instantly settles into my stomach.

Sloane is engaged to Ryder, and I have no business recalling those memories.

I hand my documents over and listen to Ryder answer the border agent's questions, nodding in agreement when she looks into the car at the three of us. Then we're on our way, as though the shoot-out on the docks earlier today never happened.

I check my phone as soon as we're through.

There's still no response to the last four messages I sent to Dagen.

"Has Dagen messaged any of you?" I look over my shoulder to the back seat.

Ryder gave Cole his phone since he's driving.

Cole looks at both phones then shakes his head.

"I don't like this. Maybe we should go back." I text Dagen one last time, threatening to do just that.

Ryder does a double take at me to check if I'm serious.

I am.

Cole chuckles from the back seat. "Relax. He's finally alone with the girl he's been obsessing over for, like, five years. He's probably fucking her on every surface he can find."

When I level an unimpressed glare at Cole, he shrugs. "What? I'm just saying, that's what I'd be doing." Then he crosses his arms, slumping back in his seat. "I miss Harlow."

As if sensing our conversation, my phone pings, and I open it to read Dagen's response.

Cole takes that as his cue and immediately dials. Then, laughing, he holds his phone in front of him before I can text back. When the line picks up, Cole says, "He was totally going to make Ryder turn around and cross back into Canada to come get you. I told him you were busy schtupping your baby momma. You're on speaker. Go ahead, tell me I'm wrong."

"Fuck off."

The tension drains from my shoulders at Dagen's response on the line, and I chuckle along with everyone else.

It feels good to laugh with them. It's been a long time.

I remind Cole to tell him about the canceled contract. As they discuss the reasons Dad would have done that, I point out a sign for a gas station up ahead, and we say our goodbyes, telling him we'll check back in a couple of hours when we arrive in Seattle.

Cole looks at his phone for a few seconds after he ends the call.

"Can you believe he's a dad?" He retreats from our conversation and reclines into the back seat.

I know my brother well enough to recognize when his question isn't meant to have an answer, and I turn my attention to the scenery around us.

My mind drifts back to the same place it does every time I sit in silence—to her.

I haven't processed what Ryder told me about Henry being Grayson's son. I love that kid like he's my own family, but I would be lying if I said it didn't crush me when I heard Ryder and Sloane were together and about to be parents.

It's not healthy to constantly return to my time with her, and it isn't fair to anyone.

Loving Sloane meant setting her free. Protecting her meant letting her go, and respecting her meant honoring the choices she made. Even if doing so went against everything I've ever wanted.

In my soul, I felt like we were meant for something else. I let her go over and over again every day. It's a constant battle because my heart refuses to cut her out completely.

Knowing that Henry isn't Ryder's changes nothing because Sloane still is.

Ryder slows and pulls onto a side road leading to the gas station. The guilt weighing on me is sucking the air out of this claustrophobic little car, so I open my window. I prepare to make an excuse at the gas station so I can wash my face and compose my thoughts when Cole's phone rings again.

"It's Dagen," he tells us before putting him on speaker and chuckling. "Hey, man. She cuff you to a tree again?"

There's no humor in Dagen's voice when he responds. "Nyla's team was able to pull the heir from the microfiche she sent them."

Ryder comes to a stop at the pump, and Cole leans forward, his smile long gone as he holds his phone between us. "Who is it?"

"You're not going to believe this. It's Sloane."

For a few seconds, we gawk at each other in stupefied silence before my brothers start talking back and forth around me, but I mentally leave my body at the news.

I'm sure they're asking questions I would have thought to ask if I was in the right frame of mind, but I'm not.

"No." I say the word with more anger than I should, and everyone stops talking and looks at me. Clearing my throat, I try again, as if I can argue this truth away. "The heir is male. Everyone says the heir is male."

"That's what we all thought. But what if we were meant to think that—as a way of throwing everyone off of her trail?"

"But those are official hospital birth records. Are you saying that someone had the foresight to forge them over twenty-five years ago? Who would do that?" I challenge them to prove me wrong.

This has to be a mistake—or a really bad joke.

Dagen is silent on the other end of the line, and I look around at my brothers. Cole has his attention on the phone, his free hand combing through his hair, but Ryder—he's looking at me with pinched lips that curve down into a piteous frown.

Dagen is the one who answers.

"Someone who worked as a nurse at the time the baby was born."

Ryder and Cole mutter profanities in stereo.

We all know Sloane's mother is a nurse.

As everything comes together, my world falls apart.

"I need to call Amara." Ryder reaches into the back, taking his phone from the seat beside Cole.

I watch him send off a text, and it isn't until he's dialing that his words sink in.

"What the fuck did you just say?"

I'm taken back to the night Ryder brought Amara to Eros

and we got into it in one of the private rooms. It tore my heart apart when I thought Sloane had come to Eros with my brother, but when I saw he had brought his old girlfriend, and behind Sloane's back, I saw red, and I lost my shit.

It hurts that she is with anyone but me, but in that moment, how little he thought of his engagement to Sloane sent me to a dark place.

"I—shit." Ryder and Cole exchange a glance, and Ryder lifts the phone to his ear.

"Hey—yeah, we're good. Are you safe? Are Harlow, Sloane, and Henry at the house?"

As Ryder pauses to listen to the answer, I start in with some questions of my own.

"Why don't you just call Sloane yourself?" I glare at Ryder before turning my anger on Cole, and I repeat myself. "Why isn't he calling Sloane?"

Cole switches his phone off speaker and lifts it to his ear. "Hey, man. Thanks. We'll call you back." As Cole waits for Dagen's response, his eyes travel to meet mine, and he ends the call with, "Yeah. I know—we'll tell him."

"Just stay put." Ryder keeps talking on the phone like the woman he's engaged to doesn't exist, and I snap.

"Why aren't you calling Sloane?"

Ryder breaks away from his call to finally answer me.

"I sent Sloane a text. She isn't responding. Amara said she's lying down for a rest with Henry."

"But why is the Scott girl with Sloane and Harlow at all? Why is she on your speed dial? And why *was* she at Eros, Ryder?" I look at each of my brothers, and Cole leans back in his seat, as if to distance himself from my barrage of questions.

"Not now, Lennox," Ryder barks.

He tries to return to his conversation, but I'm not going to let it go.

"Yes—now, Ryder."

"Just stop, okay? It's not what you think. I just need to—"

"Are you fucking her behind Sloane's back? Because if you're cheating on the woman you're engaged to, then we have a serious prob—"

Ryder hits his limit, and his composure breaks away as he cuts me off.

"Sloane isn't my fiancée. She never was."

3

SLOANE

The sound of my mother sobbing is the only reminder that I'm not dreaming as I read then reread Elia's name over and over again.

"Dad?"

His eyebrows scrunch together. He's now seemingly pained by the term.

Right. That means he's not my father.

I want to cry.

I want to scream at the two people sitting in front of me.

I want to ask why and tear this flimsy little piece of paper into a million pieces, but it would do no good.

The microfiche might still be out there.

If it is, then they'll be coming for me as soon as it's found.

"I'm going to need you to say it." I challenge my "mother" because somehow I feel like this betrayal is her doing.

My "father" attempts to step in. "Peanut, we—"

"No. You've both been lying to me my whole life. But this" —I hold up the paper—"can only be fixed by someone who had access to hospital records."

I level my stare at the woman in front of me, who, it turns out, is actually my aunt.

"You're right. We kept it from you, but it was to protect you. The woman you thought was your aunt—my younger sister—was your real mother. She wasn't in a good place when she found out she was pregnant. She knew what it would mean if her secret ever got out. What it would mean—for you." I've been close enough to the Saint family to know exactly what she's talking about, but she continues to explain anyway. "Boys in Elia's world are raised to reign. Girls are used as bargaining chips. She didn't want that for you. She didn't want you to pay for the mistakes she made."

I return to the information in my hands. "How did Elia's name get on here?"

"We had a plan, but when your mother was in the hospital, she was out of it on pain meds when the nurse came in to take her information. She answered the questions that were asked. We couldn't take it back, but I could forge a second certificate of birth and switch them out. Your mother begged me to put my name under the birth mother. She said they may come looking for you, and she was right, but they never found you. I switched your sex to male on the official certificate and listed the mother as Jane Doe, then I created a certificate to make you ours. I had no idea the original information was transferred onto microfiche before I destroyed it until—"

She stops talking and leans back and away from our conversation. It takes me a few seconds more to realize she's just talked herself into a corner, and I take a stab at finishing her sentence.

"Until I mentioned we were looking for a birth certificate on microfiche." I look between the two of them, their lack of eye contact telling me everything I need to know.

I remember the conversation clearly. I called my mother to

cancel a visit with Henry when we found out about the microfiche. It was an innocent question. I wanted to know how hospital microfiche storage worked in case she knew something we didn't.

And she knew something we didn't, all right.

She knew she had a loose end to tie up.

"Did you hire someone to steal the microfiche before we could find it?"

When neither of them speak, I lean forward and hiss, "Answer me."

To his credit, the man I've called my father all of my life inserts himself between us. "Yes, I hired someone."

"Why are you telling me all of this now?"

They share a glance with each other before my father answers me. "We got a message a little over an hour ago. The person we hired to secure the microfiche is no longer in possession of it. Peanut, you need to go. Both you and Henry are in a lot of danger, and we need to get you out of here. We're leaving the country for a while. Just until the threat on our lives passes, then we're turning ourselves in for what we've done. Come with us."

My mother stands, turning to the suitcase she left in the middle of the room. "I've packed some of your things you left here. You can't tell anyone, not even your fiancé. Ryder won't be able to help you."

I want to laugh at that.

No one can help me now.

My parents have no idea how close we really are to Elia's organization. Outside of asking how hospital procedures work, I've never spoken to them about what we've been looking into. They think my engagement to Ryder is real.

A nagging question burrows its way out of the recesses in my head, and I need to know its answer before I leave.

I stand, halting her footsteps and wrapping my hand around her arm to turn her to me so I can see her reaction when I ask the question: "Is this why you killed him?"

This is the only possibility that makes sense to my breaking heart.

The shock on her pallid face makes me recoil, and I pull my hand back from her as if she's burned me.

"How did you—" She stops talking when he rises and stands beside her, wrapping an arm around her to steady her against him.

"How could you? I loved him."

Confusion replaces the guilt on their faces as she asks, "Who did you love?"

I shake my head at her ignorance and answer, "Grayson. You killed—"

"We didn't kill Grayson." My father speaks for her as realization dawns in her widening eyes.

We aren't talking about the same thing.

"Oh my god. Who did you kill?"

Clutching the arm of the chair, I step back and let my shock take me down to sit.

They follow me down, sitting on the sofa, and I splay my fingers open across my chest, reminding myself to breathe as the room spins.

My dad tries to reach for my free hand as he answers, but I pull it away.

"You have to understand. He came to us, and somehow he figured it out. I have no idea how. He threatened to take the information to Elia if we didn't pay him. We couldn't trust that he wouldn't go to him anyway. It was our only choice."

"Who, *Dad*?" I say the term with derision.

His shoulders slump with the weight of his guilt. "Harry." When I don't respond to the name, he says another: "Scott."

I search my brain for a match, and a wave of nausea hits low in my stomach.

"Mr. Scott? Grayson's father? He died of a heart attack." As I say the words, I see the lie hiding in plain sight. My mother is a damn nurse. "It was made to look like a heart attack," I mumble to myself, meeting her guilty expression.

The people sitting in front of me, the ones I thought were my parents all of this time, killed Grayson and Amara's father to keep my secret.

Combing my fingers into my hair, I grip them tight against my scalp and rock in my seat.

"How could you—" I leave the question open because these two in front of me have done an awful lot.

When my mother answers, I observe them from a different reality I was a part of only a few minutes before.

I don't know these people.

My whole life has been a lie.

This house was always my sanctuary. After Lennox rejected me and Grayson died, I could always come home to ground myself, and none of it was real.

"She was my little sister. Of course I was going to help her. She knew that we couldn't have kids of our own, and she wanted to give you a normal life." I laugh a little too hysterically at that, and she continues, "We love you like you are our own. You *are* our daughter."

Internally, I start listing the lies and secrets. They threaten to swallow me whole, and I cradle my head while I try to pull myself out from the hellish pit that's about to overtake me.

My mother—my real mother—has been missing for a long time. My parents buried an empty casket when I was younger. I was told that it was a way for us to say goodbye.

Guilt hits me when I remember my mom standing to go to the photo sitting on top of the casket to say her final words. I didn't want to go up. She practically dragged me down the aisle, telling me it was important to say something even if we say it in our heads. I told her I did say something in my head, but I remember I didn't say a damn thing.

A whir followed by a beeping sound pulls me out of my mental descent, and I look over to see Henry holding a car and a plastic figure of a cowboy above his head.

His carefree smile knocks me out of my pity party, and I take a deep breath, exhaling my momentary lapse into panic.

Henry deserves better than me falling apart.

Grayson deserves his day of reckoning.

Grayson. All this time, I thought if we found out who Elia's heir was, we would know who killed him.

But this solves nothing.

None of this matters anymore.

What matters now is what I'm going to do about it.

Whoever is after Elia's heir will be coming for me, and whoever isn't Elia's family will be killed to get to me. I can't put Amara and Ryder or any of his brothers through something that I am responsible for, even if it is just because I was born.

I'm mad at the two people in the room with me, but I can't put them in danger either. For my whole life, they were my parents. They still are. If I take Henry and go with them, all four of us will be in danger. If they leave without me, no one will care about them if they get far enough away.

"I can't go with you, but Henry and I will leave. I need some time to think."

There's no time to cry or feel sorry for myself. Wiping my tears away, I stand and shoulder my purse, turning to Henry.

Before I call Henry over, the man I still want to call my father in my heart rises and gets his attention. "Did you pick out your favorite toys? We're going to pack them up for you."

He crosses the room to a cloth bag sitting on the dining table near the pile of toys and starts to fill it up.

"Here." My aunt hands two passports to me. "We still have them from when we drove up to Canada for the weekend with the both of you. In case you want to leave the country."

It dawns on me that I have no idea where I'm going to go. All of my safe spaces are gone.

A piece of paper sticking out of one of the passports catches my eye, and I pull it and hold it between us. "This is two hundred thousand dollars."

The check is dated today.

"It's all we could get on short notice. There's one last thing." Reaching into her pocket, she hands me a folded piece of paper. "Selina—your mom gave me this and told me to use it if you were ever in trouble. I looked at it once and haven't opened it up in over fifteen years. It's best that we don't know where you are."

I take the paper from her and shove it into my pocket unopened.

My anger at the woman standing in front of me fades a little. She lied, but I can't leave it like this. I'm hurt now, but what if I never see the people I thought were my parents ever again? What if the words I say when I leave are our last?

We are still related. We had a life together.

"I—" The only words that I can think to say are "Mom" and "Dad."

"I know, honey. We love you so much, Sloane. We packed some food and the clothes you left in your room. You take it all. We'll help you load these into your car, but you can't tell us where you're going, and you can't tell anyone you're leaving. You have to hide until it's safe to return, and I don't know when that will be. We don't have much time."

They take turns hugging and holding Henry while we stuff

everything into the trunk of my car. Then they hand him over so I can secure him into his seat.

The memory of how scared I was when I thought Grayson might be Elia's heir rattles me to my core. I circle the car, my keys in hand, and get in without a drawn-out goodbye.

I can't stick around.

Starting the engine, I throw it into drive and pull away. I can't look at them, and I don't know why yet.

Is it the lies? Is it my breaking heart? Is it the realization that there is no safe space where I can hide away?

Amara is expecting me to sneak back onto the estate like nothing happened, but nothing is the same. I promised her we'd be back, and now I'm taking her nephew away from her.

Ryder will be angry at her for helping me leave and disappointed in me for running away.

I drive for twenty minutes as everyone I know floats through my thoughts.

I don't know if Ryder or his brothers are all okay, or if Dagen made it across the border.

For a brief moment, the urge to call Lennox sits like a weight in my chest. I don't know why it's him who comes to me as someone who could help me now.

When I look at the street signs, I realize I've been driving around with no specific destination in mind. It feels eerily similar to the path my life has taken.

I pull into the first parking lot I see and pass a library and coffee shop. I park in a stall at the far end.

What the hell am I going to do?

"Mommy?"

When I look back, my son greets me with a smile that is oblivious to the world collapsing around us.

I envy his innocence.

The cooler of food sits on the seat beside me.

"Are you hungry, buddy?" I dig in and pull out a plastic bag filled with cookies, and he reaches out his hands.

As he eats, I unbuckle my seat belt and turn to the back seat, unzipping the bag my *dad* packed for him and removing a toy truck so he has something to busy himself with.

Then I crumble into my seat and watch the cars go by on the street.

So what does a girl do with two hundred thousand dollars and no place to go?

Lowering my head, I rub my eyes and try to stop my tears from coming.

Then I remember the folded paper, the one my real mom left for me a long time ago.

I pull it out and carefully unfold it, as if my mother's message will disappear if I open it too quickly.

It isn't a message.

There are no words of regret nor a final note of love and hope for me.

It's a phone number from almost two decades ago and a first name.

I can't tell if the sound I make is a laugh or a cry. It sounds manic just the same.

I reach into my purse sitting on the passenger seat and pull out my phone. There are too many text messages and voicemails to count. Scrolling through the names, I'm happy to see messages from Ryder, Cole, and Dagen. They're alive. There are also text messages from Amara, telling me to hurry back, and I feel sick all over again. I don't know how I'm going to tell her that *my parents* killed her dad to protect me.

I hold the piece of paper beside my phone as I dial.

It rings four times before there's a voice on the other end. "Hello?"

I freeze.

"Is anyone there?"

I look at Henry through the rearview mirror and take a deep breath before answering.

My exhale is unsteady.

"Hi. I think you knew my mother."

4

LENNOX

There is an eerie silence in the car that contradicts the chaos raging through me as I replay Ryder's slip. *Sloane isn't my fiancée. She never was.*

She.

Never.

Was.

"Shit. Lennox, I'm sorry. You weren't supposed to—" Ryder attempts to take back his secret and swallow it whole.

"What? I wasn't supposed to what, Ryder? Find out?" I look from Ryder to Cole.

I can't believe, after everything we've been going through, that they kept this from me. I want to tell them I'm angry that they are still lying to me, but I'm more confused than anything.

Cole is the one who speaks up.

"No. She wanted to be the one to tell you. Sloane asked us to make sure she was there when you found out. She said it was her lie, and she wanted to come clean to your face."

That sounds so much like her it hurts.

"Why were you pretending to be engaged?" When neither

of them responds, I lose what's left of my patience. "ANSWER ME!"

I'm so loud inside the car that the guy filling his gas tank at the pump in front of us startles. Then I remember I had opened the window for air. I jab at the button, rolling it back up, and return to my conversation.

Ryder still looks like he doesn't want to talk about it, but I think it is more a testament to his close relationship with Sloane.

"You have to understand, this was years ago—when Grayson was murdered. We didn't know why he was killed. We didn't know who killed him, and we didn't know if Sloane and Henry would be safe if word got out that Henry was Grayson's son. I promised Grayson I would always protect Sloane. At the time, we didn't know who to trust...."

He breaks eye contact when he says his last sentence.

The unspoken part is that this is all on me because I positioned myself accordingly, and I lost their trust a long time ago when I tried to shelter them.

They thought it could have been me.

I have no right to be angry with any of them.

Ryder thought I might be a threat, and he kept Sloane and Henry safe—from me.

It's admirable, and it's one of the bravest things he's done, because I know myself, and I know the people we are up against. This is the equivalent of taking a bullet for someone.

A random thought hits me:

"Amara is with you."

That same pinched expression from before crosses Ryder's face.

"Lennox. There are things you need to know." He exchanges a glance with Cole, who tips his chin, urging him to continue. "Amara and I are married. She almost died trying to get evidence of Grayson's killer and clear my name earlier this year. It was the night Dagen saw you standing over Harlow's dead sister. Lennox, I love her. It's always been only her. Sloane knows this, and she's happy for us. Henry is Amara's nephew. She and Sloane are as thick as thieves."

Hearing that Sloane is happy is bittersweet.

I've only ever wanted her to be happy, but, selfishly, I wanted it to be with me.

How sad is that?

I didn't think it was possible, but this car feels like it's getting smaller.

"I'm hitting the can." I don't wait for anyone to answer.

I'm fully aware of my blunt shift in conversation as I reach across my lap to open the door, but it doesn't budge. I try again, and when it doesn't open this time, my frustration boils over, and I jiggle the handle more aggressively than I would have liked.

When I finally stop fighting with the door, the car is quiet. I press all of the buttons I can find beside me, and all I end up doing is rolling the window down again.

Then the lock clicks.

I glance over at Ryder, and he's moving his hand away from a button on his door. Without a word, I open my door and get out.

The energy coursing through me at all of this information is intense, and I don't know why.

This feels like a deception, but not the kind that it should be. It's a lie, but it feels like I've been robbed of something that should have been mine, and my failure to sort out my head is bringing a new anger to the surface.

I hear Cole taunting Ryder through the cracked window as I walk away.

"That went well."

It's followed by Ryder's own impatience when he says, "Fucking shut up, you raging asshat."

There's a scuffle in the car as I walk away, but I don't look back. They need to blow off steam as much as I do, and I scan the old building for a telltale stick figure sign to point the way to the men's washroom. Thankfully, it's around the side and away from people.

The second the door to the dingy bathroom closes, I double over, bracing my palms against my thighs to steady myself. Bending further, I check under the stalls for feet, and when I confirm I'm alone, I stand and walk to the sink, turning on the cold water.

I don't recognize the person looking back at me anymore.

I've lived as a shadow of myself for years—until she came along.

Sloane came from a simple family (her mother was a nurse and her father a teacher), and she didn't give one shit about how she was perceived by the world around her. For a fleeting moment, she cared about me though, and those were the best days of my life. Those were the days when I felt that maybe I could find redemption for everything I've done.

When she shared her light with me, I felt like there was a place for me. Like she saw who I really was and, still, she could love me.

Now she's in trouble, and none of us saw this coming.

This is the very definition of chaos, and I have no control over its outcome.

I don't know how to help Sloane when she made it clear it wasn't me she wanted, and I don't know how to navigate how we relate to each other now that she is no longer going to be a part of my family.

I cup my hands and fill them with frigid water. I know how

much it's going to shock my hot skin, but I welcome it. Anything to push down these years of regret.

The sound of water rushing from the tap must have drowned out the door to the washroom opening because I don't hear my brother enter.

"She never thought it was you." Ryder keeps his distance, leaning against the first stall with his arms crossed.

When I make eye contact in the mirror, he pushes off the stall and walks to the sink beside me, holding my gaze in the mirror as I reach for a paper towel to dry my face.

It's unspoken, but we both know he's talking about Grayson's murder.

"There were times over the years when we all had our moment of doubt about you." He makes a point of turning away from the mirror and looking directly at me when he speaks next. "Some of us had more moments than others." Then he turns his attention to the sink in front of him and lowers his voice. "But not her—never Sloane."

Somehow, Ryder sharing this feels like a betrayal of Sloane's confidence, and I don't respond.

He fills the silence on his own. "Look, I don't understand what happened between you, but—"

"You're right. You don't understand." I cup my hands under the water again, cutting our conversation short.

Ryder raises his hands in mock surrender and takes a step back from our conversation.

"Got it. Look, we're ready to go when you are. Cole is going to drive. We'll be back in less than an hour with him behind the wheel. Sloane and Henry should be awake from their nap when we get back. We all need to sit down and talk." Ryder turns to leave, but I answer him anyway.

"I'll be right out."

"Sure."

When I'm alone again, I take a second look at the stranger in the room. The man staring back at me is angry; he's lost. He's a shell of the man I wanted to be when I grew up, but he's a necessary evil, and for that, I'm thankful for him.

When I return to the car, my brothers are deep in conversation like their earlier tussle never happened. That's the thing about them. They bounce back because they take each other at face value. They let each other blow off steam, then they regroup, mumble their apologies, and move on.

Ryder tosses Cole the keys as he circles the car, going for the back seat, and I shake my head, getting to it first.

I don't have it in me to be a part of their bickering for a moment longer today. They can sit up front and squabble all they want. I'm sitting by myself with my thoughts for a while.

We spend the first fifteen minutes talking about Sloane. Ryder shares a little more about the lie he and Sloane have had to weave, but I get the sense he wants to wait until Sloane is present to share more. He tells me that Sloane has always been scared for Henry. She was worried that Grayson would be named as the missing heir, which would make Henry the next in line, and Ryder was able to comfort her by telling her that no one knew Henry was his.

There is no escaping the fact that Henry is hers though, and finding this out could send her over the edge, so we have to handle it properly.

Above all, Sloane is fiercely protective of the people she loves, and Sloane loves Henry more than anything.

I wonder if things could be different between us now.

I've obsessively thought about how I could have changed our outcome. Was there one thing I could have done but didn't? Was there something I could have said?

It all comes down to choices.

She made a choice, and I honored it.

Allowing myself to drown in the memories we made doesn't change anything, and it doesn't help her out of this. What it does do is suck up the remaining time we have left on the road, and before I pull my thoughts away from Sloane, we're already pulling into the long driveway of our family home.

I hate this place.

Our mother poured herself into our home. It's big and beautiful, full of memories from my childhood. Dagen and I would spend hours in the woods and down by the creek out back. All four of us brothers lived by the pool in the summer.

That isn't why my stomach tightens the closer we get to the house.

I hate the evil that once lurked here. The demon that hid behind my mother's kind nature and sucked the good out of the happy home my family should have had.

I hate that I was too weak to stop it, so instead I became a part of it.

I hate who I am.

I want to be the reflection I see when I look in the mirror. That sixteen-year-old kid I pushed down and denied every day since I pulled the trigger for the first time—then every time after it.

By the time I step out of the car, Ryder is already talking to one of his men as Cole pulls a bag out of the trunk.

He introduces him to me as Yuri.

It isn't lost on me that I'm the only one he's introducing. My other brothers already know everyone's names. I have some catching up to do, and I don't like feeling like I'm on the outside looking in on my own family.

Yuri points around the side of the house, telling us the last time he did his rounds, Amara and Harlow were sitting by the pool, and Sloane was still asleep.

We have a lot of catching up on all sides, and I'm anxious to speak to Sloane, especially after learning all of this new information. I have a long list of broken relationships to repair, and I'm most worried about the one with her.

When I take a few steps to walk around the house, Ryder says we'll all go together, and I fall into step with Cole behind Yuri and Ryder.

Subdued laughter catches my attention as we turn the corner with Yuri leading the way, and I hear shuffling from in front of us.

"She's still asleep—oh..." Amara's face falls, and Harlow jumps up as the three of us spread around Yuri, coming to a stop in front of them.

The hairs on the back of my neck stand on end when neither of the women make a move to welcome Ryder and Cole home. Instead, they stare at the three of us then exchange a glance in uncomfortable silence before Amara snaps out of the daze she just slipped into.

"Ryder. It's so good to see you. Um..." Her eyes jump from Ryder to me, and I suddenly see her in a new light.

Amara is my sister-in-law. But more than that, she's Henry's aunt, and she stood back and allowed this sham of an engagement to continue while she lived in secret as Ryder's wife just to keep Henry and Sloane safe.

I've been nothing but gruff with her.

Cole breaks my thought when he steps past me and lifts Harlow up in a big hug.

"We told him." Ryder walks over to her, cups a few fingers under her chin, and tilts her head back to kiss her. She cuts the kiss short, and a flash of confusion crosses Ryder's features. He takes a step back, eyeing her carefully. "We really need to talk." He tilts his head toward the pool house.

I assume this is where Sloane and Henry are napping.

Harlow and Amara exchange another glance before Amara steps in between Ryder and the pool house. "Can we let them sleep a little more? Maybe you can go to the house, and I'll wake them up." Harlow nods in agreement and starts to tug Cole's arm to pull him away.

There's something about the way Amara is pushing all of us toward the house that anchors me to my spot when Yuri mutters, "They've been asleep for a while now," as though he's just realizing how much time has passed.

Ryder leans back to take in his wife before he takes a quiet step toward the door of the pool house.

"Wait!" Amara winces, and Ryder stops, raising his brow at her to continue. "She's—not back yet." Her brows knit together as a forced smile crosses Harlow's face.

They know they're in trouble.

Ryder returns to her, wrapping his hands around her upper arms and squaring himself on her.

"What do you mean 'not back yet'? You were told to stay here. Where did she go?"

"She got a call from her dad. They needed to see her. She was worried about them, and—she said she'd be back right away, but she isn't answering her phone."

When Amara tries to look away from Ryder's questioning stare, she meets my eyes, and judging by how fast she lowers her gaze, I'm not hiding my growing anger.

Where the hell is she?

"Give me her number." I pull my phone out of my jacket pocket.

Our mother once sent out a family list of emergency contacts. I added everyone but Sloane.

I hate that I never put her number in my phone, but the temptation to call her would have been too much. On many occasions, I would have been one shot of bourbon away from calling her up and having it out.

"She's not answering any of us." Ryder looks over his shoulder at me.

"Her number."

I don't know what in my history with Sloane tells me she'll answer my call, but I can't stand by and do nothing.

I dial the numbers as Ryder says them, then I listen as the phone rings: once, twice, three times.

It connects before the fourth ring.

5

SLOANE

I've been sitting in my car as it idles on the shoulder of the interstate leading out of Seattle for the last ten minutes.

I have the directions to the person who knew my mother written on the back of a receipt sitting in the passenger seat.

Henry fidgets with his seat belt as he grows restless in the back, and I reach across to the glove compartment, retrieving an old tablet and powering it up. Thankfully, it still has a quarter of its battery left, and I pull up a cartoon I had saved on it then hand it back to him in the back seat.

The screen on my phone lights up with another text message.

Nausea rolls through me when I think about Amara. She's been like a sister to me for months, and by now she must realize I'm not coming back, but I can't face her. Not yet.

My phone rings, reminding me I should just shut it off for the night, and I'm about to do just that when the name on the caller ID catches my attention.

Lennox has never called my number, not since Grayson. I wasn't sure if he even had it, or if he cared to.

I programmed everyone's phone numbers into my cell when Ryder's mother sent out her list of important numbers, but his name has never appeared—until now.

The phone rings again, startling me from my shock.

Declining a call from Ryder or Amara is one thing, but Lennox is an entirely different beast.

I told myself I had moved on.

I was fine before him, and I was fine after him.

Now, I wonder if I only felt strong because he wasn't in my life to challenge my resolve.

My addiction didn't want me back, and I was forced to move on.

But he's here now.

He's calling me, and I know it has to do with the fact that I am not where I'm supposed to be.

I wonder if Ryder put him up to it.

My will crumbles when it rings a third time, and the part of my heart that broke a long time ago answers his call.

"H-hello?" I clear my throat.

"Where are you?"

As soon as he speaks, a combination of male and female voices fill the background from the other end of the line, and I recognize them.

Lennox must be with everyone at the house.

They quiet quickly, and I imagine Lennox has shut them all down with a stern look.

When I don't answer him right away, he lowers his voice. "You know, don't you?"

A semi blares its horn as it whips by, cut off by a sports car, and I jump in my seat before I hear Lennox's muffled voice tell the others, "Her car—maybe the interstate." Then he returns to our conversation. "Tell me where you are. I'm coming to get you."

"No." I draw out the word.

There was a time when I wouldn't have denied Lennox anything, but he lost that when he didn't choose me back, and I've been keeping the peace with him for far too long.

He doesn't get to speak to me only when it suits him, and being in control of the Lucciano heir would definitely suit him just fine.

"Sloane." His timbre drops into a dark warning.

"I said no. I've been taking care of myself for a long time—on my own."

Lennox is many depraved things, but he isn't a weak man. If I draw a line, he'll stay on his side until I give him a valid reason to cross it.

"Listen carefully: don't push me. Tell me—"

I hang up.

It takes my brain a couple of seconds to catch up to what I just did. My defiance will definitely be noted in Lennox's ledger.

I can't afford to speak to him for too long at any given time. Lennox stays in the shadows, his presence just out of reach, but he's always there, and the longer I speak, the more opportunity there is for my broken heart to invite him in. It's a place he's already told me he doesn't wish to be.

My phone rings again. I decline it, but it's quickly followed by a text.

Lennox: Pick up, Peach.

I choke on my breath.

He's not fucking around.

The words on the screen swim and swirl together as tears well in my eyes.

He hasn't called me that since—

I power my phone down before another call comes in.

He deliberately used the pet name he gave me a long time ago, and I hate that none of my time away from him has prepared me for it.

Resting my forehead against the steering wheel, I inhale one deep breath after another until my heart rate returns to normal and the urge to cry passes.

Henry is still lost in his show, and I take advantage of the battery I have left on the tablet. When a break in traffic arrives, I pull onto the interstate and continue driving south.

I know this road is bringing me to the city where Elia's men are, but I have nowhere left to go.

I need time to figure everything out, and I want to know about my mother. My real mother. Not the sister as seen through my aunt's eyes, but the woman my mother was when she had me.

Still, as I drive away, I can't help but think about Lennox calling me by that name.

He used to tell me it made me his, and my cheeks warm, even now, after everything, at the memories it evokes and the power it still wields.

I love Grayson, and I miss him every day.

I struggled for a long time with the understanding that I loved two men, each very different from the other.

Grayson was my anchor in a raging sea, and Lennox was the wind that promised to lift me up and take me away.

And I lost them both.

Lennox made his choice, and he has no right to dig up the

shallow grave where I buried the remnants of my shattered heart years ago.

I've spent countless hours putting my past with Lennox behind me, and I worked hard to create a new version of him: one void of the connection we once shared, and these memories serve no purpose in my head now.

Yet, still, they come.

I met Ryder and Grayson in our last year of high school. Ryder talked about his brothers all of the time, but I only met Cole and Dagen in the first year that I knew him.

The night I met Lennox, Ryder told Grayson and I that he could get us into a club his family owned. It sounded like a fun time until we walked up to the front of the line and the bouncer told us to stay put until our identification could be approved.

Then Lennox was there, standing over us.

I didn't know he was Ryder's brother at the time, and the way he looked me over sent chills all over my body. He knew we were lying our way in, and I loved every second of his domineering stare.

I'd never wanted to be called out for my indiscretions so badly in my life.

What's the point of breaking the rules if you're not going to be held accountable for it?

That was the first time I realized I had a type, and Lennox was definitely it.

Lennox took Grayson's ID first, shoving it into his pocket. Then he turned to me, and little shivers ran down the length of my spine under his attention.

In the end, he confiscated both of our IDs then lowered his

voice with rules for Ryder. He had the bouncer attach designated driver bands to each of our wrists, and we could only order water or soda. He also told Ryder that we were to stay away from the other level, but he didn't expand on what was down there.

Then he turned and walked away.

"Your brother's no fun," Grayson had said, and I put two and two together.

The way he looked out for Ryder now made sense. He watched out for him and set boundaries to keep him safe, just like I imagined an older brother would.

But there was something else.

Something dark in the way his presence filled a room. When I met his gaze across the club, I was never brave enough to hold it—not at first.

It took many more visits before I summoned the courage to speak to him directly.

I made my way across the club, my bottle of water in hand, and climbed the steps to the second floor, where I found him in a corner, leaning over the railing, watching as the bouncers on the main floor broke up an argument that was getting out of hand.

"Your friends are down there." Keeping his eyes on the floor below us, he lifted his chin toward the corner where I left Ryder and Grayson when I told them I needed to use the washroom.

"I know. I—um, wanted to say thank you for letting us in. It's a great place." I immediately regretted the exaggerated grin on my face, but it didn't matter because he didn't look at me.

"I keep eyes on what's mine." He took a sip of the drink in his hand.

I scrambled to come up with something else to say when a

door on the main floor at the back of the club opened, and two women entered the bar, heading toward the dance floor.

"So what's down there?" I pointed at the bouncer who was still blocking the door.

That got Lennox's attention, and his eyes slowly moved and focused on my own before he lowered his gaze to my outfit. I was dressed nothing like those women who came from wherever it was the door led to, and I tugged on my shirt.

"You are not to go to the other level." The way he said it made me feel like he was used to being obeyed.

His tone grated on me, and I attempted to stand up to him by straightening when I said, "I was just asking." I had hoped I sounded more mature, but I think it came across as the opposite.

I had his complete attention.

I'd just decided on Operation Abort Mission when I turned to slink away, and his fingers wrapped around my upper arm, turning me back to him and pulling me close.

The music pumped into the club, but I heard him loud and clear when he lowered his head, his hot breath against my ear. "It's a sex club, Sloane. Through those doors are men and women who are freely exploring themselves and openly experiencing those carnal fantasies that most people are too afraid to entertain."

I tried to tug my arm away, but his grip tightened, and goosebumps crawled across my skin. I was out of my depth, slowly wading into something I knew nothing about. Shame crept in when his words made me whimper and his grin turned wolfish. He knew he struck a nerve I wasn't aware I had.

"Tell me, Sloane. What do you fantasize about? And I'm not talking about the ones you share with your girlfriends during a rousing game of Truth or Dare. I mean the ones that slither into your head when the lights are out and your fingers are knuckle-deep in your cunt at night."

I opened and closed my mouth like a damn fish a few times before I attempted to pull my arm back once again, and this time, he let me go.

I wasn't expecting him to, and I stumbled back a step. He watched me in silence, his eyes burning right through mine, exposing the dark thoughts in my head, and I suddenly felt vulnerable.

I was no match for Lennox.

Taking another sip of his drink, he projected his chin toward Ryder and Grayson once more before sending me on my way with an amendment to his rule:

"You are not to go to the other level—without me."

I spend the entire drive immersed in memories I have no business entertaining, but that was Lennox's goal when he used that name.

By the time I pull up to the address that matches the one I wrote down, Henry and I have eaten through the food that was packed for us.

It's a calm evening, and the streets are quiet. The small, one-story house sits on a corner lot, facing a park, and I lift Henry out of his seat to carry him. He's been sitting still for a few hours now, and his energy is ready to bubble over.

Pointing at the park, he wriggles out of my arms and tries to tug me across the road to play.

"In a bit. Mommy needs to talk to someone, then we'll go over. I promise."

He glances over his shoulder once more and makes a sad

face, but he doesn't pull away, and I walk us up to the front door and ring the bell.

An older woman answers the door. I expect her to ask what I want, but as soon as she looks at me, her face brightens, and she says, "As I live and breathe, you look just like her."

"Like who?"

"Like your mother, dear. I'm Cora. Come on in."

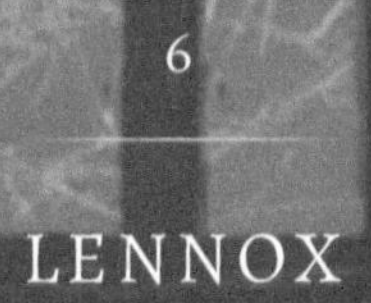

6

———

LENNOX

It was a shit move, calling her Peach in my text.

I lost the right to call her that a long time ago.

I wouldn't dare say it out loud. Not when my brothers—her friends—were standing right in front of me.

That would be admitting that I knew a part of her that she showed no one else—a piece of her that had always been mine and mine alone.

"Well? Where is she?" Ryder asks from over my shoulder.

"I—don't know. She hung up." Turning to face my brothers, I continue, "She knows."

Amara tugs on his jacket. "Ryder? What's going on? What does she know?"

"You said she went to see her parents?" I avoid her question.

"I—uh, yeah." Amara tries to hide her surprise that I'm addressing her. I don't blame her. The last time I spoke to her, I tried to warn her off of digging for Grayson's killer. She was getting too close, and she had earned the attention of my father, which is never a good thing. "Her dad called and said they had an emergency. We"—she stops abruptly, glances at Harlow, and corrects herself. "I mean, I said I would cover for her."

"We." Harlow corrects her right back. "We covered for her."

I glance at my brothers. Ryder's attention is on Amara. I can tell he's disappointed that the women went against his orders.

Cole is looking back at me, and I tilt my head toward the vehicle, raising my eyebrows.

He nods once in silent understanding.

The microfiche buyers must have been Sloane's parents. Dagen mentioned that Nyla had sent her buyers a note to update them on the status of her job. They must have panicked and called her.

"What does *she* know?" Amara asks again.

"Not here. Let's go inside, and we'll tell you everything." Ryder drops his hand to Amara's back and leads her toward the main house. As he passes his security, he motions for Yuri to join them, and Cole and I slow in our step behind the group.

"I'm coming with you." Cole holds up the keys to Ryder's car, pulling them away when I reach for them. "End of story."

When we near the steps to the house, I stop walking. "A minute, Ryder?"

He breaks his stride but nudges Amara up the stairs and toward the door, telling them to get comfortable and he'll join them in a moment.

He doesn't look surprised when I tell him Cole and I are heading over to Sloane's parents, but he does look like he wants to come with us, and I tell him to stay and bring everyone up to speed. I suggest that he attempt to reach Dagen and Nyla and have them join a video conference so everyone hears the same things, and he agrees.

Cole and I spend the drive trying to reconcile Sloane's real mother with Elia Lucciano. Cole's tech guy couldn't find any official adoption records, so the people Sloane thought were her parents all of this time knew from the start that it was all a lie.

There are no cars out front or in the driveway when we arrive. I didn't expect there to be. After ringing the doorbell a few times, I step back to look at the front door. It's a little too sturdy for my liking, and I turn toward the street, glancing up and down the block before walking around to the back door, which is older.

Placing all of my strength behind my kick, I aim my foot at the weak spot above the deadbolt, and the sound of wood cracking is promising. My second kick isn't as forceful, and the door opens through its splintered frame.

Cole hurries past me and disappears into the house as I take my time looking around.

I was here once before, when Sloane's parents had us over to meet the family and celebrate her engagement to Ryder. I wasn't going to come, but my mother had asked me to join them as a favor to her. Once I was here, I couldn't help myself. I slipped away and followed the hall to the bedrooms. I knew Sloane was an only child, so the room down the hall opposite the master bedroom could only be hers. This room held the side of her she shared with everyone around her. When her father found me in her room, I told him I was looking for the washroom. I didn't stay long after that.

"They're gone." Cole's voice drags me back to the empty home around us. "They didn't bother to set their alarm. They left fast—clothes are everywhere in the master." He looks off to the corner of the room when something catches his attention. He crosses the family room and clicks the mouse, and the computer it's attached to lights up.

Muttering something under his breath, he grabs his phone from his pocket and dials a number. "Hey. It's Cole Saint. Can you access a computer I'm standing in front of—right now? Sure thing..."

I take two steps to the door, mentally placing everyone around the room like I remember them the night I was here. My father was in an uncharacteristically good mood that night, and my mother was happy one of us was settling down.

Ryder and Amara sat beside each other, but now that I think about it, they looked no different than when they hung out as friends.

That's because they have only ever been friends.

How did I never see it?

I bite my teeth together as I answer my own question. I never saw it because I never wanted to. I was hurt that my youngest brother was happy with the woman who didn't choose me, and I couldn't handle seeing them together, so I never really looked at them.

"—for two."

I spin around, lost in my thoughts and missing everything Cole just said. A disjointed tension hovers between us as I compose myself.

"I was just—I missed that. What did you say?" I return to the family room to find an unlocked computer.

"I got in and checked their history. It turns out they were the ones who hired Nyla to steal the microfiche. The only other browser history today was to their bank. There was a large sum withdrawn from their accounts. It looks like they've decided to run."

Any sane person sitting on a secret this big would run if they had any sense of self-preservation.

"Can we trace the money that left their account?"

"I'll have Leonard check. I mean, he's done some pretty crazy shit online. We should get back to the house though."

I drove the car back while Cole handled our business. He

called and asked his tech person to look into some transactions for us. Then he called Ryder's security team and asked them to look at the tapes from around the time Sloane left to find out how she got to her parents.

It turns out she walked right through the front gate and accessed the parking lot just off the property, so she has her own car. The background noise through her phone sounded like a highway, and we have many of those all over the place here.

When we arrive and join everyone in the dining room, Amara looks just as mad at Ryder as he does with her, and I assume he's told her everything.

She turns her rage on Cole and me. "You both knew? You knew your *father*"—she spits out the word, and I don't blame her—"murdered my brother, all this time?"

Amara's face is flushed, and she's clenching her hands into fists. She looks like she's just getting started, but Ryder stands, taking her hand in his. He pries open her fingers and slides his own hand into hers. He leans close to her, lowering his voice, and says that he already explained why we couldn't say anything.

We couldn't say anything because we couldn't risk one of them losing their shit and my father deciding to tie up some loose ends. We kept it to ourselves because we couldn't risk one of them going off the deep end, but it doesn't matter now because that is exactly what's happened, and we still don't know where our father is.

"I know," Amara says as she pulls back her hand. "I know. But I'm—this is a lot, and they're in trouble, Ryder. Henry's just a little boy."

Ryder wraps his arms around her, pulling her close, and she doesn't fight. She burrows her face into his shirt. Her upper body heaves with her silent tears, and we all feel her pain.

"Why didn't she just come home?" Amara sniffles, wiping her face with her sleeve. "We're her family."

"I don't know, Blossom. We'll find her." Ryder kisses the top of her head.

"Maybe you could try calling her again." Amara breaks away and looks hopefully at me, and Ryder attempts to dissuade her.

I hadn't realized that Amara and Ryder's arranged marriage had been something they both wanted long ago. In truth, I was happy for Ryder when I found out it wasn't going to happen. My father was just using the agreement as a way to control his youngest son.

Ryder did a great job of hiding his feelings for her from everyone, and I'm impressed at how cunning he really is.

Amara was too young to know anything about Sloane and I, so her words surprise me.

"She won't want to hear from me." I keep my answer short. I don't feel like rehashing how I know this, especially since it involves her dead brother.

"I think you might be the only one she'd want to hear from," Amara mutters under her breath, trying again. It sounds like an accusation of sorts, and Ryder shushes her.

Amara has become fiercely loyal to Sloane.

I don't have it in me to sit back and let Amara's assumptions tarnish our truth.

Against my better judgment, I lay it all on the line so we can bury this bullshit once and for all and get back to what matters: finding Sloane and Henry.

"Look. I don't know what you think you know, but there is nothing going on between Sloane and me. She made her choice a long time ago. It wasn't me, and we all moved on."

Ryder and Cole look at each other before both of them turn

to square themselves on me, and everyone gawks as the room goes silent.

Cole takes a step forward. "Come on, man. Look, we know what happened." He raises his hand as though trying to calm a wild animal, and I guess that makes me the wild animal.

"What the fuck do you think you know?"

A pang of betrayal hits me in the gut when I wonder what Sloane has been telling them. I held her to high standards, and she met every one. I never thought she would distort the truth.

Ryder steps forward now, joining our brother. "Well, we don't know everything because she never wanted to talk about it, but we know she chose you." He speaks matter-of-factly, and I glare at him as I take a step back.

My confusion must be obvious because Amara takes a step toward me. Lines of worry crease her forehead.

"She—um, she told me about it once. She said she wrote you a letter to tell you that she chose you." I don't know Amara well enough to tell if she's being truthful, but she looks like she believes what she's saying. "She got her letter back the next morning, unopened. And you had written a letter of your own, telling her to choose Grayson."

"I never got a letter from her." Everyone's expressions tell me the same thing: they don't know what to believe. "I'm telling you, I never wrote her a letter."

Grayson was a good kid, but if I had thought for a moment that Sloane wanted the life I offered her, I would never have let her go.

Amara clears her throat. "She—um, she told me she still has it—your letter. She says she reads it sometimes when she can't sleep."

"Where is her room?"

Amara doesn't need to speak when she points out the

window toward the pool house in the back. It was where Sloane and Henry were supposed to be napping earlier.

No one moves when I cross the room and leave the house, walking a straight line to the building across the yard.

The door opens, and I turn on the first set of lights then hit every switch I see until I get to the bedrooms. The first room is empty. The second room must be Henry's because his toys are in a pile near the bed. Pajamas with robots on them are on top of a hamper, and a kid's book is on the nightstand.

When I open the next door, Sloane's scent swallows me whole, and I know it's her room.

I open her dresser. All of her clothes are still neatly folded, and her toiletries are in the bathroom off to the side. Everything is still here. She couldn't have known she was Elia's heir until she got to her family's home earlier today. She didn't have time to pack.

I rifle through a small credenza in the corner and return to look at the bed where she slept—alone.

Blistering rage burns through me at the thought that she was alone all of this time when I see the piece of furniture I haven't looked through yet.

Circling the bed, I sit on the mattress and slide open the bottom drawer of Sloane's nightstand. Dark thoughts flood my mind when I find a little black cloth bag tied with a drawstring at the top. Feeling through the fabric, my fingers uncover the obvious shape of the vibrator she uses to get herself off.

I open the top drawer to find a picture of her, Grayson, and Ryder when they were younger. It was taken close to the time when I first met her. Then I remove a picture of her and Grayson. It's clear from their wide grins and open mouths that they are laughing, and he has his arm wrapped around her neck in a playful chokehold. It looks like he's about to push his ice cream cone into her face and she's pushing his hand away. I can almost hear her laughter through the image.

These are all hidden away.

Of course they are. If she was pretending to be Ryder's fiancée, then she would have to conceal what was in her heart.

At the bottom of the little pile is a folded piece of paper, and I take care to open it.

My handwriting is all over the worn lined paper, and my vision goes dark.

This is my letter telling Sloane to choose Grayson and move on.

There's only one problem: I never wrote a damn word on this page.

I skip the lies written on the paper. I'll get back to them in a moment. I go right to my name signed at the bottom to confirm what I already know in the pit of my stomach.

My father never quite got my L's right.

7

SLOANE

When I arrived here with Henry a couple of hours ago, Cora quickly welcomed us into her home. Then she went about closing the blinds and locking her door.

It was clear by her reaction that she didn't just know my mother, she also knew who my father was without me having to tell her.

She invited us to stay for dinner, and Henry perked right up when she told him she had a lasagna in the oven.

While we ate, Cora told me she met my mother when they worked for Elia a long time ago, and they had become close. She glazed over what their jobs were, her eyes dancing over to Henry and back, and I got the impression she was being vague because he was with us.

We talked about what little I knew of my mother and how Selina is actually the sister of the woman who I thought was my mother all of this time. I told her that the only thing I knew about Selina was that she had been missing for a quarter of a century. The people I thought were my parents never really talked about her around me, and I was too young to remember her, so I never pushed the subject.

Cora sat in silence the whole time. It wasn't lost on me that she barely ate her food. Instead, she pushed the fat noodles around her plate every time I said something that looked like it hit a nerve.

Eventually, she changed the subject and told me about her time working with Mr. Saint, and how she'd finally had enough and asked Lennox to get her out of the bustle of their organization. She had "paid her dues," as she put it, and she wanted a quiet life, but I sensed she wanted to stay close—to what, or who, I don't know. Lennox helped her get out of Seattle and sent her to Portland to manage a restaurant for Cole.

She talked about the brothers with a tough fondness that is not extended to Elia or Sebastian.

As soon as she started talking about Lennox and his brothers, I told her I knew them very well. I told her about Grayson, and how Ryder helped Henry and me after we lost him.

After everything with Lennox ended, I never went back to their club. I wonder if I had, maybe I would have run into Cora at some point. When I mentioned this to her, she took a long look at me and said that if we had ever run into each other, she would have recognized me immediately.

When we finished, Cora stood to clear the dessert plates, and I set Henry up on the couch in the living room with his toys and flipped through the channels until I found a kid's show for him to watch. Then I returned to finish clearing and asked if we could pour another glass of wine and sit at the table to talk.

The conversation moved slowly at first. Cora looked torn between telling me everything and preserving the image she thinks I have of my mother. The truth is, no one ever gave me the chance to have an opinion either way.

I've been sitting across from her in silence for two minutes, playing with the stem of my glass.

None of this is easy, but it is necessary, and I just need to say it.

"I know Elia and my mother didn't meet at church, Cora. I just want to know who she was."

Cora takes a long look at me through glassy eyes. Her chin trembles when she says, "You remind me of her."

She lowers her head, looking into her wine as a tear rolls down her cheek, and I circle the table to take the seat beside her.

Her voice is low, so quiet I almost miss it. "I loved her." Then, when she realizes I heard her, she clarifies. "Your mother was a force. No matter what happened, she picked herself up. She never let them keep her down, and she never left any of us behind."

Cora takes a sip of her wine, then leans toward me, looking into the living room. I follow her line of sight to see Henry, sleeping on the couch as the show plays.

She takes a deep breath as she straightens in her seat.

"I started working for Elia when he and Sebastian were claiming their territory and making names for themselves. I'd been on the street on my own for a few years, and they approached me to work with their—um, girls, to manage them and make sure everything went smoothly *backstage*."

She steals a glance to confirm I understand what she means when she says "backstage." I assume it's some kind of strip club, so I nod to let her know that I get it and I'm good.

"Anyway, your mother came to us like everyone else did: She thought she hit rock bottom. The problem with that thinking is, rock bottom doesn't happen until after these men get their claws in you. By then, it's too late to pull yourself back out, and you're stuck in a vicious cycle; you get used up until there's nothing left."

"Why did you stay?"

"I was no better off than your mother. It was work for them or walk the streets. At least I could watch out for the women who passed through. The money was better—it was steady, and we were protected from everyone else."

"If I look just like my mom, wouldn't Mr. Saint have recognized me at some point?"

Cora is already shaking her head. "By the time your mother came to work for Elia, he had already had a falling out with his partner. Sebastian was living in Seattle with his wife and sons by then."

Her story sparks the image of a young Lennox and Dagen, but Cora's sniffles pull me away from thinking about them too deeply.

She places her palms on the table, pushes her chair back, and pats the front of her shirt to straighten it.

"Just a minute. I have some photos around here somewhere." Cora heads down the hall, and I walk to Henry, still sleeping on the couch. A knit blanket hangs over one arm, and I open it, tucking it around him and turning down the television so it doesn't startle him awake.

I meet Cora back at the table. The way she hugs the box to her chest tells me she treasures its contents.

"Do you—would you like to stay here tonight? I have a spare room, and we could talk some more." She stays standing waiting for my answer.

I really hadn't thought about where we would go after this, and now that I think about it, I don't know if there is anywhere I can go. I would have to show my ID, and everyone is probably looking for me, and that puts Henry at risk.

When I tell her we would love to, she sets the box on the table and reaches for the wine, pouring it into both of our glasses to empty the bottle.

She lifts the lid off the shoebox and fingers through its contents. She slides some papers off the top, then pulls out a photo, setting it facedown beside the cardboard box and going for another. Finally, she lifts a photo and smiles at it before sliding it across the table toward me. "She must have been close to your age in this one."

My chest tightens as I lift it to look at the image of my mother. She has a floppy hat on to block out the sun, but her eyes are hauntingly similar to the ones I see staring back at me when I look in the mirror.

As Cora hands me more photos, she tells me when each one was taken. It turns out, many of the women were quite close, and they either lived together or spent a lot of time together outside of the clubs where they worked. I notice that Cora has no photos from their time in the club, but I don't mention it. I imagine those are the times she wishes to forget.

We start on another bottle of wine, and by the time her stories thin out, it is after two in the morning.

We've talked about everything except the elephant in the room.

"Did you know—about me?"

"Selina came to me as soon as she found out she was pregnant. The girls used protection, but one night Elia had set his sights on your mother, and everyone knew he was never to be denied. Things were—um, different back then." Her eyes flit away briefly, and a sense of shame fills the air around us. "It was still early in the pregnancy, and she had time to get out. She wasn't indebted to Elia, meaning there would be no one coming after her if she could make the break. She knew where she stood, and she knew Elia didn't want anything beyond what he took when she was in his employment. But she knew that a child would change everything, and she didn't want what that would mean for you."

"What would it mean?"

"Honestly, if she was thinking for herself, it would have set her up for life. She would have been a kept woman. You would have been her ticket out, but for you, you would have the Lucciano name, and that meant you would be shackled to certain expectations. Most likely"—she eyes me up and down—"you would have been locked in an arranged marriage to strengthen ties with another criminal organization. In those days, women never held positions of power—most still don't. Your choices wouldn't have been your own, and defiance would not have been tolerated."

A hot tear rolls down my cheek, and the lump in my throat makes it painful to swallow. She could have had everything if she'd just told Elia about me—and she chose to save me instead of herself.

Cora places her warm hand on mine and squeezes, comforting my sadness. "Everyone else knew her as Valentina. I was the only one who knew your mother's first name. No one knew I had that information, and I never told a soul. Most of the girls used aliases, and they were paid under the table in cash, so it wasn't out of the ordinary. When Selina left, I told her to call me if she ever needed anything, and that was the last time I ever saw her."

A war starts to wage between my head and my heart. I have a question, but the answer could hold the finality I am not sure I'm ready for.

But answers are what I came here for, and that means I need to ask all of the questions.

"Where do you think she is now?"

Cora deflates as I ask the question, a dejected sigh escaping her. "I've had the same phone number for over twenty-five years. It's a bugger to keep active, and now I have it forwarded to this." She holds up her cell phone. "It's my only link to a lot of the women who've left. Out of everyone I gave my number to, Selina was the one I hoped would contact me to tell me she made it out. There isn't a doubt in my mind that if she could have, she would have." She opens her mouth to speak, but her words catch in her throat, and she swallows them down before meeting my eyes. "I think she's gone," she whispers. "I'm so sorry."

I know what she means by "gone."

A sob escapes me, not because of her answer, but because I feel it in my bones that she's right. No matter how much I look for her now, I don't think I'll ever find my mother.

"I don't know what to do," I whisper, stealing a glance at my boy snuggled on the couch.

For a fleeting moment, I feel my mother with me. I'm Elia's heir, and I'm now faced with the same options my mother was. This makes Henry Elia's male heir. He's a coveted boy who can be groomed and raised into a man who heads an empire, and I'll burn everything to the ground before I allow that to happen.

"You are welcome to stay here for a few days. I live a private life. Cole and Lennox have seen to it that I am no longer disturbed, and no one will think to come by here. Why don't you get some sleep, and we'll talk about it over coffee once you're rested. If you decide to do something else, I have a long list of contacts I can get you in touch with. I can have you both out of the country by tomorrow night if you wish."

I tilt my head to the side, doubting she can really do that, when she crosses her arms across her chest and leans back. "Favors are gold in my line of work, and I've stacked up more than enough of them."

When I lean back to tell her I couldn't possibly put her out any more than I already have, she stops me with a firm shake of her head.

"It's my story to take to the grave, but your mother saved my life once, and helping you in your time of need doesn't even make a mark against what I owe her. You have a safe place here. No matter what you decide to do, I will hide you both away forever if you wish. I love those Saint boys like they are my own, but I won't tell a damn soul about you, and that is the very least I could do—for Selina."

"I could use a place—for the both of us—for a while. Until I figure this out."

I don't have my mother.

I'm sure I never will, but for now, I have a sanctuary until I sort this out.

I have neutral ground where I can breathe, and Henry is safe.

8

LENNOX

Sloane,

*I've thought long and hard about this, and I keep coming
to the same conclusion: I want you to move on. I'm not
in a position to offer you my time or my heart, as you are
not and never will be a priority in my life. I've enjoyed
our time, but this is where it ends. My decision is final. I
don't wish to discuss this further, neither with you nor
with anyone else, and I ask that you respect my choice
and my privacy. I hold no ill will toward you, and I wish
you well.*

Lennox

M y father took a gamble that both Sloane and I
would be too hurt to speak further about the
letter, and he was right.

A shiver runs through me at what would have happened if he was wrong and one of us had broached the subject. Hell, it was on the tip of my tongue countless times.

Sebastian is not the type of man who loses, and many people who have crossed him have just up and disappeared with no trace.

Sloane may only be alive because she kept reading this forged letter, reminding herself over and over again that I didn't want her when she was the only thing I have ever wanted.

I don't know how much time has passed between when I first found this letter and when Cole clears his throat from the bedroom door.

I angle my body away from him for some privacy, and he stays where he is as I drag my palm down my face in an effort to regain my composure.

Inside, I'm fracturing.

My control is splintering apart, and I am dangerously close to welcoming the pain and rage as though they are a part of my very soul. It's what I deserve for allowing all of this to happen.

The mattress dips beside me as Cole sits, taking the letter out of my hands and reading it before muttering, "Christ."

None of my brothers knew the extent of our relationship. They still don't.

We were discreet, especially after Grayson started to show more than just a friendly interest in Sloane. I could tell she had feelings for him too, and her decision weighed heavily on her.

Sloane was young; she hadn't experienced life or love, and there was so much of her she was just starting to explore.

Grayson was her age. He was stable. If he had any demons, they were securely locked away. He was a safe choice.

I, on the other hand, am ten years older than her. I'm her best friend's brother. I manage a sex club, and my demons are saturated in blood and depravity. She knew full well what I was capable of and what I could bring out in her.

I knew that when she finally came to me, it would be with all of her heart and soul, so I set her free.

I was so sure she would return that when I saw her next, with Grayson, intentionally averting her gaze from my own, it became one of the darkest moments of my life.

I rarely allow my emotions to dictate my decisions, but when I lost Sloane, I tried to cut myself off from her. I shut the dance club down and expanded Eros, adding a lounge area where the nightclub used to be.

I once told Sloane to never go to Eros without me, and I was sure she'd honor that, especially now that she'd made her decision. So when I saw her at Eros with Ryder during the masquerade event earlier this year, I lost my shit thinking she could be so cold as to waltz into my place with no respect for what we had. When I realized it was Amara and not Sloane, I lost my head all over again.

I break the silence. "It was Dad."

I reach for the paper, and Cole lets it go.

"How do you know?"

Running my finger down the page, I point to the lower line in the first letter of my name. "You have to look closely. It's easiest to spot in my signature. Sebastian can't draw a continuous line from the left to the right."

Cole's eyebrows raise when he sees it.

It's something that, now that he knows what to look for, he won't ever be able to unsee.

Our father hurt his hand a long time ago, and the bones never healed right. It's subtle, but his thumb and forefinger can only move so far to the right before a slight bump forms in his line. It almost looks like a granule of sand got caught under the paper and disrupted the flow of the pen before it corrected and continued on.

"Why did you let her go?" Cole leans away from me as he speaks, preemptively avoiding a smack to the head, but I'm not mad—not at him.

It's a question I'll be asking myself for the rest of my life, even though I know the answer.

"It wasn't because I didn't want her. I let her go because I thought she didn't want—us." I close my eyes, suck in a deep breath of air, and blow it out, looking toward the ceiling. "Do you remember when we were in Vancouver, and I told you that Elia accused Dad of knocking Mom up to force her into choosing him?"

"Yeah."

"I left out the part where I heard Dad admit to it." I know without looking at my brother that his jaw is hanging open to some degree. "I heard him through the vent. He sounded so smug, like he'd won first place in a fucking game. Dad told Elia that he'd keep"—I use air quotes because these were his words, not mine—"'stuffing her full of bitches and bastards' until she forgot all about him."

My stomach still rolls at the way he spoke about our mother and all of us. At the time, I was too young to understand the hatred my father harbored for Elia.

"I let Sloane go because I didn't want to be like him and force her into something she wouldn't have chosen for herself." I'm not a good man, and the things I wanted to do to her are depraved, but I wasn't about to do them without her complete consent. I crumple the letter in my hands before opening my palm to glare at it, mentally willing the timeworn note to spontaneously combust from my fury alone. "I need to find her, Cole."

"You need to get some sleep, Lennox. We just returned from another country after shooting our way through half a Mexican cartel at a dockyard. Wherever Sloane and Henry are, I'm assuming they are asleep. Yuri is monitoring all of our communications, so if she reaches out, we'll know right away. Turn your ringer on in case she calls, and get some rest. You're no good to any of us if you're tired in the morning." When I stand to take his advice, he adds, "Are you sleeping in your old room tonight?"

"I'm staying right here." I point at Sloane's bed.

I want to be here in case she decides to return. The scent in the room is the only thing I have of her, and I'm not ready to leave it.

"You better be here in the morning, Lennox. I mean it. We agreed: we do this together from here on out."

"I'll be here."

Cole turns his back to me, walking out of Sloane's bedroom, and I follow him out.

"Everyone else has gone to bed. They wanted to give you some space. I need to burn off some energy." He pulls his shirt over his head and walks to a cabinet near the doors, pulling out a set of trunks. "You okay if I swim a few laps first?"

The mountain of chaos our father has created and the sheer devastation he's inflicted on his own family boils through my blood when I see the scar on Cole's back.

I'm so lost, I didn't notice Cole has already turned around and taken a couple of steps toward me, his eyes wide with worry.

"Hey, man. You okay?"

"I could have stopped him." I mutter my confession as I sit on the couch behind me before the weight of my guilt pushes me down.

"None of us saw this coming." He tries to pour reason into my dark thoughts.

"Not this." I look around the room. "I could have stopped it all."

"What do you mean?"

I shake my head, trying to push the memory away, but I've already invited this conversation in when I started speaking, and Cole waits for me to get it out.

"The first time I killed someone was the night I turned sixteen. Dad set it all up. He set me up. He took me out, put a gun in my hand, and told me to kill a guy I didn't even know. When I refused, he said he was going to send a driver home to get Dagen—or you." I try to hold Cole's rattled stare, but even I can't hide my ugly truth, so I look at my hands. "I shot him, Cole."

My brother swears under his breath, sliding closer to me. "It sounds to me like you didn't have a choice."

"But I did, and not once did I think to use the gun on *him*." I let that sink in for half a minute. I was so shit-scared of my old man that I couldn't even stand up to him while I was holding a loaded gun. "I think about that moment all of the time because everything that happened after that night is on me: I lost Sloane, Sloane lost Grayson, Harlow lost her sister, and Ryder almost lost Amara. You were attacked because of me."

"Fuck no!" Cole jumps up at my spoken conclusion. "We are not going to go down that road. Back it the fuck up." He points at me, his finger shaking with anger. "This is all on Sebastian, and he will answer for everything he's done—to all of us. I won't let him continue to destroy you from the inside out. The guilt he refuses to carry does not fall on your shoulders. That's not how this works."

Cole cuts himself off with a grunt before he says anything else. Instead, he reaches over and pulls me up to his height by my upper arms. "Lennox, the three of us are who we are because of you, not *him*. And I love who we are. We are loyal, strong—okay, sometimes Dagen is a dick, but we are damn good men."

I open my mouth to answer but am silenced when he pulls me into a hug, and I freeze in surprise.

I don't remember Cole being a hugger.

Pushing me to an arm's length away, Cole meets my eyes. "Here's what's going to happen: You are going to get some sleep. Then, in the morning, we are going to meet in the dining room and form a plan over breakfast. Then we are going to find Sloane and Henry and bring them home."

Home. The word forms a lump in my throat. Home hasn't meant anything to me in years.

I agree by stepping toward the bedrooms, and Cole lets me go.

Pulling off my own shirt and jeans, I slide under Sloane's soft covers.

I hear the splash from the pool outside as Cole jumps in. He always loved cannonballs.

The room is dark, and I stretch out under the crisp sheets she slept in only twenty-four hours ago. Knowing that doesn't bring me any closer to her, and I reach over, slide open the bottom drawer of her nightstand, and remove the little black bag I know is hiding in there.

A groan escapes me when I slip the vibrator out and turn it on. Pressing my finger against the buzzing tip, I know exactly where I would hold this against Sloane's clit to make her cry out loud. The mental image makes me bare my teeth. I turn it off and slip it back into the bag, then return it to its spot.

Everyone here adores Sloane.

They see her fierce heart, but I've seen so much more.

I've touched the jagged pieces of her soul that she tries to hide for fear they'll cut the ones she loves, but she could never cut me, because they fit perfectly with my own broken shards.

Knowing that she chose me changes everything.

I open my text messages. There's still no response, but my last message was delivered.

Good.

Now that I know the truth, my name for her stands, and I won't bury it under more messages.

She'll keep seeing the nickname that makes her mine until she responds.

I've distanced myself from Sloane long enough.

Cole is right about one thing: I need my rest, because as soon as I find out where she and Henry are, I'll be coming for them.

9

SLOANE

One day turned into two, and the longer I kept my phone turned off, the harder it was to turn it back on.

I knew there would be texts and messages, and I'm sure, by now, that my inbox is full.

Guilt trickles in when I think about how it must look to everyone back home.

If I don't check in soon, they are going to think the worst, and Amara must be sick with worry for Henry.

Now I am on my third day, and I still feel like I need more time to think.

Being away from everyone and spending this time with Henry and Cora has helped me to sort a few things out.

We've gone through all of her photographs and anything Cora can remember about her time with my mother.

My mother, and even my aunt and uncle who I thought were my parents, have sacrificed so much to keep my secret hidden. I've come to understand that none of this was kept from me maliciously, but as their way of protecting me.

Last night, I cried through the epiphany that I'm doing the

same thing for my own child because he's too young to protect himself.

There's only one thing left to discuss, and I've been waiting for Cora to return home from work so I can ask her for her advice.

Cora manages one of Cole's restaurants, and she's been going in for her shifts like nothing is wrong. She told me that she is pretty much left alone now, and it's thanks to Cole and his brothers looking out for her. But if she were to start skipping her shifts, it would raise suspicion, and someone would drop in to check on her. It would be too much of a coincidence that I went missing at the same time she decided to take a rare vacation.

I've stayed close to Cora's house with Henry. My thought is that criminal organizations don't normally cruise the suburbs, so we've been going for short walks, visiting the local library, and hanging out at the playground across the street, which is where we are now, for the second time today.

Henry is playing close by with a small group of kids as they run from structure to structure shouting something about spies, and I've been sitting here staring at the phone I haven't powered on since Lennox left me that message. It's taken everything I have not to check to see if he left another.

A little voice in the back of my head taunts me to just turn it on, and butterflies flutter furiously around my stomach at the thought.

Hoping to be saved by the bell, I look over to Cora's place to see if she's home yet, but there's no car in the driveway.

As I fidget, my thumb brushes over the button, and I turn it on, my heart rate thumping a little faster.

Lennox hasn't left any more messages. Just knowing that makes my stomach squeeze tight with nerves. His last message was a command, and so far I've ignored it.

I open the screen to start typing, but I have no idea how to respond. I write a sentence; I delete the same sentence. I try a different approach. It gets deleted as well. There is nothing I can type that will help me recover from not responding to his first message to me in years. After another try, I give up and close out of his message. Instead, I pull up Amara's long string of text messages.

I know how worried she must be. I can't offer her a lot, but I can't let her worry.

Me: We're safe, but I need time. I'll message when I'm ready.

I turn the phone off as soon as I hit send and retreat back into the real world, far away from where they can currently find me.

"Twice in two days." The words catch me by surprise, and I lift my hand to block the sun from my eyes as I look up at the woman who is speaking.

"Pardon me?"

"I thought you might have just been passing by, but here you are again today. Are you new to the neighborhood?" The woman smiles and steps to the side, taking a seat on the bench I'm sitting on.

"Oh. We're just visiting—um, my aunt." I smile and scan the playground for Henry, settling once I see him running around a slide.

The woman leans toward me and points at one of the kids with him. "That one's mine." Then she raises her voice, yelling, "Bryson, keep your hat on." We watch in silence as one of the boys breaks away from the group and takes three steps back to lift his hat from the ground before running after the rest of the kids. Then she turns to me with a smile. "I'm Irene Warfield."

I smile, leaning back in my seat. "Sloane Penner."

My stomach rolls before I understand why. I probably should have thought up a fake name.

I suck at hiding.

Her face lights right up. "It's nice to meet you. How long are you staying?" She moves her purse onto her lap, then pulls out a water bottle and takes a drink.

"I'm not sure yet. We have the rest of the summer, so we're taking it day by day."

"Where are you from?"

Her questions are so innocent, and it warms my heart. It's hard to meet friends as an adult, especially when you're at home raising a child. There are no work functions, happy-hour drinks, or chitchat around the watercooler. It's hard to find people to connect with and enjoy. I've done my fair share of circling playgrounds looking for some grown-up conversation.

Still, I can't tell her the whole truth.

"California."

Her eyebrows knit together in confusion when she says, "Oh, I noticed your plates yesterday—from Washington." She points up to the sky to indicate the state above us, not the state of California below.

I really suck at hiding.

"Right. I haven't changed them over yet. We moved out there earlier this year." I change the subject to anything that isn't me. "How do you like the neighborhood?"

Her lip twitches before she pinches them together. "I like it. People are nice." The smile on her face doesn't meet her eyes. "My husband, he travels a lot for work. Most of the kids in the area are older—high school, so the playgrounds are usually empty. Is your partner visiting with you?"

I could elaborate and weave an even bigger lie, but my

intention isn't to deceive this woman who looks like she just wants to make a friend.

"No. It's just the two of us." I smile at Henry playing with his new friends. Cora pulls into her driveway across the street, and I stand. "Speaking of which. I should get going." I don't want to brush her off or leave her to control the goodbye, so I continue, "Irene, it was so nice to meet you. I do hope we'll see you out here again on the playground."

I wait for her to agree then turn to the kids. "Henry, time to go. Dinner."

By the time we cross the street, Cora has already been into the house with one set of grocery bags, and I join her at the trunk to help her carry in another as she tells me she grabbed some food from the restaurant for dinner tonight.

Glancing over her shoulder at the playground, she side-eyes me. "That's not keeping a low profile."

"I know. I wasn't expecting her to approach me. She's nice though—seems a little lonely. She's harmless."

Cora huffs at my answer. "Lonely housewives are anything but harmless."

She cuts the conversation short when she slams the trunk and turns to walk inside, but she falters in her step, looking across the street with a scowl.

I follow her line of sight to see Irene watching us. When we both stop to look, she waves.

As I wave back, Cora plasters a disingenuous grin on her face and speaks through gritted teeth. "If you've brought the neighborhood watch to my doorstep I'll have to move. I worked hard to perfect my unapproachability."

Dropping my hand, I turn to her, trying to hold a serious expression. "You had to work on that?"

Shaking her head, she smirks then mutters, "Just like your mother."

I was going to joke some more, but the similarity she drew between my mother and me sends a happy feeling through me, and I follow her into the house with a grin on my face to enjoy it a little longer.

Once inside, she locks the door and draws the blinds, then joins me in the kitchen. I don't want to snoop too much, so I take the groceries that should go in the fridge and put them away.

She pushes the other bags to the side of the counter and opens a paper bag, pulling out food containers and setting them on the counter.

The smell of barbecue is the first thing I notice when she opens the first container. It looks like ribs.

"Is he hungry?" She nods her head toward the living room, and I answer without looking.

"Not right now. His favorite show is on. Maybe in about half an hour." I fidget with my hands for a few seconds longer. "Hey, can we talk?"

"Sure. Grab a chair. I've been on my feet all day." She takes her seat at the table, and I sit in the one across from her.

"Have you—heard anything?"

"I'm not as close to the flow of information as I used to be. People are speculating, and they are definitely looking for you, but I don't think anyone knows where you are."

"How can you be so sure?"

"Well, for starters, I don't have four Saint boys standing outside my front door threatening to kick it down." I smile at the thought. "In all seriousness though, none of those boys are in Portland. I would know. Cole usually drops by the restaurant when he's in."

"What do you think I should do?"

Cora winces at my question, sucking air in through gritted

teeth. This isn't going to be an easy answer. "I've been thinking about that ever since you called."

"Do I have options?"

Cora nods to answer my question, but the expression on her face makes me nervous.

"Okay then, what are they?"

"Well, you could leave. Try to run and stay hidden."

"But?"

"But then you don't stop running. Henry doesn't stop moving around, and you lose touch with everyone you know. You keep lying and pretending to be someone you're not. Maybe you stay hidden, but eventually someone might find you. Traffic stop, medical records, DNA...who knows how, but it may expose you. It might be best if you choose who you end up with."

"And who are you thinking? Should I go back?"

Cora breaks away from my gaze as she answers. "No."

When I stare at her for a moment too long, she explains, "God help me, I love those boys, but if you go back to them now, you will bring both sides of a war right to their doorstep. I know the Saints, and once they have you and that little boy back, they will fight to keep you with them. They are strong, and they can fight, but they can't survive if they are fighting everyone."

Everything she's saying makes sense.

If I return now, I'll be exposed. Ryder will be told to hand me over, and I know him: he promised Grayson he'd protect me, and he'll refuse. It won't end well.

"And the two sides of Elia's organization. Can you tell me about them?"

Judging by the way Cora nods in resignation, she definitely has some idea of who they are.

"Not many people know this, but the two men vying for

control of Elia's legacy are actually brothers. I've seen Cole and Dagen in the restaurant recently speaking with one of them—Creed. The conversation was tense, but it seems as though they are trying to align themselves with his side. I'm going to stop right here and say I think it's the better of the two groups. Creed's brother, Ratchet, is a crazy piece of work—like, certifiable. I keep in touch with some of the girls who worked for Elia, and I hear things, none of them good. If I had to bet my life on one side, it would be Creed's. He's more open to negotiations, and the way he runs his men reminds me of the brothers." I know she's talking about Ryder, Cole, Dagen, and Lennox.

A sense of dread washes over me as she lays it all out.

This is it.

Henry's giggle snaps both of us out of our conversation, and we glance at him clapping his hands in time with a character on the television.

I can't run forever, and I can't do that to Henry.

My mother had the right idea when she decided to fight for me, and now I need to do that for my son.

The longer I hide away, the more everyone will want to rally around me, and I won't put anyone I care about in any more danger.

I turn back to Cora, forcing the words out of my mouth before I chicken out. "And how would I get in touch with Creed?"

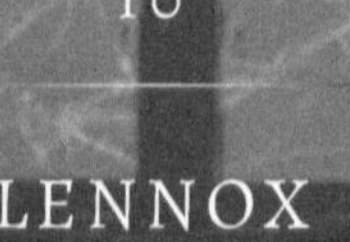

10

LENNOX

I was up early the next morning, beating everyone to the dining room, even the serving staff.

Yuri was the first to join me, following the employees into the house when they'd started their shift and were looking for a cup of coffee.

He told me that there was no activity on Sloane's number, so Cole's guy has nothing to trace yet. Then Cole joined us, and everyone else trickled in.

The fact that we were organizing instead of sitting around gave me hope—until the whole day went by with no updates.

My patience wore thin, and I had Cole check in with his tech team three times to make sure they actually knew what they were doing.

Yesterday I woke up without news for the second morning in a row, a little worse for wear. The rundown was pretty much a garbled carbon copy of the day before.

I promised Cole I wouldn't go out on my own, but I couldn't sit still, so we drove by Sloane's parents' house a second time, then we stopped in at Henry's day care—nothing.

Then, when I snapped at our security team, Ryder took me out to all of the places he and Amara used to go with Sloane. Outside of my brothers and the women in the house, Sloane doesn't appear to have any close friends she can turn to. Our little group seems to be it for her, so when I went to bed last night, my head and my heart wouldn't let me close my eyes.

Not only did I fight my demons, but I battled my worst fears and did everything I could to keep the thoughts that they were both already dead far out of my head.

I ran the perimeter of our property until my lungs felt like they would seize up, then I swam laps in the pool until the night security team threatened to wake my brothers to come out and put me down.

I was tempted to wander into the house to drink myself away, but that would have been a kindness. A drunken binge would have numbed my heart and dulled the pain I deserve to feel.

When the sun rose this morning, another day without her, my body gave out. Cole was right: I'm no use to anyone like this. I set the alarm on my phone to grant myself five hours of sleep, and I finally closed my eyes.

Now, I'm sitting in my father's old office in front of a laptop. We were able to hack into Sloane's email, and I'm scanning what little social media she has and going through all of the people in her friends list for possible leads.

Dagen and Nyla are expected back in a few hours. Because of the weekend, it took an extra two days to get their documents to them so they could cross the border. Dagen sounded like he was happy to have the time with Nyla, but I know he's worried about Sloane and Henry since he's been calling no less than ten times a day for updates.

He's been working with Nyla around the clock to try to

track Sloane, and they are looking forward to getting back here to pick up her trail.

Cole had his Dark Webb guy trace the money that left her parents' account, but it was a dead end. The check was cashed and turned into multiple drafts in smaller denominations along with a large cash withdrawal. It should have been easy enough to find her by her identification, but so far it looks like she hasn't checked into a hotel anywhere along the western seaboard.

She also hasn't left the country although her parents have. They crossed over into Canada two days ago and boarded a flight to the Virgin Islands. I've been assured they went alone, but all flights to the same destination are being closely monitored.

I shake my head, closing the tab on another "friend" in Sloane's list. I don't see the point of these stupid apps. Why would you want to keep track of the people you no longer talk to? I don't give a shit what Sally from second grade is up to these days.

Harlow is the only one who agrees with me on this subject. Amara argues that they are useful for maintaining work relationships, and Ryder and Cole say they are great for gathering intel, which is the only thing I agree with. I really think Sloane approved these friend requests just to be nice. She doesn't even post on here. To prove my point, I click on another name, and it looks like this guy has dedicated his page to trashing his second wife, who left him over a year ago.

Ryder and Cole are in the office with me, going over our next steps. We haven't reached out to Creed yet, but he hasn't tried to contact us either, and we're sure he knows who the heir is. We would be stupid to think he hasn't put it all together. By now, he's realized that Ryder's fake fiancée is his ticket to Lucciano's entire crime syndicate.

Everything from here on out needs to be handled with care.

Movement out of the corner of my eye catches my attention, and I freeze as my brothers continue talking among themselves, oblivious to what's happening.

Sloane is alive.

My heart thuds into my chest. The sound of blood rushing with each beat fills my ears and drowns out the room around me.

My phone is propped up in a charging dock beside my computer screen, and I have it permanently turned on and facing me for this exact reason.

My last text message to Sloane has gone unanswered for three days—until now.

Those three dots started dancing in the lower corner just seconds ago.

"She's texting." My voice is low, as though I'll spook her away if I speak too loudly, but both of my brothers hear me and stop talking. I wasn't clear, and they aren't sure what I'm talking about, so I elaborate. "It's Sloane. She's typing."

Both of my brothers move at the same time. Cole jumps up, trips over his feet, then runs out of the room, no doubt trying to contact his team to have her phone traced. Ryder circles the desk to my side.

"Peach." He mutters the word, and I silently chastise myself for leaving it up.

That name is mine and only mine.

He must sense my discomfort because he doesn't push it.

I count the seconds in my head, not knowing how long she needs to stay online before we get an address. The dots appear, then stop, then start again. Then finally they are gone, and there is no message.

"What the?" Ryder pulls his phone out of his pocket and checks his text messages. "She's not texting me."

A minute of no dots later, footsteps thud down the staircase at a fast pace, and Amara bursts into the room, holding her phone out. "She just texted."

Ryder and I round opposite sides of the desk and meet Amara in the middle of the room, looking at her screen.

Sloane: We're safe, but I need time. I'll message when I'm ready.

Her message was quickly followed by a response from Amara, asking her where she is and telling her she misses them both so much.

So far, that message shows as undelivered, and I assume Sloane turned her phone off after she hit send.

I'm curious about what she would have written to me, and I walk back to the desk, take my seat, and retrieve my phone, checking my messages one last time.

The dots are gone.

Bitterness hits me like a slap to the face, and I need to remind myself that only one of us knows about the forged letter she thinks was written by me. Of course she would respond to Amara, her son's aunt who she has gotten close to. Amara has probably messaged her nonstop for days.

Knowing that Sloane tried to message me says a lot, and I'm glad I saw it before she stopped and messaged Amara instead. She's seen my message, and, as far as I know, I'm the first person she tried to respond to in three days. The fact that she wishes to talk is a good sign.

We sit around for another five minutes before Cole returns to the room. I sneer bitterly when I see his defeated expression, and Ryder groans beside me when Cole says, "There wasn't enough time to trace it."

Amara tries to be helpful, showing Cole her phone as though she holds the missing piece to the puzzle in her hands.

He pacifies her with the hint of a smile, and her face falls when he explains that our team is trying to triangulate Sloane's phone, but she powered it off too fast.

I wish Dagen and Nyla were back already, as I'm sure they'd have ways around this.

I return to my seat at the desk and check my phone. My last message to Sloane mocks me. I consider sending another one, but I fist my texting fingers and refrain.

The silence in the room has reached a new level of awkward, even for me. Ryder thanks Amara for coming to us, then dismisses her, and she wastes no time leaving us to our next steps.

I decide now is as good of a time as any and forewarn my brothers. "As soon as we know where they are, I'm going after them."

"*We* are going after them," Ryder corrects me, and Cole levels me with a curt glare that tells me he agrees with our youngest brother as Ryder stands firm. "Amara and I have already discussed it. I'll be going with you."

When I look at Ryder, I still see the little boy who loved pizza night and used to run around in a onesie with safari animals all over it. I open my mouth to suggest that maybe I should wait and go with Dagen instead, but Ryder holds up his hand, demanding the floor.

"I promised Grayson, Lennox." Ryder jabs at his chest before pointing off into the distance. "I promised my best friend, before our father murdered him, that I would take care of Sloane if anything ever happened to him, and that includes Henry. Henry—who, by the way, is me and my wife's nephew. I am going with you." His last sentence is spoken as both an ultimatum and a threat.

How did I miss all of this? My brothers grew into men, and I've lost out on so much of their lives. The baby of the family got married, and I wasn't there to stand beside him on his own wedding day.

"Okay," I answer as Ryder sucks in a deep breath, ready to verbally spar with me.

"I'm not backing down, Lennox. I—" He snaps his mouth shut and looks at Cole, as if to confirm what he just heard. Cole only shrugs, sending him back to me. "What?"

"Settle down. I said okay. I need your help, Ryder."

My admission is new to both of my brothers, and they freeze in place, no doubt trying to commit this rare moment to memory.

"Okay then." Ryder looks around the room, unsure of what to do with the argument he no longer has a use for.

Cole takes a seat in front of me, propping his boots on the desk and crossing his legs at his ankles. "So what do we do now? All we know is where she's not—and that's *here*, for anyone who isn't paying attention. Unless she logs in again, we won't be able to pick up her location."

As if there is a digital god lost somewhere in cyberspace, the answer comes to me in the form of a social media notification that dings on Sloane's account, and I look at the screen sitting on the desk between us.

A new friend request.

I click on the person who sent the request only seconds ago —then my fire is back with the strength of a thousand raging infernos.

"It doesn't matter." My lips curl into a wicked grin. "I think we've got her."

My brothers flank my chair as they join me and huddle around to see what I'm pointing at.

Cole reaches over me, quickly going to work, and I let him have at it. I know nothing about how these social media accounts work.

Within a minute, he has the woman's address, then he opens a map. He inputs the address, moves the screen around, and enlarges a few things before dropping his head and shaking it in disappointment, mumbling a profanity to himself.

I exchange a glance with Ryder before asking Cole, "Do you know who lives there?"

He stands up with a heavy, resigned breath and shakes his head.

"No. But I know who lives two blocks over."

11

SLOANE

Cora and I went back and forth for an hour after I asked for a way to contact Creed. We revisited my other options, and they were all still bad ideas.

She assured me that going to Creed would—at the very least—keep me alive and protect Ryder and his brothers if I handled it properly.

Elia treated Creed like his own son, which is why it was odd to me that he didn't just leave everything to him to begin with.

Cora told me that Ratchet would use any means necessary to take control of Elia's business. She shuddered when she said that included publicly executing Elia's heir to force a sway in loyalty.

That sealed the deal for me.

She was able to find Creed's number through her contacts, and we agreed I would call him from a pay phone twenty minutes from Cora's house.

Doing this means that Cora won't be brought into my mess. She tried to come with me, but I turned her down, telling her that I needed her to protect Henry for me because I'm not taking him anywhere near this.

Saying goodbye felt like it might be final, and I hugged him tight. I told him I was running an errand and that Cora was going to look after him. None of it fazed him.

Then I pulled out an envelope of cash I'd been holding on to for the last few days and stuffed it into Cora's hand with instructions: if I didn't come back, take Henry to Ryder and Amara in the morning.

When she tried to refuse the money, I shook my head with a smile that I know held no joy. I told her she could give it back to me when she saw me again, and she finally relented.

I know Henry is safe, and he doesn't cross my mind during my drive to find a pay phone.

Who does cross my mind surprises me a little.

Over the years, I had become so good at handling rogue thoughts of Lennox that I could push them down with a smile in seconds, but for the last few days, it seems like he's all I think about. I had kicked him out of my heart, and with three simple words in a text message, he blew my walls down and reclaimed his spot.

Once I was sure I was far enough from Cora's place, I made the call. I told the guy who answered that I had information about Elia's heir, and that got me through to Creed in less than a minute.

His tone through the whole conversation was tense, and I declined his offer of sending someone to retrieve me. I had already discussed this with Cora, and we agreed it was best if I had access to my own vehicle.

The whole experience of negotiating my entry to the property was harrowing. I had to fight to keep my phone and drive onto the property with my own vehicle. It wasn't until I told them to double-check their procedures with Creed, because I was about to get in my car and drive away, that they dialed the main house and I got permission to continue on.

The house is massive, and it still sits like a speck on the land around it. The road leading up to the home from the front gate runs over a small lake that isn't crossable without some type of boat. It isn't until I reach the other side that I realize there is a second gate, where they are ready for me, waving me through as I approach.

Creed definitely didn't want to lose his chance at meeting with me.

An older woman holds up her hand, calling me toward her when I enter the driveway near the mansion before pointing to a spot beside the grand front steps.

Cora and I had also agreed that I'd turn my phone on and send a text message to myself once I arrived, so that my phone would ping off of the cell towers in the area and place me on his property—which is exactly what I do before I step out of my car.

"Leave it there." She looks at my car, then smiles at me. "He's expecting you. Follow me."

Her pleasantries do nothing to settle my nerves, and I swallow the anxiety threatening to surge up my throat.

People, most of them men, falter in their step when they look up at me as the woman leads me through the stately rooms.

She stops in front of two large doors, bracing herself to open them at the same time before turning to usher me through. I take a few steps into the room when I realize she isn't joining me, and I turn to face her.

She simply smiles that same generic smile and steps back, pulling the doors closed with her as she says, "Have a seat. He will retrieve you shortly."

I stare at the door for a few seconds longer before I turn to take in the large room I'm in. I would say, by the looks of the couches and chairs everywhere, that this is a sitting room. Men in expensive suits gather in clusters all around me, but none of them look too welcoming. They take me in, size me up, then return to their conversations like I'm a prop in the room.

I could take a seat like the woman suggested, but I already feel completely out of my element, so I stand and continue to look around.

After a few minutes, I start to think that taking a seat is probably a better idea than standing in front of the doorway when a loud voice from the back of the room bellows, "Elia's blood is present. Show some fucking respect."

The conversations stop.

Everyone in the room stands and looks toward the voice.

A man a little older than Lennox stands still at the back of the room, his eyes burning into my own.

Then, one by one, everyone in the room around us follows his line of sight, and they turn to look at me.

It isn't until all eyes are on me and I have everyone's attention that the man approaches me. His face is relaxed, confident. His suit fits him well, but it doesn't entirely hide the wolf in sheep's clothing I sense lurking just under his surface.

He exudes seduction as he crosses the room, but the reverence everyone shows him tells me he's earned their respect and fear.

A hint of a tattoo peeks out from the collar of his crisp black shirt, and I lower my gaze to more ink on his hands.

"Sloane. It's a pleasure to finally meet you. I'm Creed." I nod, indicating the feeling is mutual even though it isn't. He smiles, then steps back, holding out a hand to guide me by my lower back as he talks. "Come. We have some things to discuss."

He leads me through the sitting area and out the door at the back. As we pass the men, they turn, keeping their bodies squared on the two of us in silence as we cross the room.

As soon as I clear the last step through the threshold into the hall, the conversation picks up as though nothing happened.

The next room is much smaller than the one I was just in, and I find the lack of open space comforting.

A thin, balding man stands off to the side of the room, holding something in his hands, but I don't linger on him for long. This man has a sheen of sweat on his forehead, and I feel like I could rattle him if I tried.

No. The biggest predator in the room is Creed.

He rounds the desk, lifting a folder then returning to join me, motioning toward a leather couch with his free hand.

Opening the file, he scans the pages, looking up to meet my gaze a couple of times.

"I know you did not know your father, but you have my deepest sympathies and the condolences of everyone here."

He doesn't continue talking. Instead, he pauses, waiting for me to accept his words. I clear my throat and mumble, "Th-thank you."

Satisfied with my response, he looks at the sheet in his hands. "Your name is Sloane Benson." It's a statement, not a question.

He's also looking at me like he knows it's not.

"It—um, it's Sloane Penner." Creed takes a hard look at me, and I speak quickly to recover. "My mom. I didn't know she was my mother until recently. My aunt and her husband raised me."

He inhales slowly, deep in thought. "And your birth mother —Selina Benson—do you know what name she went by when she was employed by Elia Lucciano?"

I do know this, but only because Cora shared it with me a couple of days ago. "Yes. Her name was Valentina."

Without taking his eyes off me, Creed tilts his head toward the other man in the room, and I watch as the man pulls his phone out of his pocket and types something before returning to his statuesque pose.

"You understand. We need to verify that you are Elia's daughter."

I want to ask how they will go about that, but Creed has already waved the man over, and he joins us. He opens the little box he was holding and fumbles with a swab, taking one step toward me.

Creed reaches out his hand, blocking his path, and glares at him. "Manners."

The man straightens instantly, taking half a step back, and Creed turns to me.

"Are you willing to provide a DNA sample? We can have this all cleared up in a few hours."

I don't want to ask how they'll be able to get results that fast. I'm pretty sure these guys could wipe someone from the face of this earth in half that time.

"Uh, sure."

A fleeting sense of kindness passes from Creed when he smiles this time. He curls two fingers at the man, allowing him to approach and try again.

As I open my mouth and he takes the sample he needs, Creed explains why they have to take these precautions, and I make noises around the little piece of cotton scraping along the inside of my cheeks.

When the sample is secure, Creed sends the man out of the room, leaving us alone for the first time, and he visibly relaxes.

Creed reminds me of Lennox in his approach, and I

imagine that, given another five to ten years, Lennox could be his twin in terms of intimidation level.

"You must have questions for me."

I have a lot of questions, but I'm not sure which ones will keep me on his good side.

"Well—okay—why didn't Mr. Lucciano just leave everything to you? I mean, I can't be a better option to run—this." I point around the room.

This makes him smile, and he stands, walking to a cabinet along the wall and reaching for a bottle and a glass. "Drink?"

"No, thank you." I wring my fingers around each other before deciding to settle them, and I change my mind. "Actually, I'll have a small glass."

Creed looks at the drink in his hand and chuckles to himself. "I have a nice Malbec." He reaches into the cupboard above him and pulls out a wineglass, then retrieves a bottle of red and uncorks it in front of me, pouring a small amount into the glass.

He answers me as he hands me the drink. "Elia's successor must earn their place. Just because you are given the keys to an empire doesn't mean you are deserving of it."

"But it sounds like it was given to me." I push at Creed a little to see where I stand.

His grin is victorious. It's the smirk of someone who already knows they've won the game.

"It was given to his next *male* heir." Creed looks right through me and into my soul with his comment. I'm sure I've just turned two shades paler. "And we both know Elia has a male heir."

Henry.

Creed lets me sit with his threat for a long minute. Nothing about him has changed, and I start to think that maybe I should have chosen a life on the run.

Adjusting his jacket, Creed leans back in his chair, sliding his free hand along the back and crossing his ankle over his knee.

This man lives in chaos.

The worse it gets for me, the more relaxed he becomes.

I don't have it in me to sit here like a pet and be cordial any longer.

"My son is off the table."

"Right now he is," Creed agrees, scanning my face for a reaction. I don't give him one, and he uncrosses his legs. Leaning forward, he braces his elbows on his thighs and holds his drink with both hands. "As I was saying: Elia's successor must earn their place—and I intend to. My...rival has ways of taking control that I prefer not to entertain. A kingdom won by force is never as strong as one earned through honor and integrity. It will always be in danger of falling as soon as another self-serving tyrant comes along. I prefer to claim my place the hard way: by earning the loyalty and respect of everyone around me."

I take a larger sip of my wine than I expect to. A few drops escape down the wrong pipe, and I cough to clear my throat before I say, "You sound like you have this all figured out."

He shrugs. "Tell me, Sloane. What do you want?"

"What do you mean?"

He waves his hand around the room like I did earlier. "All of this can be yours." Lowering his eyes down my body, he continues, "I know what I want, Sloane. I'm willing to work with you so we both get what we want. So what is it that you want?"

This is my chance to pull Henry and myself out of this disaster. I down my wine in one gulp. This time, I don't choke on anything. "I want everyone to leave my son and me alone, and I want all of the people I love to be safe."

Creed looks me solemnly in the eyes. "I wish it were that easy for you, I really do, but we have a mutual problem: Sebastian Saint, and he won't stop coming for you and yours until someone makes him stop."

At first I think I don't hear him correctly.

"What does Ryder's dad have to do with this?"

"Your fiancé's father is the one who is fighting to take over Elia's organization."

I shake my head. "That isn't right. I was told it was your broth—someone named Ratchet."

Creed raises an eyebrow at my slip up, but he looks impressed that I've done my homework. "Ratchet is working for Sebastian. I thought Ryder and his brothers would have told you all of this." He monitors my face closely as he talks.

I want to hide my emotions away, but I fail miserably when what Creed is saying sinks in.

The Saints have been keeping things from me.

When it takes me too long to continue the conversation, Creed moves from his chair to sit beside me on the couch. He grabs a remote control off the side table and points it at the wall. A shelf splits open, showing a hidden television, and he plays a video.

Creed is nothing if not prepared, and I wonder what else he has to show me to sway me to join his side.

The video has no sound, and it looks like a warehouse. I hold my expression tight on my face as I look around for anything I should recognize.

Everything slips away as the time and date stamp count up in the lower corner.

Please, no.

As soon as I see the man enter, my heart knows who it is. I reach over to set my wineglass on the table beside me, and I hear a thud. I must have missed the table, but I can't look away from the screen in front of me.

Grayson.

Standing, I take shaky steps toward the screen so I don't miss a thing.

As I watch Grayson shift around, speaking with someone off to the side, tears roll in a steady stream down my face, and I'm grateful my back is turned to Creed.

Finally, Grayson raises his hands, and he falls to the ground. He doesn't move again.

This was the moment he died.

The video begins to fast-forward on its own, and I spin around on my heels, my voice raised. "Where did you get this?"

Creed stands. It's clear by the shock on his face that he wasn't expecting such an emotional reaction.

"Do you know him?" He points at the screen. His question is genuine.

He showed me this video for another reason, and he has no idea.

"He's the father of my son."

"I'm so sorry. It wasn't my intention to—"

"Wait." I hold my hand up as another man enters the frame. Then I step back when I see it's Lennox. My shock washes over me unexpectedly, and my knees buckle.

I'm moving as fast as I can to recover and peel myself off the carpet, but Creed makes it to me before I stand up, and he wraps his palms around my arms to lift me.

"Lennox—he—no!" I grip Creed right back. This man could snap me in half and toss me in the yard if he wanted to and no one would stop him, but here I am holding on to him for dear life.

The room tilts and spins as every last shred of my sanity slips away.

"Lennox didn't kill that kid. As much as having you believe he did would further my plans, I will not lie to you, Sloane."

"Who killed him, Creed? Who killed Grayson?"

Creed wanted my buy-in. I think he was trying to go about getting it another way, but this was just as effective in making his point.

"Sebastian Saint."

My legs buckle again, but this time Creed anticipates it, and he moves me to the couch to sit me back down before turning off the screen.

"He knew. They all knew who killed him."

Creed gives me a moment to catch my breath, and he walks to his liquor cabinet. When he turns around, I half hope he's holding the rest of the bottle of wine, but it's only water. He breaks the seal, hands it to me, and tells me to take a drink.

"Look. For what it's worth, if those boys didn't tell you about their father, then they must have a damn good reason. Those four are nothing like him. I merely wanted to show you what Sebastian is capable of so you never underestimate him. He will do whatever it takes to gain control of Elia's empire, and that includes using you and your son to do his bidding. Your fiancé's father is never to be trusted."

"He's not my fiancé." When Creed does a double take, I explain. "When Grayson was murdered, we agreed to pretend we were engaged to protect Henry because we didn't know who killed him. But—" I point to the screen, wondering to myself just how long everyone has known.

Creed takes a step closer, placing his hand on my shoulder and squeezing. His compassion feels like a reward for being honest with him.

He lets me sit in silence for a few minutes, and I stare at the television. It's off, but I still see Grayson lying on the ground with Lennox kneeling over him, like the ghosts of their images are burned into the screen.

I shake my head once, snapping myself away from the mental images I'm sure will come back soon enough. Then I take a few sips of water and look up at Creed.

"What's your plan?"

12

LENNOX

As soon as Cole told me who lived two blocks away from the address on the computer, everything made sense.

Cora worked with both Elia and our father. She was their madam, taking care of the women who worked for them, and she definitely would have crossed paths with Sloane's mother at some point.

Cora kept her nose clean, and she knew how to stay off everyone's radar.

I used to think she was opportunistic, that her motives seemed self-serving, like everyone else in my father's circle, until the night she overheard something she shouldn't have, and she came to me.

It was the night she heard that our father hired someone to kill Cole.

She could have kept her head down and her mouth shut, but she didn't.

After that, I realized she was just trying to survive like most of the people under my father's thumb.

When I took over Eros, my father had no legitimate excuse for keeping a madam around. Eventually, I took Cora from him in my management deal. So if he's still running women under the table, it is now without her help. I don't think she would have agreed to do it anyway. She seemed to care about the women she worked with. If she had stayed, she would have refused, and she'd most likely now just be another missing person in a sea of forgotten souls, and she damn well knows this.

I took Cora away from Sebastian, and I pushed her even farther from him when I set her up to work for Cole in Portland. It was my way of repaying her for putting herself on the line to save my brother.

And this is what I get for it.

I'm not upset she took Sloane and Henry in when Sloane felt she had nowhere else to go—that was the right thing to do. I'm disappointed she didn't call any of us earlier to come out and help her, and I'm pissed that I have to go to her.

We decided not to wait for Dagen and Nyla to arrive home before leaving to bring Sloane back. They are half an hour away, and I need one of my brothers to be at the house to watch Amara and Harlow.

Once Cole realized where we were going, his decision was made.

Cole is fond of Cora, and he's hurt as well that she didn't come to him. He also wants to make sure she cooperates once we get there because he's seen my control slipping over the last few days, and he's worried about her.

No one cares to speak during the drive to Portland, and that's fine by me.

Ryder grabbed the keys, and Cole called shotgun.

I stretched out across the back seat and closed my eyes. Once everything was blocked out, I could think about Sloane.

When I first told Sloane our family owned a sex club, I wasn't prepared for her reaction. I half expected her to withdraw from our conversation. I thought this would end my odd attraction to her, but she surprised me.

I watched her as her eyes scanned the dance floor, hesitantly making their way back to the door that was guarded by a bouncer. Her breathing deepened.

From somewhere dark inside of me, I wanted all of her. I wanted to whisper depraved things to her and watch her shiver as she imagined every one of them. Then I wanted to tie her down and play with her body until she begged me to fuck her.

One after another, kinks I hadn't entertained were lining up in my head as new things I wanted to explore with Sloane, each one dirtier than the last.

I was lost in her, and there was no way out.

I also was not about to let her go without understanding I was laying claim, so I set a rule for her.

I told her she wasn't allowed at Eros without me. It was both an invitation and a challenge, one she bravely accepted a few short months later, when she found me in the club one night.

I had been waiting for her, wondering if her thoughts about what was down there went into the gutter and if she would ever be willing to follow me down those steps. I was a walking board, my dick stiff as a pole from the anticipation alone.

I craved my little brother's friend with an intensity I had never felt before. When she came back to me, shyly asking if she could see what it was all about, I stood in silence, looking her up and down with my drink in hand.

By then she had turned twenty-one. She, Grayson, and Ryder had celebrated all of their birthdays at the club the weekend before—with their real IDs this time. Her age didn't matter. Sloane was still both forbidden and everything I've ever wanted all wrapped into one.

I watched her closely as I asked, "Have you been fucked?"

It was mostly a test, because no matter how badly I wanted to strap her to a cross downstairs, it was still important to me that she took what happened below with the respect it (and everyone there) deserved.

She humbled the expression on her face as she answered, "Yes."

"By him?" I tilt my head to Grayson, who was standing at the bar on the lower level.

She nibbled on her bottom lip, her gaze following my own. "No. Not—um..."

"Yet" was the word I sensed she was leaving off her answer. They were starting to notice each other. I could tell by the way he looked around for her when she left his side at the club.

I checked my watch.

It was just after midnight.

Leaning close enough that I could smell her over the air around us, I exhaled a warm breath into her ear before I spoke, and she shuddered.

"Tell your friends that you're tired and you've decided to go home for the night. The bar closes at two. Come back just before two thirty, and the bouncer will let you in. Wear that little sundress you wore last weekend—no panties."

I pulled away from her and looked out over the dance floor, taking a sip of the drink in my hand. I desperately wanted to touch her.

She shuffled from foot to foot beside me, and I liked that she didn't know how to play the game. I imagined everything we'd experience together would be that much better because she wouldn't be playing submissive—with her, it would be absolute and visceral.

I gave her one last chance to walk away.

"If you change your mind, it's okay. If I don't see you later, then I'll see you around." I tipped my glass to her in mock cheers.

Sloane stood still, taking everything in, her face void of expression. She briefly lowered her eyes before meeting my gaze and swallowing hard.

She wasn't taking this lightly.

Good.

She walked away without another word and returned to Grayson and Ryder at their table.

A few minutes passed as I watched them from my spot on the second floor. Then she stood and left their group, walking toward the exit.

***

"Hey, wake up. We're almost there." Cole taps my leg from the front seat.

I open my eyes, temporarily relaxed by my thoughts as they dissipate. Then I grimace when I remember where we are.

The neighborhood is quiet when Ryder pulls off the main road and drives down a street lined with single-family homes.

Cole tells Ryder to stop and park a few doors down, and I stretch on the sidewalk as my brothers get out of the car.

An area across the street is lit up, and as we approach Cora's house, a playground appears around a row of trees.

Ryder and I both halt, allowing Cole to lead us up the steps. Out of my brothers, Cora is closest with Cole.

The curtains are drawn, and he knocks three times.

If this is all a mistake and Sloane isn't with Cora, then I'll be walking over to the address of the woman who sent her the friend request next, because I'm not leaving here without her.

Metal slides along metal as the first lock opens. A deadbolt clicks, then another, then the door opens. We're still separated by the screen door.

Cora notices Cole first, but she doesn't look happy to see him.

She looks guilty.

Then her gaze drifts over his shoulder to Ryder and me.

"Cole—b-boys."

She doesn't ask why we're here. Judging by the worry in her eyes, she knows why, and she also knows that feigning ignorance won't be tolerated.

Sloane is in the house, and I settle my demons with the knowledge that she'll be with me soon.

"We need to talk to her, Cora." Cole leads the conversation, and I'm glad he came along.

The moment Cora opened the door, my skin began to crawl. The urgency to see and talk to Sloane bristles across my body.

I have so many things to tell her.

"You—can't."

"Don't make me regret removing you from Sebastian's reach." I've spoken the entire threat before I realize I've said a word, and my brothers glare at me before Cole extends his arm between us, returning to his conversation.

"Cora. We know she's here."

"That's not what I mean." She lowers her attention to the door handle she's playing with.

Henry rustles from the room behind her, and I wonder if he recognizes Cole's voice.

When Ryder hears him, he doesn't wait to be invited in.

Grabbing the handle, he gives Cora a warning glare.

She steps aside.

Ryder leads the way, following the sounds of music into the living room, and Henry calls for him as soon as he rounds the corner in front of me.

Cole hangs back in the entryway with Cora, and I stay with them.

"Cora?" Cole gives her one last chance to get Sloane out here. I'm sure he can sense my demons threatening to break free and search for her myself.

Cora lowers her voice. "She left—she went to speak with Creed."

"SHE WHAT?" I take an aggressive step toward the two of them, and Cole leans between us, blocking me from Cora as she pushes herself into the wall behind her.

Cole turns on me and steps into my space, pushing me against the opposite wall to create distance between us before reaching to the side and closing the front door behind him.

Then he returns to her and tells her to sit down. She takes another glance at me then turns and leads us down the hall, through the living room and into the dining room.

Ryder is sitting on the couch with Henry as we pass by, and Henry is showing him one of his toys. Ryder tips his chin at me, telling us he'll hang back.

Cora waits for Cole and me to take a seat before she chooses her own, and it's the farthest one from mine.

"Cora, did you know all this time?" A combination of hurt and disappointment are mixed into Cole's question.

"I only knew Selina's first name. I wouldn't have been able to lead you to her, but I'm not sure I would have if I could. I owed her for a debt I can never repay."

I ball my hands into fists under the table and shift in my seat. "And you never once thought to send her home to us?"

Ryder joins us as I ask the question, and Cora leans to the side, checking on Henry before answering.

"I did, but there were a couple of reasons she didn't want to." She eyes us all up before deciding to turn her attention to Cole to reason with him. "You know what would happen if she returned to you boys. I know you want to protect her, but you'd be signing your death warrant if you kept her from Creed, and you all know that. At least this way she has some control over what happens next, and you keep your allies."

If it were anyone but Sloane, I would see the sense in what she's saying. I know Cora has always been protective of us, and I wonder if it's because she realized long before we did that our father was a monster.

Still, this is Sloane, and I won't be quick to forgive this indiscretion.

"What was the other reason?"

I think *What?* at the same time Cora says it, and Ryder repeats himself.

"You said there were two reasons Sloane didn't want to return home. What was the other reason?"

I worry for a moment that it was my use of her nickname that made her stay away.

"She—well, she told me all about your fake engagement and your wife—Henry's aunt."

I feel Ryder's impatience when he tries to hurry her along. "What about them?"

"She wasn't sure—she doesn't know if—"

"Cora." Cole leans over the table, threading his fingers together, and she gets the message.

"Sloane feels responsible for the death of Amara's father. She doesn't know how to face any of you with that yet."

I look from Cole to Ryder. Our confused expressions are reflections of each other.

"Amara's dad died of a heart attack." Ryder challenges what she thinks she knows, and Cora shakes her head.

"No. She told me she found out the people she thought were her parents killed him and set it up to make it look like a heart attack when he found out about Selina and tried to blackmail them."

"Shit. I need to talk to Amara," Ryder mutters. Then he walks out of the room, returning to Henry as Cole stands from the table.

"You should have called us, Cora."

"Maybe so," she mumbles without looking me in the eye.

"I'm calling Creed." I stand, leaving them at the table. My phone is in my hand before I leave the house.

I double-check the number on my display when it isn't Creed who answers.

"This is Lennox Saint for Creed."

There's silence on the line before the voice returns. "Creed's in a meeting. He isn't taking any calls tonight. I've informed him that you called."

The line goes dead.

We're being pushed out of this while Creed decides how to handle Sloane. I've been to Elia's a few times, and there's no way we'll be able to waltz right up to their front door and ask Sloane to come home.

Standing in the cool evening air, I let the chill soothe the fire raging inside of me.

Minutes pass, and I'm about to throw my phone across the street when it rings. I flip it over, hoping it's Creed, but a better number pops up on my screen.

"Sloane? Where are you? Are you okay? I'll come and get you. We need to talk." I look at the phone to make sure the line didn't disconnect. The seconds are still counting up. "Sloane?"

"How long have you known that your dad killed Grayson?"

"I knew as soon as I found him." *Over two years ago.*

Pacifying her with pretty lies isn't going to keep her on the line. I really hope Cole's guy is still tracing her number.

"And that he's the one who is after me?"

"We found that out when Dagen was in Canada. Sloane, we need you to come home."

She chokes on a sob when I say the word "home," and it feels like I'm losing her all over again.

I stick my finger in my open ear, blocking out all sound as I push the phone tight against my other ear, listening to her cry under her breath. I used to love listening to her cry under different circumstances.

"I'm sorry," she whispers before she sniffles.

"What are you sorry for?"

She sniffles once more, then slows her tone, barely containing her anger. "I'm going to kill him, Nox. I'm going to burn it all down. I've made a deal with Creed to keep Henry safe. Don't look for me. You won't like what you find."

SLOANE

I've been sitting in my car in front of Elia's estate for a few minutes as a second car idles off to the side, waiting for me to drive away.

Before I left, Creed firmly suggested that Henry and I move into his large home, where he could offer both of us protection.

I told him I would think about it.

If it were just me, I would probably take him up on it, but this is about what's best for Henry.

I would be stupid to think Creed would just let me leave here without keeping tabs on me. Regardless, I know Cora's neighborhood better than his men do, and I'm confident I'll be able to get close enough to her place, then lose them in back alleys and fenced-in yards.

Creed received a message just as I was walking out—Lennox had called, and I thought I should at least talk to him before I drove back to Cora's.

I don't doubt they are trying to figure out where I am by now, and they'll most likely trace my calls. Since I don't know how that works, I'll make the call from here, so Lennox will know I'm telling him the truth when I tell him where I am.

Lennox picks up on the first ring.

"Sloane? Where are you? Are you okay? I'll come and get you. We need to talk."

Everything I want to say catches in my throat as soon as I hear his voice. It has that same dark timbre that once made me weak for him all over.

"Sloane?"

When he says my name a second time, I snap out of it and get to the questions I want to ask.

"How long have you known that your dad killed Grayson?"

He answers as soon as I'm done speaking. "I knew as soon as I found him."

"And that he's the one who is after me?"

"We found that out when Dagen was in Canada. Sloane, we need you to come home."

Hearing Lennox calling me home breaks my heart. There was a time when I only imagined my home being with him.

Tears roll down my face, but I don't make a sound as my hand holding the phone shakes, and my tears soak the collar of my shirt.

"I'm sorry." So much has gone wrong, and I'm not sure if I'm apologizing for what I've done or what I'm about to do.

"What are you sorry for?"

The image of Grayson being shot and stumbling back is on a loop in my head, and everything else turns dark as I picture Mr. Saint, all of these years, alive and walking around like Grayson's life never mattered.

That smug bastard worked Grayson's funeral without a care in the world, knowing he was the one who'd ended his life.

I take a deep breath and cut my ties.

"I'm going to kill him, Nox. I'm going to burn it all down.

I've made a deal with Creed to keep Henry safe. Don't look for me. You won't like what you find."

I power off my phone and toss it onto the seat beside me before I back up and drive out the way I came in, this time with a tail that doesn't bother to hide that it's there.

Creed and his men are working on a plan to draw Sebastian and Ratchet out of hiding and deal with everyone in his inner circle. Once Creed assumes his place at the head of Elia's organization, it will be restructured, and he's agreed to release Henry and me from any obligations while we maintain his full protection.

Until then, we all have a part to play.

Now that Creed has paraded me through his home as Elia's heir, word will get to Ratchet that I am no longer in Seattle, and everyone I care about should be left alone.

I revisit our entire conversation as I drive back to Cora's. I know Creed allowed me to leave, and he's only humoring me by giving me a day to consider his offer to move to Elia's estate. I can't imagine he will continue to allow me to roam freely while Sebastian is still out there.

I don't want to think about what it would mean for me if I were to fall into his hands.

I park three streets away from Cora's, and the car that was tailing me pulls in behind a pickup truck a few cars back. I walk with purpose up the sidewalk and slip through the gate at the side, hoping the owners of this house don't have a guard dog in the yard.

A block from Cora's, I decide to turn my phone on to see if Lennox sent me a message after I hung up on him.

There is nothing, not even from Amara, which is surprising, and I wonder if she's been instructed not to contact me anymore.

"Peach" is still the last thing on my screen from Lennox. It picks at the scabs on my heart and plays with my head, reminding me of the night he gave me that name.

I drag my feet the last half a block, trying to clear my head. My adrenaline has been heightened ever since I made the decision to go to Creed and turn myself in before he found out where I was and just took me.

Going to him first is why I have the limited freedom to come back to Henry tonight.

Using the key Cora gave me, I let myself in. The house is quiet, but the lights are on, and I walk through the living room, pausing when I round the corner to find Cora sitting quietly sipping a cup of tea.

At first, I don't understand her when she says, "Ryder, Cole, and Lennox were just here. They took Henry."

"What?" I'm already out of the room when I ask the question. I rush to the little bedroom we've been sharing.

He's gone.

When I return to Cora, the woman looks wrecked.

"How did they know?" I turn and storm into the living room, ripping the front curtains open as though I'll still see them driving down the street.

"They didn't say. They showed up, and I told them you went to see Creed. They were mad, but I thought it was under control. They said they wanted you to come home. I'm sorry, dear. I told them why you thought you couldn't. Ryder said to tell you it isn't your fault. They just want you to return to them. Lennox stepped outside—said he was going to call Creed. When he came back in, something changed. He pulled Ryder aside, whispered something in his ear, then they were packing Henry up. Lennox said to tell you that Henry is safe, they are taking him home, and he's expecting you."

By the time she's done talking, I've somehow sat down in a chair across from her.

This is all my fault.

Lennox was here at the house when I spoke to him on the phone. I told him that I took a deal with Creed. I may as well have come right out and dared him to take Henry away from me.

I pull my phone out, ready to hit redial, but I can't.

I don't know if it's my pride or the fact that I know it won't bring Henry back to me right now. No matter which brother I call, they'll all be on the same page. If they weren't, then they would have still been sitting here fighting about it when I walked in tonight.

They've all taken Henry, and I know it's because he's family to them, but I'm his mother, and I can't lose him. Knowing he'll be with Amara is the only thing keeping me from going off the deep end.

"I need to go and figure this out. I don't know when I'll be back." I look around the room, then at the bag in my hand.

Cora looks rattled. "Lennox is not to be messed with," she says with unblinking eyes.

Don't I know it?

When I left, I thought I was so far removed from his life and thoughts. I was prepared to handle Ryder and his other brothers, but now Lennox has made it his mission to have me under his thumb, and he is relentless when he sets his sights on something.

I thank Cora for taking us in and for trying to keep Henry safe. There is no fighting any of the Saints on this, and I know there was nothing she could do.

Palming my keys in my free hand, I turn to let myself out. Cora steps into my path, pulling me in for a tight hug before telling me to stay safe and return to her if I need anything.

She doesn't let go until I promise, then I tell her to lock up behind me, and I see myself out.

I take the first alley and make it almost the whole way down when my emotions boil over, and I have to stop walking just so I can breathe.

I lean against the cool stucco of a garage and wipe my tears with my shirt. My phone rings, and I do a double take at the number. Mrs. Saint rarely calls me. While we have a great relationship, it's usually Ryder that she texts, and I wonder if she's having a momentary lapse with her Alzheimer's.

"Hello?"

"Ah, Sloane. There you are." Mr. Saint's voice sounds like nails on a chalkboard now. "We've been worried about you." His tone doesn't match his words.

"I know you killed Grayson."

He's quiet on the other end of the line for close to a minute, and I stand waiting in the shadows of the alley.

"Yes. That was unfortunate." Mr. Saint lacks the empathy to support his words. "Is that what you and Creed have been discussing?"

How does he know I went to Creed? I look up and down the alley to make sure no one is stalking me.

His question must have been rhetorical because he continues, "Sloane, we're going to be family. Kristianne and I miss you and Henry. We should catch up."

"We're not coming anywhere near you, you bastard."

Mr. Saint laughs on the other end of the line. It holds no humor. His chuckle is dark and disgusting.

"You cannot keep my grandson from me."

My defenses slip, and I blurt, "He's not your grandson. Henry isn't Ryder's."

It's obvious by his silence that he didn't expect to hear that.

"Ah! This makes things easier then. You should reconsider which side you'd like to align yourself with. I can—"

"I'm aligning myself with the side that wants you dead."

"You're going to regret—"

I've already hung up on one Saint today. Why not make it two?

I close my eyes and concentrate on the sound of the traffic from the freeway a few blocks over.

I can't go back to Seattle now. Everyone is better off if I stay away.

I dial the number Creed made me add into my phone earlier.

The line connects on the first ring, and the man on the line puts me through right away.

"Sloane. Is everything okay?"

I continue walking toward my car. "Yes—um, no. I need—I don't know what to do."

There's a commotion on the line.

"Are my men there?"

"Kind of. I parked a few blocks away. I didn't want the person I was staying with to get in trouble."

"So my men are watching a house that you aren't in?"

"Well—yes."

I think he's chuckling on the other end of the line. It's hard to tell.

"I don't need a DNA test. I'll be surprised if you aren't Elia's kid. Are you able to get to my men?"

"Yes. I'm walking there now."

"Stay on the line until you get there."

"Creed, I just got a call from Sebastian. He knows I was with you tonight."

He exhales a deep breath. "Yeah. We're still cleaning up around here. Thanks for letting me know. I'll have our security pull up the cell records for this evening. We'll find out who made the call."

It's the unspoken understanding of what will happen to their traitor that makes me falter in my step.

"Oh, okay." I reach my car and look back to the vehicle that followed me. "I see them."

Creed speaks to someone else in the room with him, saying, "Do they see her?" Then he returns to me as I watch the man in the passenger's side get out of the car. "You'll ride back with them. If you want to bring your car, just give your keys to my guy, and he'll drive it. Come home, Sloane. I'll see you soon."

14

LENNOX

Just because I let Sloane go doesn't mean I haven't been watching her all of these years.

I saw how happy she was with Grayson. He made her his priority, and he never took her for granted. I would have stepped back into her life if he had.

I watched from the shadows as her world shattered when Grayson died, all the time hating myself for not getting to the warehouse sooner.

Keeping what I knew about the night Grayson was murdered away from Sloane ate away at my soul, but I never wanted her to agonize any more than she already had. She was in no position to take on my father. I've been preparing my whole adult life to stop him, and I still haven't been able to do it.

Once Grayson was gone, Sloane retreated from social situations. She spent most of her time at our old family home with Ryder. I know because I kept tabs on her while still respecting her decision not to come to me. Then, a couple of months later, Ryder announced they were engaged and expecting.

I still couldn't let her go, but she seemed to bounce back from the edge of oblivion, and I was grateful my brother did that for her.

When Henry was born, the light returned to her eyes. It was like she'd found the switch to her heart and turned it back on.

Now I've found out that not only is Henry not Ryder's, but they aren't even engaged. While we have all been searching for closure, Sloane has been consumed with finding Grayson's killer and making them suffer. I'm beginning to worry that this vendetta is about to set her down a ruinous path, especially now that she's pulled away from the people she is closest to and aligned herself with the one she sees as a means to an end.

Sloane sounded lost on the phone.

She is understandably angry and hurt, but she sounded driven by revenge, and I worry it's clouding her priorities.

This is why I made the decision to pack Henry up and bring him home without her.

While Amara was beside herself with tears of joy, she doesn't quite feel right about taking him from his mother. I argue that Henry will be here, safe and sound, when Sloane is ready to come home and piece her world back together.

Sloane hasn't contacted any of us yet, although Amara sent her a message yesterday morning that she thinks we don't know about.

I know she's confused and hurt, and she'll remain that way until she swallows her pride and picks up her phone. Our road back to each other is not going to be an easy one.

The day after we got back to Seattle, Creed returned my call.

The conversation was short.

We still wish to work together, however, and we are both laying claim to something that belongs to more than one group.

According to me, Sloane is mine, and I will die on that hill —but not before everyone else dies first.

I acknowledge that Sloane is also Elia Lucciano's daughter, which ties her to his organization, and I recognize that Creed needs her and my brothers and me to defeat Sebastian and close out his era to begin anew.

During the call, we arranged for a meeting with Creed and his heads, including Sloane. We discussed Henry's well-being since he is also an heir—the male heir—to Elia's legacy. Creed wanted to make sure that I had no interest in holding Henry as a way of taking over. The thought hadn't even occurred to me.

Then we arranged to meet with Creed's group to discuss business. I suggested Eros, and he was quick to accept. In a few days, Creed will bring Sloane back to my domain, the place where I owned every part of her, and she has no choice but to walk through my doors and face me.

I stayed with Henry in the pool house the night we got back, and I'll be sleeping out here again tonight. Henry is comfortable here, and there are reminders of his mother all over the house.

He's asked about his mom, but he's surrounded by family, so he hasn't started missing her yet. He went to bed pretty fast tonight after dinner and a swim in the pool with Dagen and Cole.

The pool house is uncomfortably quiet.

For over two years, Sloane played the happy fiancée in the main house, only to come out here and sit in silence by herself once all of the lights were out.

In the back of my mind, I wondered if she had moved on from Grayson's death. I never spoke to her about it, and she never mentioned it, so I thought she was healing.

She wasn't.

She was drowning in her grief, and now she has an outlet—a way of making the responsible party pay, and it is consuming her.

I reach over to the table beside my spot on her couch, pick up a paperback, and drag my thumb across the pages. The write-up on the back cover says it's a satire, and the blurb promises a story filled with dark humor and ridiculous scenarios. It sounds like her type of story.

Opening the book to where she marked her spot, a string of photos slips into my hand. They're the type you get from a photo booth at a fair, a row of four pictures. The first two are of Sloane and Grayson making goofy faces. In the third photo, Grayson braces his hands on either side of Sloane's face as he kisses her. Her eyes are open and as big as saucers. Ryder photobombed the last shot, and they are all a little too close to the camera, but they are smiling.

Those memories could have been mine.

It's rare I entertain feelings of envy and jealousy, but I did envy Grayson. I wanted those photos, those moments, her smile.

I set the bookmark back, careful to hold her spot, and place the book back where I found it before locking the door, turning off the lights, and walking toward her room.

I took a drive to my place earlier and grabbed some of my things so I would have clothes of my own while I was here. Stripping down, I exchange my pants for a pair of pajama bottoms and crawl under the covers and into her scent.

I envy the memories Sloane created with Grayson, but I don't hate him for it.

I can't despise him when he made her happy.

I also have memories of my own that I would never give up.

Closing my eyes, I think about the one memory I replay most of all.

———

The first night I brought Sloane to Eros, I had every intention of only showing her around and then letting her go.

Everyone at the club had cleared out an hour earlier, and the nightclub upstairs had just kicked everyone out and locked its doors fifteen minutes ago.

A couple waiters were still cleaning up when Sloane walked timidly back into the bar.

I was seated at a table, ready to head downstairs and close up if she wasn't going to show.

She surprised me when she did.

I tilted my head toward the door, where a bouncer had stood guard earlier, and she walked across the dance floor, meeting me at the entrance.

There was no one near us, but I lowered my voice anyway. "Nothing will happen down there that you don't ask for."

She smiled nervously, but she nodded her head, and it was enough for me to lead her through the door. I locked us in so I knew we would be alone. I'm no prude, but I harbored a protective streak when it came to exposing Sloane to curious eyes.

She followed me down the stairs without a word, only clearing her throat once when we reached the bottom. I gave her a moment to get used to the area. The lights weren't as bright as upstairs.

She took an interest in a few spots, but quickly looked away from others when she realized the items hanging on the walls were paddles and belts.

As I walked deeper into the club, I noticed she'd closed the distance between us as though I was her protector. I was—I still am—however, that night I was also the thing that went bump in the night, and my monster wanted to eat her whole.

The fact she stayed close to me gave me hope that the things she was uneasy about were the toys around us and not me, since she was obviously searching for comfort in our close proximity.

I showed her our public areas, as well as the stage that our exhibitionists and voyeurs frequent.

Then I led her into the private rooms, each one different than the next.

I kept my distance and allowed her to drive the tour, turning my attention to everything that caught her eye.

When we neared the end of the hall, I squared myself on her and asked if there was anything else she wanted to see or if she had any questions.

Her eyes flitted between my own and the doors to each room. Then she licked her lips and broke our stare when she asked, "Which—um, which rooms do you—uh, like?"

Keeping my hands to myself, I took two steps into her space, causing her to flatten herself against the wall behind her and jut her perky tits between us.

"Well now, that is a loaded question, Sloane. It depends on the context because I like many,"—pressing my lips against the shell of her ear, I lowered my voice—"many things." I lifted my head so I could look her in the eyes while keeping my body close to hers. "Are you asking which I've used, or which I'd like to use—with you?"

Up until that moment, I had been having fun toying with her.

I knew that, while she wasn't a virgin, she hadn't experienced much beyond vanilla sex. So when she blushed, or looked sheepishly at her feet, a surge of excitement flooded my system, and I was getting high on the chemicals I released in reaction to her.

I had no doubt in my mind that I'd be jerking off to the fantasy of her on her knees with her lips wrapped around my cock as soon as she left here tonight.

"Which have you used?"

I smiled when she chose the safe question, and I put a bit of distance between us to show her I was no threat.

"I've probably been in all of them. I can't say that I have a favorite." I didn't elaborate.

I didn't tell her that I'd never taken anyone into a room on my own. I had participated in events, and been in scenes in many of them, but not with anyone who was anything more than a distraction for the night.

With that, I ended the tour and turned, taking a couple of steps away from her to lead her out of the private area.

She didn't follow.

Instead, she cleared her throat, catching my attention and stopping me in my tracks.

"And—um, which one would you like to use—with m-me?"

This time, when I closed the distance between us, I did touch her. I brushed my hand along the length of her neck and stopped when the pads of my fingers felt the rhythm of her hammering heartbeat just under her jawline.

"Brave question for such an inexperienced little girl. Tell me, Sloane. Do you think you'd like to be bound to the bench in that last room, sucking me off while I play with that tight little ass of yours?" I traced my fingers along her lower lip, enjoying how her mouth went slack and she allowed me to push her lips the way I wanted them. "Would you like me to tie your legs open and rub your clit, forcing orgasm after orgasm, even through tears, until you pass out?"

For a moment, she looked a little pale before she took a

deep breath, and I was ready to walk away again when she spoke up.

"Would you like to?"

This was no longer a game, and Sloane was no longer a forbidden distraction. Her question sealed a lot of things, because I've never wanted to take someone into a room as much as I did right then.

I didn't answer her question.

"I told you no panties." I ran my fingers over the soft fabric of the dress I had her wear.

"I know. I'm not."

I wanted to chuckle at her answer. She had no idea what her responses were doing to me.

"Can I touch you, Sloane?"

Her eyes lowered to my hand, already on her body, before they widened in understanding of exactly where I was asking to touch her.

Nodding her head, she whispered, "I want you to," as she leaned farther into the wall behind her.

I dropped my hand to the front of her dress and slowly fisted the fabric, pulling it higher and higher up her thighs until she was completely exposed. Then I dragged my knuckles along her mound, through her soft pubic hairs and into the wet spot between her legs.

Jesus.

Combing my free hand up the back of her neck, I fisted my fingers into her hair, tilting her head back as I pushed my lips against hers and demanded she open herself for me. She did so instantly, with a soft moan.

Breaking the kiss, I licked the length of her neck, stopping when my lips were at her ear.

"Fuck, Sloane." I forced myself to pull away. "I don't know if we—"

"Please don't send me away. I don't want to go. Please—"

She had no idea what she was asking for.

Not yet.

That's when I got the idea to ease her into my dark waters.

Wrapping my fingers around her hand, I turned and led her into the last room down the hall, the one I hadn't shown her yet.

I turned on all of the lights, and she had to cover her eyes to block the brightness in the room. I flipped a couple of the switches off to tone it down and closed the door behind her.

She took a few steps in and scanned the furniture, settling on the chair I'd planned on putting her in. I joined her, then dropped my hand to the small of her back and led her closer.

"Have a seat, Sloane." I extended my hand to the chair, and she took a step in between the stirrups on either side and sat down with her hands in her lap.

I turned my back to her and walked to the cabinets along the wall. It took me a few tries to find what I was looking for, but eventually I gathered everything in a metal basin and returned to her, sliding over a stool on wheels for me to sit on.

I sat myself in front of her and placed the bowl onto a small table beside us.

"What's that for?" she asked.

I smiled, but I didn't answer. I'd tell her in a moment.

"Lean back and put your legs in these." I tapped the stirrups.

Sloane reclined, bracing her arms on the rests at her sides. Then, one by one, she lifted her feet into the stirrups, keeping her thighs together.

I tapped her knees.

"I want to see your pussy." When she didn't say yes or no, I continued, "I'm the only one here. If you don't want to, we won't."

Biting her lip, she relaxed the muscles in her legs, allowing her knees to fall open, and her dress slipped between her legs.

I ran my fingers up her calves, then slowed when I reached her thighs, inching ever closer. As I brushed along her dress and slid it up, her breath hitched, then deepened.

Just before I exposed her, I pulled my hands back and rested my palms on the insides of her thighs, staring deep into her eyes.

"I want to restrain you to the chair. Will you let me tie your arms and legs open? Nothing will happen without your permission." I lifted a pair of scissors and set them aside. Then I removed a straight razor, holding it up while running my free hand over her pubic hair once more. "I want to shave you, Sloane. Will you trust me to do this?"

She narrowed her gaze on the straight razor. I was sure there was a package of regular razors around there somewhere, but I wanted the intimacy of the sharp edge. It meant I'd have to take my time, and I didn't want to rush anything about tonight.

"I trust you." Her fingers ran along the leather strap I'd be using to bind her arm to the armrest at her side.

I went to work with her restraints, making sure they were comfortable yet unforgiving in their hold. Then I left all of my tools, but I took the basin and filled it with hot water before I returned, this time rolling my chair between her legs.

I liked Sloane in this position. She was restrained, but she was seated upright so she had a front row seat to everything I'd be doing to her.

I set the bowl back onto the table, then dropped a small towel into it. While it soaked up the warm water, I returned to her thighs, sliding her dress the rest of the way up to her waist and exposing her pussy to the both of us, forcing her to look at herself as I see her.

Her cheeks flushed a deep shade of red when I combed my fingers through her pubic hair, slowing when I touched the wet spot at her core.

The whole thing was about as intimate as I could get with her.

Fucking was easy. Creating an imprint of our time together, something that would viscerally stay with her forever, was a whole new level.

I wanted Sloane to think about that night the next time she touched herself and every time after that.

"I need you to be very still for me." I lifted the towel from the water, wringing it out and placing it over her skin to soften her pores. As the heat seeped into her skin, I trailed my fingers along the inside of her thighs, watching her legs tremble when I tickled along a sensitive spot.

She watched in silence as I lifted the towel and set it aside before dispensing some shaving cream onto my hand and spreading it between her legs. When I lifted the razor, Sloane took a deep breath, then exhaled, relaxed her muscles, and waited for me to take control.

I started at the top of her mound, holding her skin taut and gliding the straight razor over her skin, slicing away at all of her little hairs. I didn't remove everything though. I left a small rectangular patch. I worked carefully between her legs in silence, but the room didn't feel quiet. It felt alive, energized with the understanding that under everything, I was marking Sloane as mine.

I took breaks to soak the towel and clean away the shaved hairs until there was nothing left to shave. The skin around her patch of hair was smooth, and she hadn't stopped blushing since we started.

She also hadn't said a word.

Sloane watched me with wide eyes and a rough breath. I'd

caught her digging her fingers into the armrest a couple of times to try to hide her reactions.

I switched the razor for the scissors and trimmed away at the little patch I left behind.

Finally, I dropped everything into the soapy water and returned my attention to her pussy. Leaning forward, I blew a steady breath of cool air across her sensitive skin, and she shuddered.

Holding her gaze, I ran my fingers over her exposed skin and through the trimmed patch of hair she had left before I swirled into her heat and entered her.

Unexpecting, she moaned and rolled her hips to take more of my finger inside of her while she stared at me with glazed eyes set in a trance.

When she whimpered, I lost myself.

Bracing my palms against her thighs, I dug my fingers into her flesh, spreading her further, and leaned forward, flattening my tongue against her pussy and sucking her into my mouth.

She struggled to take a deep breath as I ate her like a sweet peach, without care for the juices trickling down my chin.

Her knuckles turned white as she gripped the armrest and groaned, shamelessly attempting to lift her ass off the seat and offer herself to me.

From the darkest place in my soul, I knew that if I were to take everything from her tonight, it would still not be enough, and it never was.

A creak in the floorboards from the hall startles me from my memory, and I jump from the bed to go for the lockbox where I store my gun.

I'm sporting a rock-solid hard-on, and I'm about to take out an intruder.

This moment couldn't be more awkward.

"Mommy?"

So it can be more awkward.

I recoil from where I secured my weapon as soon as I recognize Henry's voice, and I adjust myself, pushing down my fantasies of his mother for the time being.

He takes a step back, clutching a bear to his chest in sleepy surprise when I open the door.

He must have forgotten Sloane isn't here.

"Can't sleep, kiddo?"

He shakes his head before he answers, "No."

Out of habit, I scan the hallway before returning to the little boy clutching the arm of his teddy bear.

"Me neither. Come on in."

He goes straight for the right side of the bed, as though he's jumped in bed with Sloane many times before, and a stray mental image of him sleeping between us catches me off guard.

I return to my side and pull the covers over me once more. When I settle on the pillow, I look over at him, and the whites of his little eyes stare back at me in the dark.

"I miss Mommy."

I pull his covers up, tucking them under his chin.

I want to tell him I miss her too.

Instead, I smile and say, "Your mommy misses you too. We'll see her soon. Go to sleep."

Henry accepts my answer and closes his eyes, pulling his teddy bear against him in a hug.

I close my eyes once more, this time replaying my conversation with Creed in my head. They'll be here soon for a meeting, and I picked the place. I was deliberate in my choice, as well as my request that Sloane not be told about the location beforehand.

I told her once that when she comes to Eros, she comes with the understanding that she is mine, and she is never to enter without my permission.

I can't wait to watch her walk into my domain again after all of this time.

15

SLOANE

Creed was waiting at the entrance to Elia's home when I returned. He escorted me to the rooms upstairs, where a bedroom was ready for me.

Whether he had put something together at the last minute or he'd always planned to have me here, I wasn't sure, and I didn't ask.

I was in no mood to talk.

His approach was more reserved compared to when I was here earlier. He pointed out the private bathroom and told me to pick up the phone and press the number two if I wanted anything from the kitchen to be brought up.

When he was done, he excused himself, saying we would talk in the morning. He didn't ask any questions about my sudden change of heart in staying in my father's home or what had happened to make me change my mind.

I found a pair of drawstring pajama bottoms, one size too large, in the walk-in closet and an unopened toothbrush in the medicine cabinet in the bathroom.

It was tempting to order something from the kitchen since I

hadn't eaten dinner, but I knew my stomach was too anxious to keep anything down, so I crawled into the large bed and stared at the ceiling.

When I finally let myself cry, it was because I realized that Henry was safe, and it wasn't because of me.

By the time I woke up the next morning, I had one message from Amara. She sent a picture of her and Henry along with it.

Amara: Henry's here, and he's safe. I'll protect him with my life until you come back. I miss you. We have to inform security if we get a message from you.

I ordered a small breakfast to my room and ate while I looked through the closet for a change of clothes since I'd been making a habit of leaving everything I owned behind these days.

Most of the clothes I found were men's clothes, so I kept my leggings and grabbed a men's dress shirt to put over my own top, rolling up the sleeves to make it fit a bit better.

Creed sent someone to bring me to his office for a chat. As soon as he saw my outfit, he said it was unacceptable, and that Elia's heir could not walk around looking like the love child of a yoga instructor and a drunken frat kid.

An hour later, I was piling into a car with Creed and two of his men and heading into town to meet up with some sort of personal shopper for the family.

She was nice enough, I guess, although I think ninety-three percent of her job description involved sucking up. The two men we traveled with took turns watching the SUV we arrived in and walking around the store while Creed stayed close by me, making suggestions for various outfits. Holly, my shopper, approved most of them as she grabbed clothes off the rack and held them up to my body to gauge size and check the color against my face and hair.

I questioned a couple of the fancier items, but Creed just brushed me off, saying we had some upcoming commitments we'd need certain looks for.

I didn't care what he picked up, as long as I got some clothes I could actually wear.

I made my way into a new section of the store, and I exchanged a glance with Holly when I found the items I really wanted to add to my pile. She side-eyed Creed, who had gotten sidetracked in the lingerie section, then returned to me with a sly wink and started adding a fitted leather biker jacket and a few boho-urban tops along with some fitted pants. Then she pointed at a gorgeous pair of boots like she could read my little fashionista mind.

Creed seemed to trust her judgment, and I walked out of there with everything I wanted, along with some of the more revealing items he'd picked out. I have no doubt he wants to use some of them to parade Elia's lost heir around his social circles.

We stopped by a private hospital to visit a man he only referred to as Ghost to discuss his situation and when he would be transferred back to Elia's estate.

On the drive home, Creed joined me in the back seat to ask me what happened after I left him yesterday evening. I didn't go into a lot of detail, but I did tell him that my son is safe with Ryder and his brothers, and that is where I wish for him to stay for now.

He grew distant for the remainder of the drive.

I spent the rest of the day shadowing Creed as he handled business and entertained guests.

Creed's men came and went, but as it grew later in the evening, the rooms thinned out. I found a large reading room and chose a couple of books to take up to my room. Reading makes me tired, and I needed a distraction if I was going to stop thinking about Henry and everyone back home—Lennox in particular.

I had become so immersed in the book I was reading that I didn't hear Creed until he spoke.

"Tell me about your relationship with the Saint boys."

Flipping into a seated position from my stomach on the bed, I snap the book shut in surprise, and Creed raises his hands to show me he didn't mean to startle me.

He waits for me to start speaking, an invitation to enter my room, and he takes a seat in a chair off to the side of the bed.

I think about it for a moment before I answer.

"Well, I told you about Grayson." Creed nods in confirmation. "Grayson, Ryder, and I were best friends. Ryder is like a brother to me."

"And are all of the Saints like brothers to you?" Propping his elbows on his knees, Creed temples his fingers together under his chin, running his two forefingers along his lower lip.

"Um, yes."

I focus all of my thoughts on Cole and Dagen.

Creed watches me closely before he asks the same question a different way:

"All four of them?"

"I'm—um, closest with Ryder, Cole, and Dagen."

"And what about Lennox?"

"What about Lennox?"

"Is he like a brother to you too?"

I glance down at the book in my hand, suddenly concerned that I've lost my page. I open it and start thumbing through the chapters as I answer. "Lennox didn't know that my engagement to Ryder was fake until recently, so he thought I was going to be his sister-in-law."

My skin prickles as I try to look anywhere except at Creed. I'm sure he's unimpressed at my evasive answer to his direct question.

Eventually, he sighs and stands.

"Don't stay up too late. We're heading up to Seattle in a couple of days, so you'll spend tomorrow making sure you have everything you need." Creed turns to leave, and I stand.

"We—I'm going to Seattle with you?" Creed pauses in his step and turns to face me, watching as I fidget with my pajama top as I build up the courage to ask, "What are we doing there?"

He steps toward me until he is a couple of feet away. Tilting his head, he smiles, but it isn't kind. There's something lurking just below the surface of his grin, and I can't place it.

"We have a meeting with the Saints. Your presence, as Elia's heir, has been requested." He takes one step closer to me, lifting his hand to brush along the hairline on my forehead as he lowers his voice to an intimate level. "Is there anything I should know, Sloane? Anything at all?"

Up close, Creed is an intimidating man. His sex appeal is off the charts no matter who you are, and he has this way of commanding the space around him without lifting a finger.

I do my best to look him in the eyes and shake my head, but I can't find my voice to answer him.

He mutters, "We'll see," with a smirk before turning, saying good night, and leaving me to my thoughts.

I don't see Creed again until close to lunch the next day, when he knocks and lets himself into my room without waiting for an invitation.

I have my clothes out on the bed to pack, and I'm about to

ask him how long we'll be in Seattle before the look on his face sends chills through me.

"What is it?" I drop the jacket I'm holding and turn my attention to him.

He takes a few steps into the room and closes the door behind him.

"We have reason to believe Sebastian Saint is going to make a play to abduct Henry today."

I glance around the room as though Henry's with me, then I stop and stare at Creed, shaking my head in confusion when I realize he isn't here.

Then the meaning behind Creed's words almost knocks me over, and I stagger two steps to the side as he reaches out to steady me.

Sebastian is going to bring an attack on his own sons to try to kidnap Henry.

I grip Creed's forearms and pull him toward me, getting in his face. "We need to warn them."

Then I release him and reach for the phone I haven't turned on in a couple of days.

"We've already tried them. There's no answer. We think it's happening right now." There's a soft knock at the door, and Creed tells whoever it is to join us without looking to see who it is. One of his men walks in carrying a few empty bags, and Creed tells him all of my clothes are in the closet and to pack everything before he looks at me, pointing at the pile of fabric on my bed. "Put all of those clothes in a bag and meet me downstairs in five minutes."

As his guy heads toward my closet, he tosses one of the bags onto the bed, and I pick it up. "It'll take hours to get there."

I talk while I stuff clothes into the sack, and Creed turns to walk out of the room. He says over his shoulder, "We aren't going by car."

After I squeeze the last item of clothing into the bag, I run into the bathroom and stick my arm out, then pull, dragging all of my toiletries off the counter in one go. What falls into my bag, I'm taking. Everything else clanks onto the ground, and I'll deal with it when I return. Then I run out of the room and down the hall toward the stairs and out the door.

As soon as his guy sees me, he waves me over, and I move away from the rows of bikes and cars toward an open field. A heavy thumping sound draws my attention to the sky as a helicopter appears from behind the estate, lowering onto a pad in the middle of the field.

I stop to look toward the house. Creed is just exiting, his men flanking all sides as they shout information back and forth before he reaches me.

"Their security went offline fifteen minutes ago. We'll be there in just over an hour."

I hold my breath when the corners of my eyes start to sting, and Creed waves his men away.

Sensing my panic, he steps close to me. "We don't know anything. Until we do, we work on getting there."

What he doesn't say is why he's invested.

It isn't all because of Henry, although I know he respects Elia enough to protect the family he left behind. But if Sebastian sent someone, then he's exposed himself. I'm sure Creed wants to get his hands on whoever it is, to send a message and possibly learn Sebastian's whereabouts so he can end their war once and for all.

Regardless, if it protects Henry, I don't care about Creed's reasons for helping me, and I follow him onto the helicopter, taking my seat and buckling up.

Then, as we lift off the ground, I sit back and mentally prepare myself to face everyone I just ran away from— including Lennox.

16

LENNOX

When Amara took Henry up to the main house for lunch, I took advantage of the break and grabbed a shower.

I thought once we got Henry back to his home that he would stay close to Amara. He is, but it isn't lost on me that he's been following me around.

I've always been the one who kept my distance.

I stood on the fringes of our family functions.

So to have him seek me out just to sit and watch a movie, or to play with him in the pool, was new. It was new for everyone, and I caught my brothers sneaking glances at us out of the corners of their eyes.

My phone is ringing when I step out of the bathroom. I walk into the main area of the pool house just in time to see Yuri at the sliding door, his arm raised to knock on the glass.

Waving him in, I answer. "Yeah."

The head of my security clears his throat on the other end of the line. "We have reports that both the property and fire alarms are going off at Eros, and the fire department has been called. They'll need to speak to you. Would you like to meet me there?"

I tell him to give me a minute, then nod to Yuri to speak. "Our systems glitched about ten minutes ago. It's fine now, but it's out of the ordinary, so I wanted to bring it to your attention."

"Where is everyone?" I ask Yuri as I put the phone on speaker and set it down, pulling my shirt over my head.

"Dagen and Nyla are working with their teams to try to locate your father. They said they'll be back in a few hours. Cole and Ryder left to check out a lead. Amara and Harlow are inside with Henry."

"Convenient," I mutter to myself before returning to my call, telling my head of security, "You go ahead and meet with them. I'm going to hang back here and check something out." Then I hang up.

Holding my forefinger up to Yuri to ask for a minute, I head to Sloane's room, open the lockbox, and retrieve my gun.

When I return to the living room, I speak quickly. "I think we're about to have some company." Checking my firearm, I keep the safety on and tuck it into the back of my pants, concealing it with my shirt. "Here's what's going to happen. Get on our open lines and have one of our security guys meet me inside the garage at the side of the house. Announce I am leaving the property to go to Eros. I'm going to walk over there as though I'm leaving, and your guy is going to drive away in the empty car. I'll go into the house through the inside door."

Yuri keeps his eyes on me and lifts his walkie talkie. "Who's at the gate?"

It crackles before a response comes through: "It's Jackson, O'Brien, and Nowack."

"I've got a run for Nowack. Lennox has business at Eros, and he's taking a driver. I need him in the main garage in five."

"Sure thing."

Yuri cuts the conversation.

I point toward the door, then we both walk out of the pool house together, heading toward the house.

Inside, I'm a ball of nerves, and it's unlike me. Then I realize it's because I'm worried about Henry. I can't take him off the property because I don't know if there's an ambush waiting for me out there.

I try to keep my expression calm and talk as though we're discussing the weather as we cross the yard.

"As soon as you get back to your building and Nowack is gone, lock the front gates, and contact Ryder, Cole, and Dagen on our secure line. Tell them I think we're under attack. Have them get back here and call in everyone on our payroll."

It might be a hunch, but the fact that all of my brothers are gone, there is an issue at Eros, and we have a system glitch is just too much.

Yuri turns off his walkie talkie and slides it into his pocket. Our lines aren't as secure as I'd like them to be, and he knows this.

When we reach the front of the house, we separate. Yuri walks down the driveway to the security gate, and I circle around the front to the garage on the other side.

I've never met Nowack personally, but he straightens when I enter the garage. He's already gathered the car keys from the wall, and he's standing beside the vehicle he's hoping to drive.

"Not this time. I need tinted windows. I'm not going with you." I toss him a different set of keys, and he doesn't seem to care.

I tell him to drive to Eros and pull around back, then park and stay in the car and off comms until Yuri contacts him. I stress the importance of maintaining the appearance that I am in the car.

I step into the shadows at the back of the garage then open the door. Nowack pulls out and drives away before the door closes, and I slip inside the house.

I know I might be overreacting, but it isn't like my father to be quiet for so long, and I wonder if he knows we have Henry, and that Creed and Sloane are coming here in a couple of days.

It could push them to try to make a move for Henry now, while they still can. Granted, it's a desperate move.

I walk at a brisk pace to the dining room to look for Amara and Harlow, but they aren't there. Two women look up from their spots around the table as they clear away plates of food. One of them asks if they should keep some lunch out for me.

I shake my head and tell them to leave everything for now. I tell them to gather any staff they can find and lock down in the kitchen. Their pleasant smiles disappear, and they hurry out of the room.

I turn and get two steps into the front foyer when a blast sounds from outside, rocking the ground I'm standing on.

I yell "LOCK DOWN!" as loud as I can to no one in particular as I run to the front doors, and the staff runs from where they were and heads through the dining room.

Yuri reaches the steps as I open the door. Out of breath, he points to the wreckage at the front gate. "They cut our lines. We have nothing. I got a call out to Cole, then everything went dead."

I pull him into the house with me and tell him to make sure our staff is secure in the kitchen, then I yell up the stairs.

"AMARA!"

She appears at the top of the stairs, but she's alone. "It's Henry. I don't know where he is. We were playing hide-and-seek. I'm calling, but he won't come out."

Harlow joins us from the library. The worried expression on her face tells me she doesn't know where he is either.

"Stay together. Keep looking. Tell Henry that you give up. That's how I got him to come out last night. When you find him, go straight to the basement. Did Ryder show you the panic room?"

Harlow runs up the stairs to Amara as she tells me she knows about the room, and they run off together.

I step to the side of the window and count four cars getting through the gate that's been blown open. The rest of the vehicles are bottlenecked at the end of the driveway as our first wave of security shows up to push them back.

Two of the vehicles drive across the grass and around to the back of the house, which is fine by me. Ryder beefed up security as soon as we found out what our father was up to, so they'll be waiting for them back there. My assumption is confirmed the moment I hear rapid gunfire coming from around the back of the house.

"HENRY!"

I can't slow what is about to happen, but I can try to get him safely out of harm's way before I start killing every motherfucker I see.

A loud crash in the dining room catches my attention, and I take a step toward the source of the sound when Harlow hits the top of the stairs with Henry wrapped around her. She runs down as fast as she can as he holds on for dear life.

When she's halfway down the stairs, Amara turns the corner and follows them down.

The door bursts open behind me, and someone barrels into me. I hit the ground already pushing to get back up, and Harlow just makes it around us when I reach for my gun, but it must have fallen loose.

The guy who took me down reaches for Harlow, but she's too fast, and she's running for the basement door when I return the favor and tackle him to the ground.

Henry is our priority.

Once we lock him safely in the panic room, I will rain hell down on everyone around us.

The man I'm fighting matches my size, and he slides his weight on top of me. Before I can push him off to get up, he straightens, and I notice the knife in his hand one second too late.

He raises the knife above his head. My only option is to block the stab, and I hold my hands between us, hoping to catch his wrists on the way down.

Before he brings his weight down, he's knocked off of me when Amara runs right at him and uses all of her weight to knock him over, and I get free.

I knew Amara had some experience with self-defense—I experienced it firsthand once at Eros, but I didn't know how skilled she was until now. Rolling off him, she tumbles and immediately gets up into a fighting stance. She runs for the knife, kicking it away from the three of us as I charge at the guy to move his attention off Amara.

As we fight, the guy scans the room, his eyes jumping between Amara and me. Then he draws his gun and yells at Amara to get on the ground.

Neither of us are willing to go down, and he points his gun at me.

A gunshot blast tears through the room around us.

When I realize I wasn't hit, my stomach sinks, and I look at Amara, who is staring back at me, wide-eyed and shaking her head.

The guy drops his gun and clutches his upper arm as red seeps into his jacket sleeve in a steady flow.

When I look over to make sure Henry is okay, a disheveled Harlow stands at the edge of the room. Henry cries as he clings to her body, and she's holding the gun I dropped.

I'm glad Cole took my advice and taught her how to shoot.

I turn on the guy, now slumped against the wall, and hit him with my hardest punch. He goes down like a sack of sand.

I get Amara's attention. "Lock yourselves in the panic room until we know it's safe."

"I can fight. I'll stay and help you." Amara tries to wave Harlow and Henry down the stairs, but I grab her arm and coax her to the stairs as well.

"I know you can fight. Probably better than all of us. That's why I need you with Henry."

She hesitates and scans my face, and I wonder if she thinks I'm blowing smoke up her ass to get her to safety.

I'm really not.

I know Ryder would probably shoot me himself, but if Henry wasn't here, I would have Amara as close to my side as possible to make sure I had the best chance of getting out of this alive.

Amara runs to Harlow, and they all disappear down the stairs before she yells up that she's locking the door, and I head to the front to take in the damage.

Blown out cars and bodies litter the driveway leading up to the house, but the yard is quiet. Cole's truck is just entering our property, and I turn my attention to the inside of the house. It doesn't look like many intruders got through our doors.

The one Harlow shot is still alive, and I'm hoping there are a few more, because I have some questions that need answers.

Remembering the commotion in the dining room earlier, I open the doors to find Yuri. His shirt is ripped, and blood pours from his lip, but he's standing—and he's smiling.

I stare at him in confusion.

"I got you a little present on my way back from the kitchen," Yuri says, wiping the blood from his face on his sleeve before pointing at the chair that's turned away from me at the head of the table.

Walking around to the front, I stop and stare at the man who's knocked out and tied to the chair with a mixture of wrath and disbelief.

Ryder and Cole enter the room behind us, and I look over my shoulder at them while pointing at the unconscious one in front of me.

"Henry, Amara, and Harlow are safe in the panic room. We need to get them out, then set this one up in the back room and get him ready."

My brothers exchange grim looks. I'm telling them to get him ready—for me.

What they both think I'm capable of is just the tip of the iceberg when it comes to what I've done to protect my family.

This has gone on long enough. I'm taking my family and my life back piece by piece, even if I have to carve it out of the flesh of everyone who stands in my way—which is really going to suck for Ratchet when he wakes up.

17

SLOANE

Creed had our pilot fly over Ryder's family home on our way to his reinforcements in Seattle.

The yard looked like a war zone, with charred cars and tire tracks spread across the front lawn. The one thing that wasn't present was law enforcement, which I found to be oddly comforting.

As soon as we landed, Creed took my bag and tossed it to the first guy who met us, then he ushered me into the back of an SUV.

I sat quietly by Creed's side, watching him rally and organize his men as we drove back to my home.

The view from overhead is nothing compared to the sight when we stop at the front gates. We're behind a vehicle carrying the men Creed brought with us in the helicopter, and we stay in the car as they cautiously approach what's left of Ryder's security.

Yuri glances over the guys' shoulders and toward our car. He sees me. I look away, my guilt pulling my gaze into my lap

as I consider what would be happening right now if I hadn't
snuck off the property to see my parents when they first called.

I brought all of this trouble here just by being who I am.

As the men escort Yuri to our car, Creed rests his palm on
my leg, offering one squeeze to let me know he's here. I pinch
my lips together and nod, not lifting my eyes.

I flinch when someone taps the window and my side rolls
down. Yuri leans into the car and waits for me to look at him.
When Creed squeezes my thigh again, I look up and gasp when
I see his face.

He went a few rounds with someone, and judging by his
cuts, I'm not sure if he won.

Yuri's expression is tight but kind. "Henry's safe."

Standing and returning his attention to the men with him,
Yuri doesn't wait for my response, and I release a shivering sigh
of relief.

My body vibrates with nervous energy as our car pulls
through the gates, and Creed takes his hand back.

"We have some unexpected business inside. You'll
accompany me. I know you don't want to be a pawn in this
game, and that's fine. But it means I expect you to be the
queen."

He stops talking when we come to a stop outside the front
doors. I slink down in my seat and scan the area for signs of
Henry. As badly as I want to hold him in my arms and run
away from everything, I'm not ready for him to see me like
this.

In a strange repetition of history, I'm now becoming the
parent who gives up their child in the hopes that they will have
a better chance at a normal life.

I follow Creed's lead and open my door, rounding the car to
stand quietly at his side as he approaches Cole and Ryder, who
are standing on the front steps.

They reflect each other's expressions with a mixture of worry and remorse as they glance my way.

Ryder looks like he wants to say something to me, but Cole taps him on the chest once and shakes his head. We're here on official business, and lines are drawn between us. Until we sort this out, I'm part of Creed's side now.

I want to ask about everyone, but even something as innocent as that might be seen as a slight considering how high tensions are right now.

I listen as Creed and Cole talk. We are permitted entry as a sign of good faith, but only two of us are allowed to enter the house. Creed tells Cole that he's bringing in his own gun, and that once they are done questioning Ratchet, he wants him dead.

I remember Cora telling me that Creed and Ratchet are brothers, so his words shock me. Keeping my head still, I lift my gaze to him before looking away.

Ryder steps aside, and Cole leads us through the front doors. The place is a mess, but the damage is all cosmetic, and a streak of dread spirals through me at a blood smear along one of the walls.

Cole walks to the steps that lead to the basement, and I fix my gaze on the top of the staircase to the second floor, wondering if I'll see anyone else before I go downstairs.

I know where these stairs lead, and my stomach drops with each step I take.

Ryder showed me the panic room a long time ago. There are also a couple of other areas down here that Ryder told me haven't been used since his father moved out.

Cole knocks twice on the door, then waits a couple of seconds before opening it and stepping back so we can enter. I follow Creed into the room to find Lennox standing quietly beside a table and wiping his bloody hands on a rag.

His eyes are fixated on me as I walk into the room, and my heart rate increases when I sense that if I wander too close to him, he'll pounce on me.

Ratchet sits bound to a chair, his body slumped forward and held up only by the rope tied around him.

Creed glances over his shoulder at me with great interest before he turns to address Lennox. "Thank you—for seeing us. Is everyone okay?"

Lennox answers without taking his eyes off me. "We lost one guard. Some needed medical attention."

Thankfully, Creed asks the question I want to ask. "And the boy?"

He's avoiding using Henry's name, and it's helping me to hold it together.

Lennox isn't so kind.

"Henry, Amara, and Harlow are safe. I've instructed them to stay in the pool house while you are here." Then he pauses and takes a step toward me. "Henry misses his mother."

I break our stare.

Creed steps between us, halting Lennox's advance. "That is easily solved. We'll take the boy back with us."

I wasn't expecting his response, and I look up, widening my eyes from behind Creed and hoping Lennox sees the resistance written on my face.

"Henry will stay here. You are no less a target than we are, but we've proven that no one will get near him on our watch."

Creed considers his words before turning to defer to me, and I nod once tersely in agreement.

Then he gestures to Ratchet and changes the subject. "What has he given up?"

"*He* is right here, brother. Why don't you ask *him* yourself?"

I thought Ratchet was unconscious. I take a step away from him as he lifts his head, glaring at each of us.

When Creed turns his attention to Ratchet, Lennox lifts his phone and taps the screen a few times before setting it down as Ratchet looks at me. "So this is Elia's whore kid, hey?" He smiles at me through bloody teeth as his eyes rake down my body, and my skin crawls.

Creed doesn't entertain Ratchet's insult. "You're not walking out of here. Tell me where Sebastian is, and we'll do it quick."

Lennox turns his attention away from me to look at the tools on the table beside him, and I examine him in a new light. I knew he could be vicious, and I knew he had the potential to be a savage predator, but watching him in this element makes me feel shaky on my feet.

I'm so lost in Lennox's pull that I miss Ratchet's answer, but I assume it isn't good since Lennox steps in front of him and hits him so hard across the jaw that his head snaps back and the two front legs of his chair lift off the ground before thumping back in place.

A cold sweat prickles across my skin as I replay Creed's words in my head in his same detached voice:

You're not walking out of here.

Is he going to kill him in front of me?

I shouldn't care.

Ratchet attacked the people I love, and he tried to take Henry. I shouldn't give a shit about him, but now that I'm standing here, I realize that wishing someone dead is a lot different than watching it happen.

Lennox breaks the silence. "I don't think he knows." He stares down at Ratchet, the corner of his mouth ticking up in a malicious smirk. "Isn't that right? You can't give my father up because he never trusted you enough to tell you where he was hiding." Ratchet's glare turns sour, and Lennox keeps taunting him, this time bracing his palms on his thighs and leaning over to get in Ratchet's face. "There are men who my father trusts to know his location, but you are not one of them. That must sting. His own lap dog doesn't know how to get home."

"FUCK YOU!" Bloodied spit sprays from Ratchet's mouth when Lennox pokes at his sore spot.

Lennox straightens, seemingly satisfied that he made progress, as he turns to Creed. "He doesn't know Sebastian's location. He would have given him up before I cut his finger down to the stump."

The room tilts to the side as I lower my gaze, narrowing it on Ratchet's hands. I hadn't noticed one was bandaged until now.

A little voice in the back of my head tells me not to take another look at the tools on Lennox's table, but I can't stop myself. Sure enough, I see something that I overlooked earlier. Pieces of one finger, cut at each of the three joints, sit beside each other.

I force my gaze to Creed, who is staring solemnly at his brother. It's the look of someone who is coming to terms with saying goodbye. He asks, "Did you get *anything* out of him?"

Lennox shrugs, telling him that he has some information about their family's business, as well as a possible lead to a bigger fish in Sebastian's organization. Then he tells him he doesn't think there's anything else to tell.

After half a minute of silence, Creed slowly reaches for his gun. Lennox doesn't flinch or make a move to challenge him.

This is it.

I take a deep breath, preparing myself to expect the gunshot so I can remain strong and unmoved when they kill him in front of me.

What I'm not prepared for is Creed turning to offer me the gun, handle out.

When I lock eyes with Creed, his expression is cold and dark. "You want to be more than a player. It's time to claim your throne."

Lennox adjusts his stance, and I catch his expression as a flash of unease crosses his face.

A cold sweat washes over me as I take the gun.

Creed tilts his head to the side to look at me before lowering his voice. "It's okay, Sloane. Point the gun at his head and shoot."

As I lift the gun and point it at Ratchet's chest, I bite the inside of my cheek until I taste blood to try to settle my nerves.

His instructions seem so simple: point and shoot. Is this how they do it? Do they take their heart out of it and reduce everything to simple, detached steps?

As if sensing my weakness, Ratchet stares me down. He's challenging me to do just that. Kill him and destroy myself.

"I don't want to do this," I whisper to myself, as though some divine being will hear my words and pull me out of this moment.

Ratchet hears me and sneers, baring his bloody teeth.

"Sloane." Creed's voice is firm and demanding, and Lennox stays silent, his attention focused on my every move.

I try to tell myself that Ratchet would have killed Henry if he was told to, that he broke into my home to go after my family. My hand shakes as I reason that he won't hesitate to do it again. Then I tell myself that this is one step closer to filling my obligations and earning peace for Henry.

I raise the gun to Ratchet's head, and he refuses to look anywhere but at me.

Closing my eyes, I take a deep breath in through my nose and out through my mouth before steadying my nerves.

I almost drop to the ground when the blast of a gunshot grates against every nerve in my body. Tears spring from my eyes, and I choke back a scream as blood splatters across my front.

The scene in front of me is horrific, and the first two things that hit me are: Ratchet is dead, and I'm not the one who shot him.

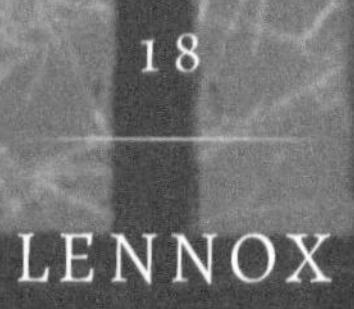

18

———

LENNOX

The moment I saw Sloane enter the room behind Creed, I knew something was off.

When I limited the number of men allowed down here, I expected to see just that: men.

This shouldn't have come as a surprise.

Creed is an extremely calculating businessman. He's methodical, and he has a reason for every move he makes.

As the minutes ticked on, it slowly became apparent that his reason for parading Sloane through here was me, and I might have tipped my hand when I insisted that she be present at our official meeting in a couple of days.

He watched us like a hawk as we spoke, and a hint of satisfaction crossed his face when Ratchet insulted Sloane, calling her a whore again, and I stepped over to beat his remorse out of him.

Sloane didn't seem to notice the second derogatory comment, and I assume it's because this whole situation is overwhelming her.

But Creed saw everything.

The color drained from Sloane's face when I allowed a glimpse of who I really am to show through. I left the pieces of Ratchet's fingers on my table to fuck with his head, so he would give up my father, but it became apparent that Sebastian wasn't as loyal to Ratchet as Ratchet was to his master.

Our father pitted the four of us brothers against each other, and in the end it didn't work. He must have thought he'd hit the jackpot when Ratchet came along, willing to do anything he asked for scraps of his approval and empty promises.

This broken man sitting in front of us could have been any one of my brothers if we hadn't been strong enough to see beyond Sebastian's manipulations.

When Creed made the decision to end things, I felt relief.

As much as I wanted to see Sloane these last few days, I never wanted her to see me like this. I've always done what needed to be done, and I'm aware of how abhorrent that makes my soul. I never deserved someone like Sloane, and now she sees every disgusting flaw.

I had gotten everything I could out of Ratchet, and the sooner he died, the sooner Sloane could get out of here and try to put this behind her, although I knew in my heart that witnessing this would haunt her. The despair in her eyes in that moment will forever stay with me.

Then Creed made a move I didn't see coming.

He turned his attention to Sloane and held his gun out to her.

He wanted her to kill Ratchet.

Rage bubbled from the pit of my gut as I watched her face fall even further. She paled once she realized what was being asked of her, and I clenched my jaw to hold my apathetic expression on my face.

I sacrificed everything for my family, and now Sloane is being told to do the same thing to protect hers.

The moment Sloane murmured, "I don't want to do this," I broke inside. I thought I had shattered a long time ago, that there was nothing left of the little boy who killed a man on his sixteenth birthday, but I was wrong.

Hearing Sloane say the same thing I said to my father when I was told to kill a man for the first time will stay with me for the rest of my days.

Creed says her name, trying to coax her along. Granted, he's taking a different approach than my father did, but the end result will still be the same.

Sloane will be broken, and Creed will have his obedience.

Creed is cementing Sloane's loyalty. He's going to use this to confirm his position as Elia's successor.

It's the fastest way to pull in anyone in his organization who wasn't sure which side to take, and it's a smart move. However, this now involves Sloane, and whether she is aware of it or not, she is under my protection.

Sloane lifts the gun in her trembling hand and aims it at Ratchet's head. Closing her eyes, she takes a deep breath.

I react quickly.

Reaching for my gun on the table, I swing my arm around and fire a bullet into Ratchet's head, killing him instantly before Sloane can open her eyes and watch everything as it happens.

The castoff from Ratchet's gunshot wound is unavoidable, and droplets spray into the room, some landing on Sloane as she seizes, her tear-filled eyes shooting open.

Dropping the gun on the table, I take advantage of Sloane's shock to cross the room to Creed, grabbing him by the shirt and pushing him back against the wall. He braces his hands against my arms but makes no move to fight me.

"NOT HER!" I yell in his face.

He can't take her from me. I won't allow it. After losing her, then losing her over and over again every time I had to watch her be with anyone but me, I won't let her go.

Never again.

Creed doesn't look surprised. He merely smirks and says, "The clip is empty."

The tension is shattered when we hear Henry's voice on the other side of the door. "Mommy?"

I swear under my breath.

Sloane gasps, shoving her hand over her mouth and stepping away from the door in a panic. Her eyes flit around the room in horror at everything she sees.

I hold my forefinger up to my mouth, telling her to keep quiet.

Creed observes in vested silence as I walk to the door and yell through it.

"Sorry, kiddo. Your mom isn't here. Is anyone out there with you?"

There's a moment of silence before Ryder yells back, telling me he's got him now, and they are going out back for a swim.

When I turn back to everyone in the room, Sloane looks like she's at her breaking point.

"I need to see him."

She takes a few steps to the door when I turn and block her way. "That's not a good idea."

She tries to step around me. "Just for a minute. I just—"

I hook my hand around her arm and haul her to the side, holding her in front of a mirror and forcing her to take a good look at herself.

Sloane's eyes are wild when she narrows her sights on the blood splattered across her tear-stained face. The skin on her cheeks is blotchy from stress. Instinctively, she lifts her hand to try to rub Ratchet's blood off her, and the gun she forgot she was holding comes into view.

I'm not sure if Creed notices, but her body sways then pulls away from me. She's moments from passing out. I tighten my grip and hold her upright, shaking her and spinning her to face me as I lower myself so my eyes are at her level.

"Henry is okay, Sloane. You both got what you came here for, and now you need to leave so we can clean up." I turn my attention to Creed, who's been watching us this whole time. "Isn't that right? You came here so Sloane could kill Ratchet, and that's what she did."

He understands the threat in my tone. I'm telling him to parade a blood-covered Sloane in front of his men for show. It doesn't matter who killed Ratchet. What matters is that everyone thinks it's her: Elia's blood and heir under Creed's orders.

Creed steps forward, taking his gun from Sloane and exchanging the clip for one that is loaded before holstering it and reaching for the door.

Since they first stepped into the room, I've wanted to separate Sloane from Creed, and my chance comes when he reaches for the door.

When they first joined me in the room, I fired off a text to Dagen as soon as Creed was distracted and told him to have Nyla at the top of the stairs, waiting for him to exit.

If Creed wants to use Sloane against me, then I have no problem using Nyla against him.

When the door opens, Nyla calls, "Jonah?" from the top of the stairs.

Creed thought his sister had died years earlier, and he hasn't had a chance to talk to her yet.

"Lady Bug?" His demeanor changes, and he takes a step out of the room without thinking.

I use the break to pull Sloane back and shut the door, locking him out.

She stumbles with me easily, still numb by what happened earlier.

"I'm not done with you." I walk her to the nearest wall and pin her back to it as I retrieve a piece of paper from my pocket, holding it in front of her face.

She knits her eyebrows in confusion until she realizes I'm holding the letter she thinks I wrote, then she snaps out of her daze. Her body goes rigid, and she tugs, embarrassed that I know she kept it. She tries to get free.

She hasn't wanted to face this for years.

"Don't, Lennox." She pushes me, but I don't budge. "Please, just don't. I can't."

"You can't *what*?"

Her bottom lip trembles as she blinks rapidly, fighting to hold back her tears. "I don't know what more you want from me. I did what you asked. I didn't want to, but I did what you told me to do. What more do you want?"

When she reaches out to grab the letter back like it's the only thing she has left of me, I crumple it in my fist, refusing to let her read its lies even one more time.

"I never wrote this letter, Sloane, and I never got the one you wrote to me."

"I don't understand." She chuckles nervously, as though she thinks I'm lying to her. When I don't break my scowl, she asks, "Then who wrote it?"

Someone knocks on the door.

"I don't have time to tell you how I know, but it was my father."

For years, my father has manipulated his sons' lives. He agreed to an arranged marriage for Ryder because he wanted to control him. Now, when I look at his decision to cancel the arrangement and send Amara away, I wonder if he knew all along that Ryder had feelings for her. It's the only thing that makes sense now.

He knew Sloane was becoming my saving grace, and he waited until he could drive us apart. Then, to punish me for pushing back all of these years, he fully supported Ryder marrying Sloane. He was over the moon when he thought Henry was theirs. He knew it would eat away at me until there was nothing left.

"Tell me you chose me."

Another two knocks startle Sloane, and she looks over at the closed door. Wrapping my fingers loosely under her jaw, I pull her attention back to me.

Creed can wait. That's what he gets for pulling his bullshit in our house.

"I did, Nox. I chose you. I loved you both, but I chose you," Sloane whispers, lifting her slender fingers to rest them on my hand, which I've lowered to her throat.

"Let me be clear: you chose me, and as far as I'm concerned, it still stands. So when you ask me what more I could possibly want from you, the answer is *everything*, Sloane. I'm going to take everything because you were always mine to have."

I tighten my grip around her throat enough to make her open her mouth in surprise, then I lean into her, brushing my lips against hers before crushing them into her and kissing her as I've wanted to for years.

Sloane's hand drops away from mine, and she allows me full access to her, just like she used to.

Another knock on the door, this time with more strength, warns me that my time has run out.

I break the kiss and take a step back, giving her room to breathe.

Then I say the words I don't want to say. "You need to go with Creed."

Confusion crosses her features as she shakes her head. "But we—"

"Creed is waiting outside this door to walk you back out to his men. He needs to take over for Elia, and we need that if we have any chance of stopping Sebastian. If you stay here and break away from him now, it would start something between us that nobody wants, and Henry is still on the property. As much as I hate to admit it: Cora was right. This is our only option."

As soon as I mention Henry, she snaps back to the present.

She nods, then she looks right through me when she says, "I hate him, Nox. I hate your father for everything he's done to you and all of your brothers. Sebastian took you away from me, then he took Grayson away, and now he's trying to take Henry, and I'm going to kill him for what he's done."

Her words rattle me because I absolutely believe them, and now I need to make sure I get to Sebastian first.

When she takes a step to the door, I reach for her arm with my parting words: "I'll see you in two days—at Eros."

Sloane trips in her step, and I can't stop the sadistic grin spreading across my face.

The last time she was at Eros with me, I had her strapped to a St. Andrew's cross with a vibrator fastened against her clit while I paddled her ass. I edged her so hard that when I finally fucked her, she passed out when I pushed her to come for the third time.

Judging by the flush in her cheeks and her failure to meet my gaze, she's remembering exactly that.

Then I open the door and guide her to an impatient Creed, who is waiting in the hall with one of his own men and Cole.

The wicked smirk Cole levels me with tells me everything I need to know.

Creed handles Sloane carefully, telling his guy to make sure he gets her to the car, then he squares himself on me. "A word, Lennox?"

I step out of the room, closing the door behind me. Then I point toward the stairs, telling Cole to see everyone out and give us some privacy.

We watch until his feet disappear up the stairs before Creed speaks. "Are you trying to lay claim to something that isn't yours?"

"No," I answer matter-of-factly.

"Good. I'm glad we understand each—"

"I'm laying claim to something that is mine."

"Care to explain how your brother's fake fiancée is of your concern?"

"No. But I will tell you that, as long as you keep her safe, it won't get in our way of working together. We are all as loyal to your claim for succession as we always have been"—I take a slow step toward Creed and slow my voice—"but Sloane is mine, and I'll be taking her back."

"I see." Creed glances toward the stairs in thought before continuing, "And Sloane feels the same way?"

When I don't answer the question, Creed chuckles to himself, then turns to walk toward the stairs, pausing before he takes the first step. "I'll send someone for Ratchet."

"Understood."

Then he leaves without looking back. The thunk of his boots on each step is the only sound in the room with me as I think about how good it feels to have Sloane in my sights once again.

19

SLOANE

We arrive at our accommodations before I notice we've driven away from the Saint estate.

Everything after the moment Lennox kissed me again, after all of this time, is a blur.

In my defense, I'm pretty sure no one spoke in the car, and I used the silence to wrap my head around the fact that Lennox never wrote the letter I punished myself with for years.

I don't need to have the note to recite every word of it, like I have over and over again.

I snap out of my daze and look up at the large house. It's much smaller than Elia's place in Portland, but it's still heavily guarded.

I snap out of my thoughts when Creed steps up to me and cups the side of my head with his hand, rubbing his thumb along my skin as his men stand around him in silence. He stares keenly at the spot he's rubbing on my cheek as he speaks to one man in particular. "Take Sloane's things and escort her to the room that is made up for her. Have the cook send dinner up, then meet me in my office in twenty."

I'm unable to turn my head, as Creed still has me firmly in his grip, but I shift my eyes to the man holding the bag I packed in haste. He nods and steps back, allowing me to walk with him.

I return to meet Creed's gaze to find him looking into my eyes. Tilting his head toward my ear, he lowers his voice. "I'm going to take your phone for the time being. Get some rest, Sloane. I'll send for you when I'm ready."

Then he drops his hand from my face and holds it out, waiting for my phone. When I pull it out of my pocket and hand it to him, he steps back, turning his attention to the man closest to us and walking toward one of the other cars in our convoy.

The man with my bags has already turned and is walking up the stairs without me, so I follow behind him into the building.

Inside the place, the men look at me in silence. The few women present do a double take when they see me, but they don't say a thing.

Maybe I should make an effort to get to know some people here.

"Hey. I'm Sloane," I say, trying to catch up to the guy in front of me when he turns to walk down an empty hall.

He laughs under his breath, but it isn't malicious. "I'll stop you right there. We all know who you are."

"I figured you did. I was saying that to get your name. You know, like make a friend."

I follow him into a room, and he drops my bags on the bed before turning to look at me. When he takes in my face, he scans near my jawline before meeting my eyes.

"Make a friend, hey?" His tone carries a hint of amusement, and I feel like a dork. He flashes a pretty-boy smile at me, and it feels deceiving. The men I've encountered around

Creed are hardened. I almost feel more comfortable with them because at least you know what you're getting. I get the impression the man standing in front of me could charm a woman into tying herself up for him to kidnap.

"You can call me Scout." Shaking his head, he turns to leave, saying, "Creed said you were funny," under his breath.

"Creed likes my sense of humor?" I spin in place to ask, and I catch him off guard. I'm not sure I was meant to hear his observation.

He openly grins at me. "I think he meant as in *odd*, but—yeah, you're funny too."

Then he closes the door, leaving me on my own.

I unzip my bag, pull out the toiletries I shoved into it, then cross the room to an open door that leads to a washroom to set my things on the counter.

When I look at myself in the mirror, suddenly the last ten minutes make sense. The way Creed touched my face as he stared at me, the looks from the women and the way Scout paused to look at me just now. They weren't looking at me—they were looking at Ratchet's dried blood splattered across my face and neck.

Somehow I had forgotten about the blood. I saw myself in the mirror when I was with Lennox, but his kiss wiped the memory from my mind. Until now.

My reflection conjures the sharp bang of the gun when I closed my eyes. When I opened them again, Ratchet was dead. His eyes were open, staring off to a corner of the room.

Lennox killed him right in front of me.

He killed him so I wouldn't have to.

I turn on the tap and start splashing my face, not waiting for it to warm up. The dried blood mixes with the water and runs over my skin, and it reminds me of the blood running out of Ratchet.

A wave of nausea hits me, and I launch myself to the side, aiming for the toilet. I just get the seat up before I throw up, then I heave a few more times.

I can't look at myself in the mirror.

I shut off the tap water, spin, and open the shower door, turning the shower on. Then I pull my clothes off and leave them in a pile before stepping under the spray.

I scrub my hair, face, neck, and body, then I rinse and do it again.

By the time I step out of the hot shower, my skin is raw and red.

Creed leaves me alone for dinner, and for most of the evening, and I don't bother to search him out.

I'm left to hope the time on the nightstand clock is correct. Regardless, it's dark outside, so it should at least be close to the ten o'clock it says it is, and I decide to get ready for bed.

Creed and his men probably have more pressing things to handle, and I'm sure I'll hear from him in the morning.

The moment I step out of my bathroom in my pajamas, there's a knock at the door.

Scout enters when I call out, but he stops one step into the room with his hand still on the doorknob. "Creed will see you now."

I look down my front at the tank top and thin pajama pants I'm wearing. "Just give me a second to—"

"He'll see you as is." Scout does that thing again when he turns around and walks away, leaving it up to me to follow him.

I pad down the hall behind him in my bare feet, but when we reach the main area, there is no one around. Unused rooms are dark, and it looks like everyone has settled down for the night.

Scout knocks a few times on the door, then enters.

The room is cozy. Flames flicker in the gas fireplace off to the side, and Creed sits in a chair, his attention on something on his phone.

As he stands, he sets his phone on the table beside him and lifts a glass, taking a sip of its contents before waving at me to join him.

As I close the distance between us, Creed dismisses Scout, telling him to get him a discharge date on Ghost.

I turn to the door before he leaves. "Thank you, Scout."

The two men look at each other for a moment before Scout curls his upper lip and shrugs. Then he leaves us. When I return my attention to Creed, he's openly looking at me in disbelief.

"Why are you looking at me like that?"

"You called him 'Scout.'" He raises an eyebrow and tilts his head.

"Yes."

Creed speaks more slowly, as if to clarify. "Scout told you that you can call him Scout?"

"Yes. That's his name, isn't it?"

"No—actually, it isn't. It's the name that very few of us get to use. Elia gave him the nickname himself." He looks at the closed door for a few seconds before looking back at me. "Let's just say that, including you, I can count on one hand how many people are allowed to call him that—and two of them are dead."

Then he finishes his drink and points to the couch. When I sit down, he joins me, closer than he's ever sat before.

"I asked you a question a while ago, and I believe we need to revisit the answer you gave me."

"Wh-what question is that?"

Creed is not a man who beats around the bush.

"Is Lennox like a brother to you?"

I thin my lips into a smile. "He and I—um, it's complicated."

"I think you'll find that it really isn't as complicated as you think it is," he challenges me.

"I don't know about—"

Creed unfastens the button holding his jacket together and leans forward, snaking his hand up the back of my neck and pulling me to him. The way he moves is calculating. He commands the room and everyone in it with ease. I should be no different, but I am, and that is because of Lennox.

When he presses his lips close to mine, I throw my palms against his chest and lean back, trying to buy some time.

He loosens his grip.

"So he isn't like a brother then." It sounds less like a question now and more like the findings of a science experiment.

"No. But it is hard to explain."

"You're his. You belong to him, and he knows it."

"I did—I do. It's just—hard to understand."

He stares at me, allowing me the chance to speak some more, but I don't. After a minute, he stands and crosses the room to fill his glass before pouring one for me and bringing it over.

I take a sip and cough, but the burn feels good after everything that's happened today.

When he joins me on the couch again, there is a comfortable space between us, like he didn't just try to kiss me.

"You're not—disappointed?" He cocks his head in confusion, so I explain. "You tried to kiss me, and I didn't..."

He chuckles. "No, Sloane. That was a test. If I wanted you,

I wouldn't have failed." He winks at me while he takes a sip of his drink.

Creed is in the deepest of deep ends of the alpha male pool, and I have no doubt that what he said is true.

"Way to make a girl feel special," I mumble into my glass. Creed's laugh is easygoing.

I always loved the way ice sounds when it clinks against glass, and I swirl my drink, then look at Creed. "May I ask you a personal question?"

He takes me in as he seems to consider the wide range of questions I could ask him, then he simply says, "You may."

"What happened between you and Ratchet? Wasn't he your brother?"

If Creed is surprised by my question, he doesn't show it.

"Now that is a story. Yes, Ratchet was my brother, but he lost his place with me." He stops talking as though his answer is done. I shift in my seat, tucking my legs under me and settling in, as if to remind him that I currently have nowhere else to be. He sighs.

"Fine. Almost two decades ago, I fell into Elia's organization. I started making good money. Carson—Ratchet was younger than me, and he liked what he saw. He wanted what I had, and he asked to be introduced, so I brought him in.

"Ratchet didn't like starting at the bottom, which was where I was working at the time. We all pay our dues, and we earn our place. But he wanted it to be given to him, and it wasn't long before he met others in the organization who shared his views. An attempt was made on Elia's life, and he lost his second-in-command. I happened to be there, and I took two bullets pulling Elia out of the ambush. I knew Ratchet was responsible, but there was no proof. Elia agreed with me. Ratchet had started to build a devoted following, so it wasn't easy to just get rid of him without an uprising, but it slowly got worse. Then, when Ratchet crossed paths with Sebastian, he finally thought he'd found a way to take everything away from me. Sebastian lied to him, told him what he wanted to hear and pandered to his egotistical greed. Ratchet couldn't see past his own jealousy and contempt for me, and he ate it all up."

He stops to take a sip of his drink. "I mourn the loss of my brother in a different way because, to me, Carson died a long time ago. Ratchet has tried to have me killed, and he put someone who I do consider a brother in the hospital. I recently reconnected with my sister Nyla—she was the woman at Ryder's place who called me Jonah. Anyway, Ratchet tried to kill her, for no other reason than to spite me. I lost my brother a long time ago."

"That was a lot more than I was expecting you to share."

He tips his glass to me. "You are Elia's heir, and you are our family. You should know the history you are walking into."

"And Lennox? Does this change anything?"

"Are you asking me if Lennox is in danger?"

I nod.

"Not from me. Lennox is a better man than Sebastian ever was. He understands family and loyalty, and we share many views. He's a strong ally." He pauses, lowering his voice and talking to himself. "We'll need to figure you two out." Then he looks at me and continues our conversation. "Lennox knows very well that waltzing in here and claiming you in front of my men won't fly. It will be seen as a challenge for power, and I can't allow it. That being said, as Elia's successor, I owe it to him to make sure you are taken care of."

"What does that mean?"

"It means: let me do what needs to be done. I told you I would ensure your and Henry's freedom once this was all over, but I need your compliance to finish what we started. Can you do that for me?"

20

LENNOX

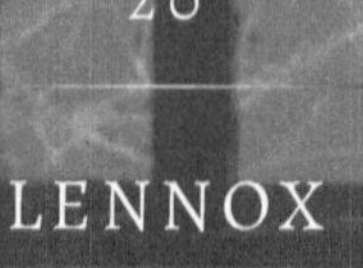

I wasn't going to contact Sloane again until I saw her at Eros, but when she left here earlier, covered in Ratchet's blood and looking like she was going into shock, I had to make sure she was okay.

Ryder and Amara took Henry out to the pool house a couple of hours ago to get him ready for bed, and I've been staring at my phone ever since.

Fuck it.

Send.

Lennox: I need to know you're okay.

There's no reply for twenty minutes, and I check the clock. It's only 9:30, although Sloane could be sleeping off her shock. Finally, those three dots dance on the screen.

Sloane: This is Creed. Sloane is fine, but I have her phone for the time being.

Lennox: Thank you for letting me know. Ratchet is in transit as you've requested. Delete these messages from her phone.

Sloane: Already done.

Creed and I are a lot alike. I would have taken her phone as well. There's no telling what she might do in her fragile state of mind after watching a man's execution today, and she does have access to Sebastian's phone number.

I stand, stretching out the muscles in my neck, and walk to the liquor cabinet, where I pour myself a glass of bourbon.

My father always drank rye whiskey, but he never cared for scotch or the sweeter taste of bourbon, so that's what I developed a taste for. I never drank rye again after my sixteenth birthday.

"Going that good, hey?" Dagen watches me from the door as I pour an extra two fingers into my glass. Then Nyla pokes her head into the room, and I call them in.

"It's been a day." I take a sip and point to the couch and chairs, asking them to join me.

Dagen steps away from Nyla as she takes a seat on the couch. He walks to the cabinet and pulls out a bottle of wine that was opened earlier, pouring one glass. He takes a sip, then joins Nyla, handing her the glass.

"Have you heard anything about Leon?" Nyla tries the wine, then sets the glass on the table between them.

I could tell Leon had a soft spot for Nyla when we were up in Canada. They seemed to get along well. Then, when he was shot, she ran to make sure he was okay. I'm pretty sure that sealed her new-best-friend status with Leon for the foreseeable future.

I've been in touch with Leon over the last two days. Once he was out of surgery and recovering, I got him access to a phone, and he's been texting daily updates.

"He's recovering, but he's being stubborn about it. He says he's ready to be discharged, but his doctors say it'll be another week at least." Nyla hides her smile when she takes another sip of wine.

Something's been eating away at me all day, and I don't want to put it off any longer. "Listen. It's going to come out that Sloane shot your brother, but I want you to know that it was me, and I'm sorry that it was someone you knew."

I'm careful not to say that I'm sorry I shot Ratchet, because I'm not. I'm only owning my regret that it affected Nyla.

From all of the stories Dagen has told me about their time in the wilderness, I owe Nyla for saving his ass on more than one occasion.

Dagen slides a little closer to her and wraps his arm around her. She sets her palm on his thigh, then sets her glass on the table.

"Thank you, but I have to admit that when I heard he was dead, I was relieved. It sounds awful, but I didn't think Vaughn or I were going to be safe until he was gone. It was just a sick feeling that wouldn't let go of me."

Considering Ratchet was caught making a run for Henry, I don't blame her.

Dagen reaches for the wineglass and finishes it before standing and walking to the wine bottle. He speaks over his shoulder as he fills up their glass. "We have some stuff to talk about as well."

Nyla and I wait for a few seconds as Dagen returns to his seat and leads the conversation. "We—but mostly she"—he points at Nyla—"discovered that Dad's presence is required to finalize some of his financial affairs in town. For this particular transaction, he can send a proxy in his place, and the person scheduled to attend is—"

"Please tell me it's his accountant or lawyer."

Dagen points at me with a smile. "Bingo! Accountant. The best part is, no one knows we know about it. They've scheduled the meeting for tomorrow evening."

"They must know we'll be at Eros meeting with Creed then. They're hoping we'll be distracted." This doesn't give us a lot of time to plan anything. "What if I'm the only one who meets with Creed and his group? I can message him and have him increase his men around the building to make up for everyone's absence. I'll make sure he doesn't tip off anyone as to why though."

"Where will we be?"

"I want you two here with Yuri, Amara, and Harlow to watch Henry. I'll add more security detail on the grounds tomorrow night—and Ryder and Cole will head up Paulie's capture."

Paulie Myers has worked as my father's accountant for as far back as my memory takes me. Few people know where all of the figurative and literal bodies are buried, and he is one of them.

He used to be a hands-on guy within my dad's organization, but in the last decade, he slipped into the background as my father became rightfully paranoid that he might one day become a target.

I stand and stretch, wringing today's events out of my tense muscles. "I'm going to get some sleep. It sounds like we'll be busy tomorrow. Can you update Cole and tell him to meet us in the dining room early so we can figure this out? I'll mention it to Ryder."

"Will do." Dagen stands and holds his hand out to Nyla to steady her while she joins him, then he leads her to the door.

Once she walks through, he stops and looks at me. "We're going to find Mom, and we're going to stop him."

Dagen's comment sends a chill through me.

I hadn't thought a lot about our mother because I assumed she was safe, but I really don't know how far Sebastian will go to get what he wants. He has already tried to kidnap Henry, and he's just a kid.

The thought stays with me for my entire walk back to the pool house.

Amara is sleeping with her head on Ryder's lap when I enter. He combs his fingers through her hair as he stares off into space. We have a television in the room, but it isn't on.

"You okay?" I ask.

He looks over and smirks sardonically. "That's a loaded question."

"Well then, here's another: what are you thinking about?"

"We're worried about Sloane." He looks down at Amara, and she stirs but doesn't wake up. "I wish she'd come to us when she first found out."

"Yeah." I lean back into my chair. "Me too."

"Word is that she killed Ratchet." Ryder eyes me cautiously.

"That is the word." I neither confirm nor deny.

"But that's not what happened?" His tone is accusatory.

"How do you know? Do you think you know her that well?"

"Well, yes, but I've also been getting to know you. You wouldn't let her do that." Out of all of my brothers, Ryder was the furthest removed from me. He's the one I never got to know as he grew up.

"What makes you say that?"

"Because I wouldn't let her do that, and I'm starting to realize we're a lot alike." Then he chuckles to himself. "I think that's why I find you infuriating. You remind me—of me." He pauses, uncertainty flashing across his expression before he continues, "I'm going to take a stab in the dark here, but when you thought Sloane chose Grayson, you let her go because you truly thought she was better off without you. You sent her away to protect her and shield her from you and all of our family bullshit."

I stare at him for a long moment in silence before asking how he knows all of this, and he looks at Amara sleeping in his lap. "Because that's why I sent her away."

The similarities between our stories shock me.

When Sloane made her choice, I never held it against my youngest brother's best friend.

"Grayson was good to Sloane. He was a good choice." I envied Grayson. I wanted what he had, but in my heart, I thought she was getting everything she wanted, and I wanted that for her—even if everything she wanted wasn't me.

Ryder nods. "He was a good choice. No one is disputing that, but he wasn't Sloane's choice. He knew that, and they worked through it, and they loved each other."

"I know."

Ryder stares at me as if contemplating his next words. "There are a lot of things I wish I could take back, Lennox. There are a lot of things I would have done differently if... What I'm trying to say is: the night I brought Amara to Eros, you told me that none of us deserve Sloane. I'm starting to think maybe one of us does—and I just want you to know that."

Ryder and I have never talked like this before. When he announced his engagement to Sloane, I backed away from my family even more than I already had. This sounds like Ryder's version of a blessing, and it is a huge step forward in repairing the damage between us.

"I missed your wedding." How much I lost out on will always be a sore spot for me now.

"Don't worry. I was on so many painkillers that I kind of missed it too." Amara opens her eyes and gives me a sly smile. She sits up and stretches, then leans over and kisses Ryder on the cheek before looking at me. "I know my brother, Lennox. Grayson would be at peace knowing Sloane was happy."

Then she stands and takes two steps toward me, leaning down and placing a kiss on my cheek. "I never thanked you for being with my brother after he died."

When she stands and meets my eyes, hers are filled with tears, but she smiles before turning to Ryder. "Walk me to the house?"

Ryder stands, and I tell him we've got some things to discuss early in the morning, but it can wait.

Ryder and Amara have given me a lot to think about, and I want to check on Henry then crawl into bed. I quickly learn they are both the same thing when I find Henry splayed out sideways like a starfish and taking up most of Sloane's bed.

When I slide under the sheets, he latches on to me, then settles and falls back to sleep. I close my eyes thinking about Sloane and what will happen when she shows up at Eros after all of this time away from me.

SLOANE

I woke up with butterflies in my stomach this morning.

Tonight is our meeting at Eros.

While I'm not sure who will be there, I got the impression that Lennox will definitely be in attendance.

Eros is Lennox's domain.

It was always the place where he ruled, both over the club and over me.

I never went back there after I got the forged letter from Lennox. I couldn't bring myself to drive down the street it was on, and years went by.

I changed—at least, I think I did.

Maybe I just hid.

I'm a mother now. I drink vanilla mocha lattes and take my son to day care. I talk about the weather, thrift stores, and the new speed trap in front of the mall.

I'm not the same girl I was, but I know, without a doubt, that Lennox is the same man.

He's dominant, confident, predatory.

He may want who I once was, but my reality has grown up and toned down.

"You look deep in thought. You didn't hear me knocking?" Creed stands in the open doorway to the room I've been staying in while we are in Seattle.

"Sorry. No. I was—it's not important. What's up?" I stand from my chair and wave him in.

"You have visitors." A mixture of excitement and curiosity fills me. I've been a little bored here, and I'll take any company I can get. "Come with me."

He walks at a leisurely pace, and I have to slow my step to keep myself from looking excited. As we stroll through the place, Creed tells me that, while he has some business to attend to, he'd like Scout to be present in the room.

I know trust is earned, and I have no problem with it. I'm not here against my will, and I'm not trying to escape. It isn't my intention to deceive Creed in any way.

I stop him before we go into any rooms. "May I ask you something? It's about my mom."

The half-second pause from Creed tells me he wasn't expecting me to ask about her. "You may."

"It's just that I gave you her name, and I'm assuming you looked into her." I pause so he can confirm, and he nods. "Well, I was hoping maybe you could tell me more about her—um, some time. And maybe you could tell me some things about my dad too."

I've had a lot of time over the last week to sit by myself and think about things.

We don't choose where we come from, and my past was a lie. I could dwell on it, or I could take advantage of the people who knew my parents and learn a little of my own history.

A smile tugs at the corners of Creed's mouth when he tells me he'd be willing to share what he's learned about my mother, and he's happy I want to know about Elia, but it will have to wait for a couple of days while we wrap up our business here.

Creed has the door open before I realize I don't know who's waiting for me. Ryder turns from the window he's standing in front of, and I hurry into the room to greet him.

Scout stands from his chair off to the side of the room, and I stop mid-step when Amara rises from the couch to turn and look at me.

I'm so happy to see her, but I know it isn't reflected on my face. A sudden rush of guilt makes my stomach churn, and I steal a glance at Creed, who is still at the door. I wasn't ready to face her, and the urge to run away in shame causes me to take one step back.

Amara's eyes go wide, and she walks toward me. "Wait, Sloane. Please don't go. They"—she looks at Ryder—"they told me what you found out. Sloane, I don't blame you. I miss you so much. Can you come in, and we can talk?"

When her eyes fill with tears, I close the distance and reach out, pulling her into me. "I'm so sorry. I just—I didn't know what to say. Your dad and brother were killed, and it's all my fault."

Amara breaks our hug. "Hold up. That's a lot to unpack, but Grayson wasn't killed because of you."

I'm not prepared for that.

"What are you talking about?"

Ryder takes a step toward the couch. "Sloane, come and sit down. Lennox sent us to check in with you. There are things you don't know. We should have told you, but we were trying to —shit, we were trying to fix it. We were all trying to make it right, and it went so horribly wrong." He glances over at Scout, who merely looks at me then away, as though our conversation doesn't concern him.

"Ryder." Creed gets his attention. "I have someone outside

the door. See him when you're ready to talk, and he'll show you the way to my office."

Amara tugs my arm, pulling me to the couch with her. Then she hugs me again, and Ryder takes a chair off to the side. When she holds me at arm's length, she scans my face before leaning in close. "You tell me right now if you're not okay, and I will get you out of here. I don't give a shit what anyone says."

"Amara," Ryder warns, and Amara feigns innocence before looking over her shoulder and offering Scout a half smile. He stares back at her warily, then he shakes his head and looks out the window.

"I'm fine. Really, I am. Can we get back to, um, why was Grayson killed? I assumed he must have found out about me."

Amara crosses her arms and looks at Ryder. I get the impression she knows the answer, and she isn't impressed that the information was withheld from her.

Ryder unbuttons his jacket and slides forward to the edge of his seat. "Grayson was looking into some financial abnormalities within our family business. It turns out our father had turned over some shares to an unknown party, which means that neither our father nor my brothers' combined shares hold majority. And since we will never see eye to eye, if those shares fall into the wrong hands, we could lose everything. Sebastian killed Grayson to keep that information from reaching us."

"Who has those shares now?"

"Well, Elia does. Creed doesn't have the details on where they are yet, but we think they are wrapped up in his will so no one will know until the reading. His will stipulates that it isn't to be read until his successor has been decided and confirmed. I don't know what that means or when it will be. But this is why it is important to us that Sebastian isn't successful at taking over Elia's organization."

I screw my eyes shut and take a deep breath before staring my friends down. This is a lot of information to take in. When Amara reaches for my hand, my sadness rises up.

I meet her eyes. "Still. My parents killed your father."

"And that is something they will answer for. Not you. Look, I'm not going to sit here and claim my parents are angels. It took me a long time to see it, but they were opportunistic—my mother still is. None of this is your burden to carry. You are my family, and you mean more to me than either of them. My mother still hasn't tried to reach out to me, and I'm her only living relative—well, besides Henry, but she doesn't know about him." She hugs me again, and this time I hug her back just as fiercely.

"Let's talk about happier things. So, Lennox. What's up there?" She winks with a wide grin, cutting the tension in the room.

"Hold it right there. We're not discussing Lennox," Ryder interjects.

Amara shoots a fake look of shock at Ryder. "What? All I'm saying is that guy has been focused on nothing but her since she left." She turns her attention back to me. "He's kind of intense. Like way more intense than..." She holds up her hand as if she's blocking herself from Ryder's view, then she points at him, making a wild face.

"Okay. That's it. We are not talking about"—he leans over to Amara, pointing at his mouth to emphasize his words—"*my brother.*" He stands. "I'm going to talk to Creed. Behave yourselves." Ryder takes one step away then turns and glares at Amara. "I mean it. You won't like what happens on the way home, Blossom."

She snickers as he leaves the room.

They've come a long way since we met with her at her

office in Portland. I was worried she was too far gone to find her way back to Ryder after all of this time.

So much has changed.

"Seriously though, Sloane. Lennox was a wreck when he found out about the letter you thought he wrote you. I've never seen him like that. He went from apex predator to wounded woodland animal like *that*." Amara snaps her fingers. "I thought brooding, stalking Lennox was scary—this was so much worse. Lennox's weakness is you."

"I don't know about that. We happened a long time ago. I ended up with Grayson, and we have Henry."

Amara opens her mouth to speak, then snaps her lips closed before trying again. "Wait. Do you feel—guilty?"

My first instinct is to deny, but as I'm reeling back and preparing myself to shake my head, I realize that is exactly how I feel.

I feel like I moved on with my life based on a lie, and that makes everything that happened since also feel like a lie. But it wasn't. I loved Grayson, and we had Henry together, and I wouldn't give up the moments I had with him. I still miss him, and that's okay.

"I—I think I did, and I didn't realize it."

"Sloane, you need to open yourself up to life and take what you want. Grayson lived his life, and he loved you, but he's been gone for over two years. I know it feels like it sometimes, but you didn't die with him. If you still choose Lennox, then embrace it. Don't spend your time punishing yourself for it. I never thought I would find Ryder again, and when I did, I was so focused on not getting hurt again that I hurt myself. We all love you, and we want you to be happy."

"I worry about Henry," I confess. "I worry we've confused him too much. The only thing in his life that wasn't a lie was me. He doesn't know Grayson is his dad. We needed him to call Ryder that so no one would know, and he'd be safe. But then there's Lennox, and—"

"And you'll figure it out, but figure yourselves out first. Everything else will fall into place. You know, Lennox and Henry have gotten kind of close since he brought him home. Lennox sleeps in the pool house with him every night."

"Really?"

"Yeah." Amara laughs. "Henry even calls him Lenny. He says they are 'Henny and Lenny,' you know, because he's still working on sounding his R's. Lennox let him, but when Cole tried to call him that, Lennox put Cole in a headlock until he turned purple." Her lips widen into a goofy grin. "It was great."

This time when I laugh, it feels like the mental break I needed to put my pieces back together. I had been so wrapped up in stress and worry, and it turns out my life is still here, waiting for me.

"So tell me about Dagen and Creed's sister."

Amara's face lights up, and my anxiety passes as our conversation becomes natural, familiar. She starts with a bang: Dagen is a father to a four-year-old little girl, and he is over the moon about it.

I sneak a glance at Scout, who continues to look out the window, pretending not to eavesdrop. But the corner of his mouth ticks up in a smirk when Amara tells me a funny story about their time in Canada.

"Hey. Before I forget: Harlow wanted me to ask if you've seen James. She hasn't had a chance to talk to him lately."

"I met him briefly in Portland. He stopped by to check in, and Creed introduced us. Really nice guy. He seems fine. He wasn't with the group that came out here this time though."

The door opens, and Scout stands from his spot.

Creed enters first, followed by Ryder, who walks to Amara's side as we stand up.

"I'm afraid we've got to end the meeting here. Ryder, thank you for updating me on everything. Tell Lennox I understand, and I'm on board." He walks closer to Amara, taking her hand and kissing the back of it. "It's a pleasure to finally meet you. I'm sorry we'll miss each other this evening. Speaking of which, Sloane needs to get ready. Darius will show you out." I look around the room for a new guy, but only Scout steps forward. That must be the name everyone else calls him.

Amara turns to me and hugs me again, raising her voice so everyone can hear her. "We'll talk soon. I'm serious though. You tell me if anything is wrong, and I'm coming to get you." I think she's trying to look menacing as she flits her gaze between Creed and Scout. Ryder drops his hand to her lower back and uses her name as a warning.

I love how fierce she is.

"She's funny too." Scout chuckles as he walks to the door.

Amara turns to me with a smile and leans into me as she lowers her voice so only I can hear her. "He thinks I'm joking?"

I whisper back, "Hard to say. I think he means funny as in 'odd.'"

Ryder shakes his head, wraps his fingers around Amara's hand, and pulls her with him. Then he leans over to kiss me on the forehead, saying, "We're all here for you. We'll talk more another time." Then he leads Amara out of the room behind Scout.

Once they leave the room and we're alone, Creed turns around, holding out a small bag. "Your outfit for Eros tonight."

I chuckle as I take it, but he doesn't laugh with me. "Are you—it's the—this is a small bag."

My comment and confusion don't seem to faze Creed, so I open it and pull out the fabric, holding it between us. "It looks like a bib. I'm not sure this will cover me."

"It's what you'll wear." Creed smiles as he says it, but his definitive tone is meant to block the objections sitting on the tip of my tongue.

I take another look at the sleeveless dress. The fabric is a matte beige; the shade matches my skin tone. There doesn't appear to be any back to it, and the sides each have wide slits that are held together by small strands of diamonds, I can't even attempt to wear underwear with this, and it will barely cover my ass. "I'll look naked in it."

"Goody for everyone there." Creed's gaze rakes down my body.

"I can't believe you would buy this for me," I mutter, hooking the "dress" over my arm.

"I didn't buy that for you. It's a gift—from Lennox Saint."

LENNOX

*E*ros hasn't opened its doors for the evening yet, and the phone has been ringing off the hook. It turns out, when you send a notice to your club members informing them that attendance has been limited for the night and only those who see an invite in their member account are permitted, everyone wants in.

Thankfully, I had called in my staff early to set everything up. I've had to assign a bartender to answer phones. That was a couple of hours ago, and now that we're getting close to opening, the calls have dwindled.

The lights will be turned off in a couple of minutes, so I circle the club to make sure everyone has what they need and knows their jobs for the night.

Ginny slides a drink to me when I approach the bar.

"How are the calls?" I ask.

"Haven't had one in"—she taps the front of her phone to check the time—"wow, ten minutes. I guess they're getting the message."

"Did you have any problems?"

"No. I told them tonight is a private event, and you'll be revoking the membership of anyone who asks to speak to you to dispute your final decision."

I hold my drink up in salute to her. I knew there was a reason I put her on the phones.

The lights go out, and the first few trickle in through the door. Normally, it would take a while before people showed up, but I pushed the opening time back a couple of hours. I didn't want to sit here waiting around for my company to arrive.

When I reviewed our lists to see who to allow in tonight, I chose most of the members who joined while I ran Eros, not my father. Some are business associates, but most are only interested in the lifestyle they can freely explore within our walls.

I left off anyone who may still be loyal to Sebastian.

Everything in this club is the way I made it. Our father created Eros, but I turned it into what it is today. He had a limited and somewhat dark vision of what this place should be. Once I got my hands on the club, I slowly changed the layout and amenities, and I added new rules for the protection of everyone.

Now, with his limited shares, Sebastian has no say in the way I run Eros. He started showing up less and less until it was only for special functions. This is probably part of the reason he wants to get his hands on the majority of the shares. He would waste no time taking Eros back and turning it into the cesspool he envisioned it would be. I'm pretty sure he'd use it to traffic sex and drugs, and he's probably already sold it to the Mexican cartel in theory.

I won't let him have it.

This is where Sloane and I existed.

I wanted more, but I appreciated what we had. I wanted to have her with me in all things, but I couldn't risk exposing her to my father. Sebastian saw her parents as a notch above the help. Her mother was a nurse, her father a teacher. They had nothing Sebastian wanted or could exploit.

I would often leave the back door to the club open after closing, so Sloane could find her way to me, and this is where we were ourselves and we were together.

My only rules were that we were both honest in all things and there was no shame. She was my sanctuary, and I never told her, but I loved her.

I'm sitting on a stool with my back to the bar, and I'm on my first drink when Darius enters and scans the club before spotting me. I don't bother to look directly at him as he approaches, but I know he's making a beeline for where I'm sitting.

When he's a few feet away, Ginny sets a glass on the bar, waiting for his order. He points to what I'm drinking, then takes the seat beside me facing the bar.

"Everything okay?" It's unusual that Creed would send his guy in here without him.

"They're in the car out front. They'd like to see you." Darius takes a sip of his drink and hums in approval.

I take another sip and keep my eyes on the people filing in. "Tell Creed I'm waiting in here."

It takes a few seconds for Darius to speak again, and when he does I realize it's because he's choosing his words carefully.

"It isn't Creed." He looks down and speaks discreetly into his drink. "Sloane needs a moment of your time."

That's a different story.

I stand from the bar and walk to the entrance, nodding at some of our patrons as they meet my eye. The bouncer at the front stops what he's doing and holds the small line that's forming back so I can step out of the club to the car parked at the curb.

Creed is standing at the front of the car, talking to one of his men. When he sees me, he circles the car, placing himself between me and the door to the back seat.

"You wanted to see me?"

"She seems—distressed. She's telling me she's fine, but, well, I don't need to tell you the importance of appearances."

I step to the side, glancing around Creed at the tinted window of the back seat, then reach over and knock twice on the glass.

Sloane rolls down the window. A black jacket is zipped all of the way up to her neck, no doubt hiding the gift I had Ryder take over to her earlier.

Even fully covered, she's captivating.

I make two attempts to get her to meet my eyes, but she doesn't. She wrings her fingers together in her lap and bites her lower lip.

"Hello, Sloane."

Her eyes get a little closer to mine. "Lennox."

"Are you okay?"

"Yes. I'm fine."

I challenge her. "No, you're not."

When she doesn't meet my gaze this time, my gut twists as I'm hit with an epiphany.

I know what's wrong, and it sends a thrill through me. Bracing my forearms on the window, I lean into her space in the car, keeping my eyes on her.

Now we both know that we both know she's avoiding me.

I lower my voice. "My rule, Peach. We are honest in all things."

Ever so slowly, her eyes meet mine. The tone of her voice falters with uncertainty. "It's just that"—she glances past me to the front door of Eros—"you said I can't go in there…"

"Without me."

After all of this time, our connection is still imprinted on her heart, our souls are bound, and we're both holding on to each other.

Seeing Sloane as she is right now—waiting for my permission so she can walk into Eros, that it is upsetting her to enter without me—is empowering.

"You are here because I invited you, and I look forward to seeing you both inside at my table. Don't keep me waiting."

Sloane swallows and smiles in relief as I stand and exchange a glance with Creed. "How many of your men will be joining us?"

"Inside? Only Darius, but we have more than enough waiting outside."

The news is welcome. Creed fully trusts few men, and having fewer in the club with us means I can take more liberties with Sloane.

"I'll see you at my table when you're ready."

As I enter, I pull aside one of our hostesses and send her to the front to escort Creed and Sloane to me once they check their coats.

A smirk finds its way across my face when I remember what Sloane should be wearing under that heavy jacket of hers.

Darius is where I left him.

I stop to have Ginny pour me a new drink since I left mine unattended, and I order a round for my guests to be sent over. Then I turn and make my way to my reserved table. Darius trails about ten feet behind me.

Once we both take our seats, I relax. "How's Ghost?"

Darius unbuttons his suit jacket and crosses his ankle over his knee. He scans the room but doesn't settle on any of the scenes unfolding around him.

He keeps a close eye on the entrance as he answers. "He's

good. It's going to be a bit of a road to recovery for him, but hey, at least he still gets to make the trip."

I drink to that.

Darius stands out of respect, and I join him when Creed reaches the table with Sloane standing behind him.

"Are you going to hide back there all night, or are you going to show me the gift I sent you?"

Creed smirks to himself then takes a half step to the side, and Sloane steps the rest of the way out from behind him.

She fills out the dress better than I ever could have imagined. I specifically chose this for her so she couldn't wear anything underneath. It's worth every dollar I spent to see her nipples harden under the soft silk fabric after all of this time. The lights are dimmed, but I can still make out every single curve.

A waitress approaches, carrying a round of drinks for everyone. Creed takes his and a glass of red wine, handing the wine to Sloane. He points to a seat on the couch then takes the spot beside her, and Darius waves off his drink, instead asking for a club soda. The waitress sets mine on the table then steals a glance at me. I shake my head, telling her I won't want another after this.

Creed, Darius, and I settle in our seats. Once we are still, it's obvious Sloane is fighting with the small piece of fabric covering her from me. I watch in amusement as she pulls the hem down, trying to cover her thighs. She stops for a moment, seeming pleased with herself, then notices she's pulled the top down a little low, and she's in danger of showing everyone her nipples.

She balances holding her wine and adjusting herself until Creed covers her free hand with his own, telling her she looks fine and everyone here appreciates either view.

That gets me Sloane's undivided attention, and I flash a

wicked grin, dragging my tongue along my upper teeth as though I'm already savoring the taste of her.

Then Creed turns his attention to me. "You asked for a meeting."

It isn't a question, but I answer it anyway. "I did. In light of the discovery of Elia's heir and your inevitable succession to his throne, I wanted the chance to acknowledge and reinforce our alliance."

As I finish talking, my phone lights up with a notification— it's the one I've been waiting for. When the waitress returns with Darius's drink, I read the message.

While my attention is on Creed and Darius, for business, I take the occasional look at Sloane as she sips her wine and looks around the club. She's never been to Eros when it's open. I always had her here after hours to protect our privacy.

Every moment I had with her was ours and ours alone.

"We appreciate the gesture, Lennox. Elia always valued our joint efforts. He saw you and your brothers as strong allies, and I still do." Creed takes a sip of his drink. "Do you have anything else for me?"

I check my phone. "As a matter of fact, I do. It turns out Sebastian's presence is required for an important meeting here, in Seattle. He's sending one of his advisors in his place as a proxy, and, as of five minutes ago, Ryder and Cole were able to intercept his second-in-command, Paulie, while he was on his way to the meeting. I'll be chatting with him later tonight."

Sloane scans my face for the meaning behind my words. She must realize it means I'll be interrogating him later when she takes a larger sip of wine.

"Do you need anything from me?" This is Creed's way of saying he wants in without stepping on my toes.

"Not at this time, but I do have a request." Creed looks surprised for a moment before he covers it and asks me to continue. "Elia's heir is a woman." I shake my head and tsk, hitting every misogynistic button there is. "You are primed to lead his men. Allow me the opportunity to further our joint efforts. I'll bring you Sebastian's head in exchange for Elia's daughter's heart."

Sloane nods along like she's paying attention until she gets to the point of my bargain. "Wait. What?"

Creed holds up his hand to silence Sloane, and she scowls, not liking our turn of events one bit. If I've learned anything about Sloane, it's that she is her own woman, and she makes her own choices. Even if her choice is me, she wants to be the one who makes it, and the daggers her eyes are trying to stab me with prove it.

"That would be one way around our predicament, wouldn't it?" I'm not entirely sure, but I think Creed looks impressed as he runs my offer through his head, searching for downsides.

Sloane takes advantage of his silence. "Do I get any say—"

"No." Creed and I answer her in unison, and Sloane's jaw drops as she stares between us. Darius chuckles into his club soda.

Creed finishes his drink. "I can't offer this to you only. You understand that, right? You run the risk of someone else finding Sebastian first and stepping in."

"Just give me a head start. Sebastian is my father. Allow me a grace period to kill him first, to show my family's loyalty to our alliance."

Creed starts nodding before he speaks. "I can work with that. You have a two-week head start. If Sebastian is still in the wind, then I'll have to open it up or remove this offer from the table."

"Done." I extend my hand, and Creed shakes it.

"Until then, we should get going." Creed stands, reaching for Sloane's arm to help her up.

Darius finishes his drink and rises with them, but I stay seated.

"We're not done here."

Creed looks down at me. "What else do you want?"

I set my drink on the table, aware that Sloane is watching my every move.

Slowly, I stand, adjusting my jacket and stretching my neck. I allow my gaze to run freely down Sloane's body, taking in every single inch of her. Spit fills my mouth as I imagine exactly what else it is that I want.

Then I look at Creed and answer simply: "Her."

SLOANE

"We're not done here." Lennox stares at me shamelessly from his spot on the couch. Holding a drink in one hand, he rubs his thumb along his fingers on his lap as I stand, looking down at him.

I was so close to getting my long coat back, but Lennox still has more to discuss.

"What else do you want?" Creed holds a hand up, halting Scout from getting us out of here.

By the way Lennox is looking at me, I may as well be standing here naked.

Then he sets his drink on the table and stands. As he rises to his full height, my mouth goes dry. He turns his attention to Creed, answering, "Her."

I chuckle incredulously under my breath, but my laughter quickly dies when both Creed and Scout look at me, and neither of them share my humor. "What? You can't be serious. I'm standing right here." I point at myself. "You're talking about me like I'm a—"

I snap my mouth shut.

I don't want to say it.

I'm Elia's heir, and I'm a woman. In their world, that makes me an expendable asset.

I know Lennox, and I thought I was getting to know Creed. I was sure neither of them thought this way, but it won't stop them from using these archaic traditions to get what they want.

If Creed is affected by my plea, he doesn't show it. Instead, he turns his attention to Lennox.

"The deal was for Sebastian's head, and I don't have that yet."

Lennox shrugs, tipping his head to the side. "You limited the number of your men inside my club to only Darius. That tells me you already anticipated this scenario and are prepared to allow me some time."

Is this true?

I look from Lennox to Creed for confirmation as they stare each other down. Creed's cheek clenches as a slight smirk pulls the corner of his mouth up. Then he looks at Scout and points to the seat. "Join me for a drink before we go."

Scout returns to his chair, and I try to casually sit down with them. Without skipping a beat, Creed wraps his fingers around my upper arm and keeps me standing while he speaks to Lennox.

"You have until we finish our drinks." Then he nudges me toward Lennox, who takes hold of my free arm.

Lennox leads me through Eros without a word. I look over my shoulder at Creed and Scout as I tug the back of my dress down to cover my ass as we walk away. They've already turned their attention away from me.

My nerves tickle just below the surface of my skin, heightening my sensitivity as butterflies fill my stomach. I haven't felt this nervous since the last time I snuck into Eros after hours years ago.

Lennox holds my arm in a firm grip yet keeps me behind him by half a step, so I look like I'm being dragged along like a disobedient child.

We earn the occasional glance from people around the club. The men watch in amusement, and most of the women won't meet my gaze.

As we get farther away from Creed, my anger begins to bubble up, and by the time Lennox opens a door to a private room down a darkened hall, I'm ready for a fight.

"What the hell are you doing?" I pull my arm away and point at the door as Lennox closes it behind us.

He casually crosses the room as though my discomfort is of no consequence to him. It's clear he isn't going to answer my question when he opens a cabinet and turns his attention to whatever is inside. He speaks over his shoulder. "I should ask you the same thing."

"What?" I cross my arms, partly because how dare he, but mostly because my nipples are hardening under this little scrap of fabric.

"Are you under the impression that being Elia's heir makes you invincible? Because it doesn't. It makes you a pawn, and I intend to take full advantage of that to take what I want."

"Wh-what do you want?"

I can always tell when I ask Lennox the right question because he stops what he's doing and turns around, staring through me with fiery determination.

"I thought I made myself clear, Sloane. I want you." He lifts his hands, and I notice too late the strap he holds between them.

"Oh, hell no—"

"Do you think Creed will just step aside and allow you to make the rules? That he'll allow you to dictate his actions? I gave you the chance when you were running away to come back to us—to let us help you. You wanted to be a big girl, and you made your own decisions. Now it's time to accept the consequences."

"You don't understand, Nox. I—"

"No. It's you who doesn't understand, Sloane. You put yourself in danger. You put Henry in danger, and you've started something I'm having a hard time stopping. Creed will allow you some freedom, but even he can't let you go now."

"I didn't know that when—"

Lennox holds up his hand, telling me he isn't done talking.

"I want two things: I want my father dead, and I want you, and you are getting in the way of both of those things by foolishly trying to fix all of this on your own. Whatever guilt you feel, whatever you think you are atoning for, you need to get it all out of your head right now, because we are all in this together, and I won't allow you to continue to defy me."

"But I wasn't yours."

"You were always mine, and now I've officially laid claim to you with Creed. Denying me leaves you open to other options that might pique his interest should he get backed into a corner. So I'm going to mark my claim and send you out there with a message for you and everyone else."

"A m-message."

He stalks toward me, pinning me to the table behind me and tossing the strap on it.

It's hard to hide my nerves when I'm practically naked. The fabric covering my chest stretches as my breathing deepens.

Lifting his hand between us, Lennox dips his finger under the dress at the swell of my breasts and runs it along my skin, causing goosebumps to rise and meet the pad of his finger.

"That you belong to me, Peach, and I will kill anyone who tries to take you from me."

I shudder when his hot breath tickles along my neck.

His tone effortlessly switches from commanding to comforting. "Tell me you chose me, Sloane."

My confession is delivered on a husky breath. "I chose you."

Revisiting this after all of this time is bittersweet.

I loved two men once, and I chose one of them.

My time with Grayson was never a lie, but admitting this to Lennox feels like a betrayal because I wouldn't have had that time with Grayson, and I wouldn't have Henry, and I wouldn't give up either of those things.

Lennox lifts his head enough to hold my gaze.

"Now tell me you choose me."

"I choose you, Lennox."

Thick air fills my lungs when his hand roams higher until it circles my throat. His fingers tighten, holding me in place as his other hand tickles my skin under the hem of my dress between my legs.

"You shaved your pussy."

My face flushes with heat, and I'm sure I'm turning bright red in front of his eyes. "I—yes."

"Do you usually shave now?"

I can't move my head, but my eyes break away from him and wander around the room. The first night Lennox brought me down here, he sat me in a chair and shaved then trimmed me. It was the hottest thing I had ever experienced in my life.

The chair isn't here, and this isn't the room it happened in, but I can't help but look for it anyway.

When I return to Lennox, he doesn't bother to hide his confidence, but he is waiting for me to respond.

"No. I don't." He lets me sit in silence with my answer.

Now we both know I shaved for him today.

"You'll grow it out for me." He tugs me forward by his grip

on my throat and licks along my lips. My nipples rub freely along the silk fabric, and I grip the table behind me to steady myself. "I'll shave you when I'm ready."

Lennox continues to feel my smooth skin, but he doesn't go any further, and when he pulls his hand away, I slide my feet closer together, clenching the muscles in my thighs to alleviate my arousal.

In one motion, I'm spun around and bent over the table. I settle facing the strap he placed here earlier. He allows me to place my palms on the table on either side of me, but he holds me down with his hand at the back of my neck.

"Shh. Stay still for me, Peach. We both know this is going to hurt you more than it hurts me, but I remember you liking it that way."

"I—I don't know if I'm that person anymore."

His deep chuckle catches me off guard.

"I'll be the judge of that." His free hand traces over the skin along my spine, dropping lower until it runs over the thin silk. Then he lifts my dress at the bottom, pulling it up and over my ass before sliding his fingers between my legs. "If you weren't still mine, you wouldn't be as wet as you are, and, baby, you are soaked."

My legs tremble as a shiver runs through me and the strap is removed from my line of sight.

The snap of leather against my skin fills my ears before the heat of the strike registers, and a combined gasp and groan escapes me.

It's been too long.

I told myself I shouldn't want these things as a way of coping with not having them.

"Tell me you choose me."

"I choose you."

Smack.

"Tell me you choose this."

"I choose this."

Smack.

His clothing scratches along the reddened skin of my ass as he leans his body over mine, and I shudder when he tells me he wishes he had more time to properly tie me to the table.

"Do you want me to stop, Peach?"

I relax my muscles and step my legs out so I can feel the sting the next time he spanks me. "No. Please don't stop. Please—harder."

Releasing his hold on my neck, he slips his hand along the front of my thigh and between my legs, rubbing loose circles along my clit. I stay on the table for him and lift my ass higher, propping myself on my tiptoes.

He brings the strap down stronger than before, and all I feel is relief as I cry, "Yes."

His fingers increase, and I hump my hips to chase my orgasm.

"That's it. Show me who you answer to. Come on my fingers while I whip your ass."

He works his fingers against my clit a few more times until bliss takes over and I scream into the table. I'm sure this last strike is the hardest one yet, but I don't feel a damn thing outside of euphoric surrender.

I space out for a few moments, riding high. My pussy clenches around his fingers as he slowly rubs them inside of me while I ride out my orgasm. Lennox stays with me through my fall, whispering low into my ear and telling me how good I am.

When I'm ready, he helps me to stand from the table and turns me to face him.

I'm transfixed by his hand as he lifts it to his mouth. His full lips wrap around two of his fingers, and he sucks me off of him.

"Just as sweet as I remember."

"Holy shit." I meant to think that, but, judging by the amused smirk tugging at the corner of Lennox's mouth, I'm pretty sure I just said it out loud.

Tangling those same fingers in my hair, he angles my head up to him and kisses me, pushing his tongue past my lips to make me taste myself on him. I groan into the kiss, reaching out to pull him closer to me.

Lennox surprises me when he breaks the kiss, groaning in disappointment. "I wish we had more time."

He bows his head and takes a step toward the door.

Panic overwhelms me when I realize he's about to end this and send me off with Creed, and I'm not ready to leave. Not now that we've found our way back to each other; I'm afraid we'll lose each other all over again.

"Wait. Please." He stops at the door with his hand outstretched and turns to face me. "I—I don't want to leave."

I close the distance, pushing his back against the door, and Lennox cups his hands over my ass. I hiss at the sting, but that doesn't mean I don't love how it feels, and I wrap my legs around him. Lennox spins us both, slamming us into the door that's now at my back before he reaches for his zipper.

In one rushed motion, he frees himself and pushes his length all of the way inside me as we moan in unison.

"You're the only one who gets to hurt me, Peach. I want to feel your need."

I wrap my arms around him, digging my nails into his skin.

There is nothing tender about the way we fuck. Lennox is rough and possessive. He consumes and he conquers every inch of me, and I willingly beg him to take more.

I want to feel all of this for a long time. I want to ache tonight when I close my eyes. I want to wince when I sit down because it will remind me of him—it will remind me of us, and I need this to keep me going until I can be here again.

"Fuck—yes—" Lennox drops his forehead against mine as he pounds into me, and I dig my nails in, desperately pulling him as close as I can get him.

My second orgasm builds at a furious pace, and I sob, begging him to fuck me harder. Lowering his head, he drags his teeth along the base of my neck, then over my shoulder before licking a long line back up to my ear.

His breath is hot, his voice a growl. "Sing for me. Show me how happy this body is to have its master once again."

Something deep inside of me snaps.

I scream as my body shakes and white light flashes across my vision. When Lennox increases his grip on me, it feels like he's holding us together. He's keeping us from shattering apart, and I clutch onto him for dear life because I know, this time, I will break without him.

Crushing his lips against mine, Lennox thrusts inside of me a few more times before he pushes deep and tenses, and he joins me in my descent over the edge.

We're both panting and out of breath by the time I mentally return to the room. Lennox has his arms wrapped tightly around me as he holds me up, his cock still seated inside of me.

Sliding out carefully, he loosens his grip, asking, "Can you stand?"

I have no idea, but I tell him I'm fine, and when he lets me stand on my own, I go down like a sack of potatoes, but I don't hit the ground. Lennox catches me before I fall and steadies me against the door.

"I don't have much time, but I don't want to let you go until I know you'll be okay." Lennox searches my face as he speaks.

I know what he's saying. He's worried he can't give me aftercare like he used to.

"I'm scared, Nox, but I'll be okay."

He looks like he doesn't like my answer.

He brushes strands of hair off my sweaty face before kissing my forehead. "Promise me, if you aren't, you'll ask Creed to let you call me. He will do that for you if you need. He… understands these kinds of things."

"I will." Lennox stares at me in silence. "I promise."

He nods, finally accepting my answer when a loud knock rattles the door from the other side.

It's Creed. "Time's up."

LENNOX

After Sloane left with Creed and Darius, I took a seat at my private table and zoned out, lost on the high of having myself buried deep inside of her as I fucked her into the door.

I left a couple of marks low enough on the back of her upper thighs so that when she walked ahead of the men, there would be no misunderstanding who she belonged to.

What first attracted me to Sloane was her innocent energy. Now it's evolved into this beautiful, raw need, and it's all for me.

She's mine, and she chooses this.

We've found each other.

The last hour flew by in a blur. I heard no sound. Bodies moved around me, but I wasn't present. I was back in that room, doing a whole list of depraved things to Sloane.

It wasn't until Ginny approached my table to remind me we were closing in five minutes that I looked up to find the last few members leaving.

I told her I would be meeting Ryder and Cole shortly and

to leave a bottle and some glasses on the counter before she closed up.

Then I sat here by myself and enjoyed the silence.

I wish I'd had more time here with Sloane. I've never let her go after something so intense before. My intention was to clarify my place with her, but when she pushed me against the door, I silenced every little voice in my head that told me to send her away, and I took everything just like I said I was going to.

My only regret is that I couldn't hold her and talk with her after. I knew I was pushing my time in the room, and Creed wouldn't allow me to take more than he granted.

The side door leading to the alley creaks on its hinges, and I stay seated, enjoying my last few sips of scotch.

I strayed from my usual favorite tonight because I know scotch is Paulie's drink of choice. Being the kiss-ass he was, he never asked for it around my father, but when he came by on his own, this is what he would order.

I've made it a point to learn everything I can about those closest to Sebastian.

Paulie reluctantly crosses the empty room, stopping five feet from my spot, and looks around. "It's been a while."

I'm not sure if he's referring to stepping foot in my club or speaking with me, but both are true.

I take a sip of my drink. "It has. Sit down."

I open a brand new bottle in front of him, and Paulie notices the label of his favorite scotch when I slide an empty cup between us and fill it. He hangs his head a little lower. "Well, shit."

Ryder and Cole stand behind him without a word as Paulie reaches out and lifts the glass to his nose. He savors the smell before looking behind him at my brothers and raising his drink. "I taught your brother this. You know, your father never understood civility. We may not be good men, but we can be honorable among ourselves."

"There is no honor for men like us, Paulie." I take a sip of my drink.

He agrees and gulps his down. The glass clanks against the table, showing a slight tremor in his hand as he leans back in his seat.

Outwardly he looks calm, but Paulie knows this is his last supper of sorts.

He won't be walking out of here alive.

When I was almost seventeen, I tagged along with Paulie on one of his jobs. My father wanted to make sure I didn't freeze in front of his men again, so Paulie was tasked with babysitting me until Sebastian was satisfied I'd pulled my head out of my ass.

Paulie's target was some poor schmuck who'd gotten stuck between a rock and a hard place, and there would be no other way out for him but death.

My father had a murder rap that wouldn't go away. Prosecutors latched on to some random witness and wouldn't let him go. They went so far as to threaten this guy if he wouldn't testify, telling him that they'd force him to and he'd be in danger anyway. The only way they would protect him was if he cooperated with them, and he did.

In the end, they failed to save him. We waltzed right in through their front doors and took him from under their noses.

Paulie asked the guy what he'd like to drink. To his credit, he asked for some really expensive shit and a pack of smokes. We sat there while he enjoyed his last drink, then Paulie put a bullet in the back of his head. When he was done, Paulie poured the rest of the bottle out before smashing it on the rocks, saying it was bad luck to drink a dead man's drink.

"You could tell me where Sebastian is."

I've known Paulie my whole life. I already know extending this olive branch is a waste of breath, but out of respect for the only person in my father's organization who remotely looked out for me, I make the offer anyway.

"I could tell you where he was yesterday. When I left for the meeting, they moved again. I won't get his new location until the paperwork is signed, and we all know I didn't make it to that meeting." Paulie notices he's piqued my interest with one of his words, and he answers my unasked question. "Your mother is doing well."

"Where was he yesterday?"

"He had chartered a yacht off the coast of Antigua. They've been spending time on the water and at a villa on the island. They left shortly after I did."

"Did they fly out?"

"As far as I know." When Paulie answers, I nod at Cole, and he pulls his phone out of his jacket and sends a message off as Paulie points to the bottle on the table. "I know I don't deserve it, but can I have a little more?" When I consider his question, he keeps talking. "Look, I get it. I either have a message or I am the message, and I can't give you anything else. I can't do Sebastian like that. No matter what I do now, I know I won't see the sun rise, but if I cross him, he'll kill my family. My sister is a kindergarten teacher on the East Coast. She has three kids, and she has no idea what I do. I won't do that to them."

"What were you here to sign?"

"Some documents for the completed transfer of Saint's Wharf."

It makes sense that he would be mostly interested in the docks, especially now that we know he is working out a trafficking agreement with the cartel.

I refill his glass. "Drink it down, Paulie."

There is a reason for every move my father makes.

He sent Paulie because he knew he was the only one in his whole organization whose death would stay with me if I got my hands on him. If he'd sent that weasel of a lawyer, I would have taken great pleasure in torturing him, even if I was sure he had nothing to give me.

"Give me a moment." It isn't a request, and I don't wait for his response.

I stand and walk to my brothers, who are standing ten feet behind the couch Paulie is seated on. He doesn't bother to turn to watch me.

"The flights?" I look at Cole, and he taps his pocket where his phone is.

"I sent it off. Webb will get us a list of every passenger and aircraft out of there." He looks over my shoulder, then lowers his voice. "You sure you're good?"

I'm not good, but there is no other option. This war has already started, and none of us will be able to stop what's coming.

"I'll be right out." I tip my chin to the exit.

"We're not going anywhere." Ryder crosses his arms, refusing to leave.

I turn to face Paulie's back. He's still where I left him, sipping his last drink. I grab a cushion off a chair as I approach the back of the couch and pull my gun out.

In a second, I lift the pillow, setting it on the top of Paulie's head, and aim my gun directly downward.

The best I can offer him is no warning and no suffering.

The glass drops from his hand and clatters across the floor.

Paulie slumps to the side, and I drop the pillow on top of him before turning to face my brothers.

"We need some guys in here to clean this up and burn the couch." I holster my gun and turn to my brothers. Cole is already typing away on his phone. "Ryder, you have the best business sense out of all of us. I need you to stop the wharf transfer. Get our lawyers on it. If we can, cripple Sebastian. He might slip up. And I want a list of flights that Sebastian and Mom could have been on. And one last thing..."

I don't want to do this.

Paulie deserves a better death than this, but he's right: he either has a message or he is the message.

I pull a burner phone out of my pocket and lift the pillow from Paulie's head. I snap the picture, then glance at the photo long enough to make sure it's clear. Then I send it to Sebastian.

The phone rings in seconds, and I put my father on speaker.

"Who's there with you, boy?"

On instinct, I want to cover for my brothers and tell him it's just me, but Cole beats me to it when he says, "We're all here." Even though Dagen isn't, he is in this with us from here on out, and he wouldn't want to be kept away from sticking it to our father.

"Mark my words: by the time I'm done with all of you, you will beg me to take the company back from you. Every single one of you has something you would give your life for. Think long and hard before you challenge me. No one—NO ONE— will be spared." By the time he's done speaking, he's yelling.

The line goes dead.

"Do you think he's talking about Mom?" Worry lines cross Ryder's forehead.

Being the youngest, he's the closest with our mother. She once told me how much she likes chatting with him through text message, and I got the impression they spoke almost daily.

"We need to find them." I glance at Cole. "Get me their travel information as soon as you have it." Then I swing my attention back to Ryder. "Call Yuri, tell him we are on high alert for now."

I check the time on my phone. It's almost three in the morning. At the very least, most people are asleep, and we'll have to wait until morning to get answers. I glance once more at the man slumped over on the couch before picking the bottle off the table and the glass off the floor.

I cross the club and walk to the sink behind the bar, pouring the contents of the bottle down the drain before smashing the glass in the sink.

I've gone from one extreme to another in the span of hours, and I am mentally and emotionally drained.

A stray thought enters my mind, catching me by surprise and chasing the shadows away.

I'm looking forward to getting home to Henry, crawling into bed, and fighting him for what little sliver of mattress he lets me have in his crazy-ass sleep positions. Then I'll close my eyes and replay all of the depraved things I did to his mother only hours ago.

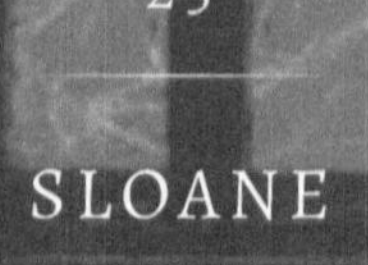

SLOANE

I cough to cover my shock at the price of the dress in my hands as the personal shopper assigned to me holds up a wrap in a lively shade of chartreuse from across the clothing store. She pinches her lips as though she's sucking on something sour before turning around and walking away.

"That look of disgust better be because of the godawful garment in her hands," I grumble to myself, but Creed chuckles behind me. "Seriously. I can pick out my own clothes. There's a gorgeous red gown, like, right there." I point to the rack twenty feet away. "I think she's avoiding it on purpose because I didn't like the canary yellow one she thought would be"—I hold my fingers up in air quotes—"'the one.'"

Now Creed laughs louder.

Each dress she's asked me to try on for the last fifteen minutes has been "the one." Personally, I think it's all their old stock that didn't sell last year.

"Please, Creed, can I take you to a thrift shop? I know a really good one that carries a huge line of vintage designer dresses."

He's halfway through telling me that we're shopping here because he can have the store closed during our visit when he reconsiders. "I'll make you a deal."

I spin in place, sizing him up with a wary stare. "I get the impression you like making deals."

"Ones that work out for me—yes." He walks across the room, grabs the red dress off the rack, and checks the label before closing the distance between us.

"What's the deal?"

He looks at the dress in my hands. The shopper asked me to try this on five minutes ago, but I've been putting it off. I already know I won't like the puffy sleeves on it, and getting undressed for something like this feels like a waste of time.

He takes the dress from me and hands me the red one.

"We'll find you a dress here first. It will be perfect, and it will be something you are in love with. You do that for me, then I'll have Scout stop in at this thrift store you won't stop talking about."

I'm energized by a second wind. I can do this, but I'll need to start getting a little more aggressive with the salesperson who's determined to dress me in this store's ugliest colors.

"I can do that." I take the dress and hold it up. He picked a size larger than what I wear, but it looks like it will fit.

I take a few steps toward the changing room when he adds, "There is one other thing, but we'll talk about that later."

I freeze.

If I've learned anything from these men, it's that I need everything in writing ahead of time.

Creed is ready for my mind to go to the worst-case scenario, because he's answering me before I ask the question. "You wish. Get your mind out of the gutter, Lucciano. It's—personal. I'd like to talk about it in private. You can say no."

The shopper enters and frowns when she sees Creed

holding her dress choice and the red item in my hands. I step behind the curtain and pull it closed before she tries to replace it with something else. Then I raise my voice and answer Creed: "Deal."

I'm a bit disappointed when the dress doesn't fit right because that means I'll be here a little longer, but when I leave the dressing room to return the gown, Creed is waiting for me.

"I told her to bring a rack of this year's styles and not to waste my time. Did you like the red one?"

I hang the dress on a nearby rack. "Sadly, no."

Our shopper returns with a coworker, and together they push a rack taller than them into the area. Creed must have made an impression on my shopper, because immediately I notice a difference.

Shades of gray, cream, and dark blue dominate the rack, and each one is elegant and unassuming. I would wear any of these and be over the moon.

Creed notices my spirits lift and smiles appreciatively at the women, who excuse themselves to give me space to shop.

"Tell me again what this is for? I want to make sure the dress is a good fit." I take my time looking at the front and back of each dress before sliding its hanger over and moving onto the next.

"It's a wedding reception. The daughter of one of our largest overseas shipping partners is marrying an American. The reception is a place for appearances, and it's a way of showing our commitment and support. It is also your final appearance before we declare our successor. There will be many different groups in attendance. Some are not our allies, but you will be safe with us."

I choose a one-shoulder gown in a midnight-blue-to-black gradient with a slit to the mid-thigh on one side. It's simple, elegant, and won't upstage the bride, which should earn points with her father. It also goes all the way to the floor, which is a welcome change from the one I wore to Eros two nights ago.

Creed nods his agreement, and I take it to the changing room, sliding the curtain behind me.

As I try on the dress, I wonder if Lennox has been invited to this wedding reception.

If the bride is a shipping magnate's daughter, then there's a good chance he'll be there, since his family has a lot of property on the docks.

Who am I kidding?

I hope he's there.

I want him to see me in this dress.

I want him to look at me like he did the very first time we saw each other. That's a high I'll never be able to replicate. I fell for him hard the moment I laid eyes on him, and he looked at me as though I was already his.

Since this is the dress I want, I open the curtain to model it. The two saleswomen defer to Creed, who tells me it looks stunning, which makes me smile.

I retreat into the changing room, saying over my shoulder, "This is the one. I'll be right out."

They retrieve the dress as I change back into my own clothes, and it's wrapped and ready at the front counter when I join them. A hunch gnaws at me, and I decide to test my theory.

"Thank you, Uncle Creed." I nudge him with my arm, and he does a double take in confusion.

The woman who wasn't much help earlier perks up at that. Suddenly, her frown gets turned upside down into a wide smile as she tells me how gorgeous the dress looked on me.

Once we're settled up, they unlock the front door and let us out.

Two of Creed's men who were waiting outside of the shop

follow about ten feet behind us, and Creed waits until we are away from the store to ask, "Mind telling me what that was about?"

"That woman in there totally wanted you. She thought we were together. That's why I was getting the ugly dresses at the beginning." I cock my head to the side with a sly smile, proud of myself for reading the room correctly.

"Her? Please. She's younger than you are." He shakes his head.

I lower my voice to make sure the men following us can't hear me. "It doesn't change the fact that she wanted to jump your old-man bones."

This earns a laugh from Creed.

My relationship with Creed has evolved since we left Lennox at Eros a couple of days ago. I hadn't noticed any tension between us at the time, but now that there is a lack of it, I can safely say it was there before.

Lennox made his claim painfully clear when he spanked me and handed me back to Creed and Scout.

I was told to walk in front of everyone on the way out, and I wasn't allowed to wear my jacket until we were in the car. Anyone walking behind me would have seen his marks on the back of my legs, because I could sure as hell feel them.

Sitting in the back seat with my strapped ass was an entirely different experience. Every bump and turn made me wince. Getting out of the car was particularly difficult. The muscles in my butt had settled into the seat, but they ached all over again when I released the pressure and stood.

Creed and Scout were both completely aware of what happened, and it settled some things I hadn't realized were hanging between us. Lines were drawn, and we all fell into our groove. When Lennox stepped up and claimed me, the pressure of where we all fit vanished.

Now, I'm able to joke around with Creed—when his men can't overhear us, of course.

"What was the other part of the deal you wanted to talk to me about?"

Creed takes the garment bag from me, draping it over his arm. He glances behind him at the men following us as he hooks his arm in mine.

They give us a little more space.

"I was hoping you would help me pick out a gift."

He surprises me, and I attempt to stop walking, but he keeps me moving with his arm in mine.

"Is this a lady friend?" I'm made painfully aware of how dorky I just sounded when he looks at me like I'm ridiculous.

"It's—for my niece. She's four. I've never met her. I'd like to give her something...meaningful, but I'm not usually around kids, and you have a son."

I'm reminded how much I'm missing out on. In a crazy turn of events, Dagen is with Creed's sister, and they have a daughter. Creed and the rest of the Saint boys have a niece.

I miss my family.

Not the one who pretended they were my family, although I hope they are okay. I miss Amara and Harlow and the brothers. I miss Henry most of all. I should be at home with them, meeting the woman who handcuffed Dagen to a tree.

"Anyway, I don't expect to see her until this business is all dealt with. I'd like to have something ready—for when I do."

"Sure. I'd love to. There's a toy store around the corner, if you'd like to stop on the way back. I'll even give up going to the thrift store for this."

Scout is leaning against the car as we approach. When he sees us, he stands and greets us. "Your sister called the house. She was hoping you could stop by for a visit. She says she's at the Saint home and they are expecting you."

Creed looks from Scout to me. From the few conversations we've had together, I get the impression that he is keen on restoring his relationship with his younger sister.

I take the garment bag from him. "Why don't we hit the toy store later this week? It'll give me time to think about a good gift. We're done here, and I have a dress." I hold the bag up to show him I'm good to go.

Creed curls his fingers at the men behind him before speaking to Scout. "Take Sloane straight home. Owens will ride with you. I'll take the other car. I'll be in touch when I arrive." He points to the SUV with tinted windows that's parked behind Scout before turning to me. "I'll take you up on your offer later this week. Thank you, Sloane."

Even though I want to, I don't ask Creed if I can tag along. He knows Henry is there, and I want to see him. At the same time, I'm not sure I have it in me to leave him again. It sounds as though Creed will be named in Elia's place soon, and this may all be behind us fairly quickly. When it comes to Henry, I think with my heart, and Creed thinks with his head, so I need to let him make this choice.

One of the men follows Creed to the SUV behind us, and he's already opened the door when I realize I forgot to ask him when and where this wedding reception is going to be.

It doesn't really matter since I'm kind of on everyone else's schedule these days, but I don't like being in the dark.

Scout opens the trunk, peeking his head around the side to call me over, and I lay my new dress flat inside before taking the back seat for myself.

Creed's car pulls away first, and Scout makes a U-turn, taking us in the other direction. The men talk together in the front seat as we drive through the shopping district, and I rest my head against the headrest as I make a mental note of a few new stores that have opened up. I miss shopping with Amara, and Harlow is all about the thrift stores.

I wonder if Creed will see Lennox at the house and—

The car crashes violently to the side, and in an instant I'm both spinning and weightless. I think I hear the screeching of tires and horns, but I can't bring myself to open my eyes, as we're still hurtling around, and I'm jerked from side to side in my seat belt.

The air is pushed out of my lungs, and it's hard to take a full breath when we settle. My head feels heavy while the rest of me feels suspended. When I open my eyes, I see Scout's hands above his head. It takes me a second to notice mine are above my head too.

I don't remember the name of the man with us, but when he unbuckles his seat belt, he falls up.

We're upside down.

Glass crunches under his hands as he fights to get out of the car. I reach for my own seat belt, fighting to get it open.

The man from the front seat meets my eyes and tells me to wait as he reaches into his jacket and pulls out his gun. He doesn't have enough time to look outside before I hear a gunshot, and his body goes limp in front of me.

Scout isn't moving, and I hope he's alive. I hold my seat belt together to ease the tension, and then I'm able to unfasten it and crawl along the roof toward the front seat.

Owen. I think his name was Owen. His gun is too far away from me, and I know I'm running out of time when I hear, "She's in the back seat."

I reach around Scout, check inside his jacket, and grab onto his gun. Strong hands wrap around my ankles from the side of the car, and they tug me hard, dragging me over the glass all around me and cutting my clothes and skin. I try to kick him off, but more boots appear around the vehicle.

I can't fight all of them.

One final, harsh tug, and I'm yanked out of the car through the back side window. The shards of glass embedded in my skin sting as I roll onto my back and point the gun at the first man I see.

"Fucking bitch!" He reacts faster than I do, lunging forward and slapping the gun away from me before the back of his hand lands hard across my face.

"Got her." A vehicle screeches to a stop beside us. The sound grates into my eardrums. I'm hoisted up and pushed inside. Only one of them speaks to me. "Sebastian is looking forward to seeing you."

LENNOX

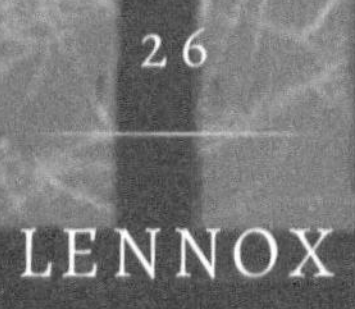

I've asked Ginny to manage the club for me again tonight. I haven't been able to return, and I'm not sure if it's because of my memories of Paulie or Sloane. Either way, I'm happier hanging close to Henry.

Ryder took yesterday away from the office, and I sat out by the pool while he taught Henry how to swim. I had to remind myself a few times that Ryder isn't his father. Old habits are dying hard, especially when Ryder is so good with him.

Watching my youngest brother give everything to that little boy, even though our own father only taught us to take from the world, gave me pause.

Sebastian's attention was conditional, his affection nonexistent. If it wasn't for our mother and each other, I shudder to think where we would be.

Ryder reluctantly returned to the office today, and I've been sitting in the garage, watching Cole work on his bike for the last hour so we can catch up on our progress.

Cole had his guy check every flight out of Antigua on the same day Paulie left. It turns out there were just over twenty departures. Some passenger lists were easier to obtain than others, and our parents weren't on any of them. I'm sure my father isn't stupid enough to travel under his own name, so Cole now has his guy matching passport information and photos against the manifestos.

My phone vibrates on the table beside me, and I put it on speaker. "It's Ryder. Cut the engine."

"Hey."

Ryder speaks quickly. "I heard from Mom!"

"What? How?"

"She started texting again. She says she's at home." Cole and I look at each other, and his shock matches my loss of words. "I called her. She says she's sitting in her living room."

"With Dad?" Cole grabs a rag.

"No. She says he left yesterday, and he hasn't been back. I'm going to get her and bring her home."

"Wait." Red flags are popping up all over the place, and I immediately think about Henry. We were ambushed the last time everyone took off on their own missions. "What if this is a trap? You can't go there alone."

"I'll go with him." Cole looks at me, then back at the phone in my hands. "Stay where you are. I'll meet you in front of your building in fifteen minutes."

I don't like how fast this is moving, but, at the same time, if my father has given us a window, he might not see us coming for her. If we can safely get her away from him, it'll be one less thing he can hold against us.

"Okay." I relent. I want to be able to go with them, but I won't leave Henry. I point a finger at Cole while Ryder is still on the line. "You have to stay together, and get out of there if anything looks off."

"Fifteen minutes," Cole says and reaches over my phone,

disconnecting the call. He turns back to his bike, saying it's good to go, and he climbs on.

"You are not taking your bike." I cross my arms.

When Cole turns to challenge me, he reminds me of a much younger version of himself. "Oh, come on. I've been dying to tell Ryder he has to ride on the bitch seat." He reaches back, tapping the pillion. "That's like reason number three of why I bought her to begin with."

While I'm enjoying being included in my brothers' ongoing battle for supreme dominance, we are running out of time, and I don't think Cole has figured out the simple math yet.

"And how are you going to get both Ryder and our mother on your bike?"

Cole dismounts, hissing a profanity under his breath and walking to the keys hanging on the wall.

I tell him to take one of the men he trusts at the front gate with him, then send Yuri a text to update him on our situation. When Cole pulls away, I head around toward the pool, where I left everyone else with Henry earlier.

Henry sits on Amara's lap, shivering in an oversized towel as water soaks through and into Amara's pants. She only holds him tighter.

"Listen. We should get everyone into the house for a while." I look at Dagen but make sure everyone can hear us. "Mom texted Ryder. It turns out she's at their house, and Dad is missing." While we are all excited at the thought of getting our mother back, we stare at each other cautiously, unwilling to accept this as good news. "Cole has gone to meet up with Ryder, and they're going to bring her here. For the time being, we should lock down and stay together."

Amara continues to rub warmth into Henry's arms through the terry cloth. "Hey, what do you say we get you upstairs for a warm bath?" She leans to the side to look at Henry's face, and he smiles through shivering lips. I step forward, lowering myself to my knee, and Henry takes the cue, flinging off his towel and climbing onto my back for a ride to the house.

Amara walks ahead with Harlow and Nyla as Dagen joins me. "I don't feel good about this."

He took the words right out of my head.

"Yeah."

There's nothing else to say. I hate this feeling. Sebastian would never give our mother up if he didn't have something else to hold against us, and now we get to sit around and wait.

Henry finished his bath in record time when Dagen suggested we watch a movie once he's out of the tub.

The women had fun with it and went crazy with the popcorn. Harlow even broke into Cole's candy stash, saying she'll take one for the team to a fit of laughter.

As we went through our old box of movies, Henry asked which one I liked best when we were kids. I didn't have the heart to tell him my father never kept any of my favorites, so instead I picked one I knew Dagen used to watch all of the time.

The movie is half over when Cole calls to tell me they have our mother and they're bringing her home. There was no resistance because there was no one else there.

Sebastian always surrounds himself with security, but our mom told them he took everyone when he left yesterday, and he left her there alone. One of the maids showed up to work today and helped our mother find her phone so she could text Ryder.

While they were there, Cole got confirmation from his web guy that a private plane had been chartered from Antigua to

Seattle, making one stop on the way to refuel, and I'll bet it all that my parents were on it. That means Sebastian has been right under our noses for a few days.

A call from the gate comes in, and I disconnect with Cole to answer. It's Yuri, who tells me Creed is at the gate, asking to see Nyla, and he seems confused.

I give him the go-ahead to drive through, then I return to the media room to ask Nyla to join me outside. Dagen excuses himself as well and follows us out.

A black SUV with tinted windows pulls up, and Creed steps out of the passenger side. Two men exit the car with him but stay near the vehicle as he approaches us.

Nyla steps out of the house as soon as she sees him. "Jonah?"

"I got your message." He ascends the steps.

"What message?" Nyla asks. She looks over at me confused, like maybe he's talking to me.

"You called the house. You asked to see me." As he answers, he glances over his shoulder.

He's thinking the same thing I am.

Something isn't right.

"I'm happy to see you, but I didn't call."

"Where were you when you got the call?" As I ask, I look over to the vehicle.

If Sloane is in there, then we now have everyone in one place, and we've become sitting ducks once again.

"I was out with—shit!" Creed pales in front of my eyes, and my heart sinks along with the expression on his face.

Turning his back to us, he rips his phone out of his pocket and holds it to his ear. There must be no answer, because he hangs up and dials another number, speaking almost instantly.

The two men standing at the car startle and approach our group when Creed raises his voice.

"FIND DARIUS AND SLOANE RIGHT NOW!"

A cold sweat washes over me at the mention of her name.

Creed listens for a few seconds before barking orders. "Someone called Darius to tell him my sister wanted to see me. I want that person brought to me—no, alive. I have questions for them first."

One of the men with Creed holds up his phone, saying, "Owens has a tracking app on his phone." He swipes and taps, then holds out his phone between us, showing a map. They are on a popular street, but the pin isn't moving.

"Lennox, care to join us?"

Creed doesn't have to ask me twice.

I look between Dagen and Nyla. "Someone stays with Henry—always."

"I'm coming with you." Dagen takes the first step, but I stop him.

"I'll be okay. I'm with Creed and his men. Henry needs all of you."

Dagen takes another step forward. "What if this is how Dad separates us?"

I open my mouth to answer when my second phone vibrates in my pocket, and my blood runs cold.

I held on to my burner phone after I sent the image of Paulie to my father, and there is only one person who has that number.

It isn't a phone call. It's a photo of Sloane in a car. She glares at the camera with hate in her eyes and a bruise forming on the side of her blood-smeared face.

"Wait!" I holler to Creed, who turns and stalks back to join me.

I clench my teeth until a sharp pain shoots up my temple. I deserve all of the pain in the world for failing Sloane, and it still won't compare to the hell I'll inflict on my father for what he's done.

Three little dots dance below her battered image, and we wait huddled around my phone for the message.

Unknown: Now it's my turn.

My heart breaks.

For the second time in my life, I've lost Sloane, and a cold chill snakes its way down my spine.

My father is right about one thing: I may just beg to give him everything to get her back.

27

SLOANE

I'm jolted awake by sharp stabs in my arms when I try to stretch.

The rhythmic *drip, drip, drip* from the corner of the room makes me shiver. When I reach my arms to my sides to push my face off the floor, dirt scrapes across my cheek like wet sandpaper.

My bones are cold.

Varying shades of gray cover every surface in the room. Light filters through a dirty window at the top of the wall, but that won't be my way out since it's secured with bars and there is nothing that I can stand on to climb up and look out.

It feels like I'm underground.

Drip, drip, drip.

Taking a deep breath, I push my shaky arms and sit up. My vision wobbles to the side and the room tilts, but I steady myself in time.

Everything hurts, and there are too many afflictions to count, so I tuck my knees and try to stand.

A sharp sting takes my breath away, and I follow the

searing pain to my arms. Dried blood coats thin cuts, and when I touch my arms, pain travels through my body. I was dragged across glass shards. Some of them must still be in my arms.

I add that to my list of things I need to deal with.

Drip, drip, drip.

Turning toward the sound, I pull one foot out from under me and push up through the agony, walking toward the closest wall to brace myself. It's cement; there's cement everywhere.

The men who took me mentioned Sebastian. Judging by the hue in the sliver of sky I can see through the grimy window, it must be after dinner.

My stomach growls. Great. I'll add it to my long list of what isn't going right today.

Drip, drip, drip.

The sound grates on my nerves, and I glare in its direction.

I was mistaken.

The room isn't empty. There is a cracked sink and mirror in the darkened corner.

I walk the perimeter of the room, unsure if I should attempt to stand without support, until I reach the sink.

Rusted water drips from the tap, and I tighten it, stopping the flow. A light flickers above the mirror, flashing my ghostly reflection back at me. It's like something out of a horror movie.

I look like death.

I'm pale, and the smears of crusting blood on my face are not doing me any favors. I'm pretty sure the blood didn't come from my face, and I look at the cuts on my arms for confirmation.

I feel the backhanded slap all over again when I look at the bruise high on my cheekbone.

Instinctively, I reach for the medicine cabinet. The door opens on a high-pitched squeal but offers me nothing else.

I close the cabinet and return to looking at myself.

I'm still alive. This is the one single thing that surprises me the most.

I was told by everyone, over and over again, that if Sebastian got his hands on me, he'd kill me.

So why am I still breathing?

The shuffling of footsteps from outside the door breaks my thought, and I turn toward the door. There is nothing to protect myself with, so I prop my ass against the sink and lean on it to look stronger than I am.

"Ah, there you are." I have no food in my stomach, but that doesn't stop it from rising up into my throat as Sebastian takes a few steps into the room. He's smiling at me as though I should be happy to see him. Another man enters but stays near the door. "And how is my fake soon-to-be daughter-in-law?" He takes a couple more steps before asking, "Did I get that right?"

"Where am I?"

His sick smile doesn't meet his eyes. "The only thing you need to know is that you are with me now."

"I'm not with you. You killed Grayson."

The smell of Sebastian's nauseating cologne fills my nostrils when he steps into my space, souring my stomach. He lowers his voice. "I'll tell you a secret." He looks into my eyes as he speaks. "I killed your mother too."

My vision goes dark. His sneer is the only thing I see, and I lunge for him with tears in my eyes and rage in my heart. "YOU BASTARD!"

He was expecting me. He moves fast, stepping to the side and pushing me forward. I'm too far gone to correct myself, and I skid across the ground, angering the glass shards in my arms.

When I sit myself up, my words are out before I have the chance to consider them. "I won't help you." Tears roll down my face. "There's nothing you can do to make me help you."

"Never say never." He mockingly chastises me as he puts some distance between us, waving to the man standing silently at the door.

The guy steps out of the room, and I listen as Sebastian watches me intently.

There's a brief pause, then scuffling as the heavy door opens again and he pushes someone else into the room. They hit the ground with a grunt, and I push myself along the floor until my back hits a wall.

From my spot on the floor, I can't make out who it is until they roll over and sit up.

"CORA!" I crawl the long way around the room to avoid the men and sit myself between her and everyone else.

"I'm sure I can think of something I can do to make you help me." Sebastian's eyes wander over my shoulder at a groaning Cora, and I lean over, blocking his view of her.

"What are you going to do?"

"We. You haven't been paying attention. It's what are *we* going to do?" When I don't play into his game, he continues, "You will be on display at a dinner I'm attending. It will kick off my challenge for Elia's empire, and it will solidify my standing with a few key organizations." He seems to muse to himself. "Elia Lucciano's heir and my puppet." Then he squares his frame on me. "If you are anything less than my quiet, pretty little toy, then Cora will die slowly—in front of you."

Crossing the room, he stops a step in front of me and crouches down, gripping my chin painfully hard to make me look him in the eyes. "Or I will give you the chance to make it quick by killing her yourself."

I tug my head back, aware that when I release myself, it's going to hurt. But having him touch me is worse.

He chuckles as he stands up.

"How am I going to attend a dinner looking like this?" I hold up my arms, and he studies me with disgust, curling his lips into a frown.

"You'll attend naked if I wish it, but you have a point. It would look better if Elia's heir wasn't beaten into submission—which is a shame because that's how I like the women I use." He turns and walks to the door, no longer looking our way. "You have five days until the reception. I'll have a first aid kit sent in to help hide your wounds. For now, dinner is here."

As sick as our conversation made me, I'm still aware I need to eat. I can't afford to lose the little strength I have.

Moments after he leaves, the door opens a crack, and two fast food bags are tossed in.

I leave Cora where she is while I gather the brown paper bags and return to her side, opening each meal and flattening the paper to set the food on top.

"Are you hurt?"

When she doesn't answer me, I look up to meet her wide eyes.

"Good God. What did they do to you?" she gasps, scanning my face.

"Oh, right." I rub my fingers over my cheek, pulling them away to look, but nothing comes off. "It's all dried. I think the blood is from my arms." I lift my hands to show her my lesions, and she looks woozy, so I recover quickly. "It's not as bad as it looks, but I need to get some glass out of my cuts once I get the medical kit. Are you hurt?"

"Nothing like you. They just knocked me around a bit." She turns her attention to the food on the ground between us. "I'm not sure we should eat that."

"You heard Sebastian. He needs me alive for the next five days at least." I take a bite out of both burgers before stuffing a few fries from each container into my mouth. They've been sitting in the bag for a while. "For now, I'll try everything first. Let's give it fifteen minutes. If I'm not twitching on the floor, then we should be good to finish it."

Cora stares at me, expressionless, for half a minute before she starts to chuckle. She sounds a little delirious, but since her tone matches my mood, I join her.

When we've released enough tension, Cora wipes her eyes. "You got fight in you, kid. Selina would have been so proud of you."

I force my food down, tears springing to my eyes as the lump clears my throat.

Now I want to cry. "He said he killed my mom."

She lowers her eyes to the ground, and we sit in silence with his confession while we count out the fifteen minutes.

When I'm confident enough time has passed, I account for what I already ate and separate the food into halves, sliding hers over. "I'll ask for water when they bring the first aid kit. How long have you been here?"

"I might be missing some time, but I think they grabbed me a few days ago. This is my second day in this building. I woke up here, but the room they had me in had a mattress on the floor. Are we still in Portland?"

I start to shake my head, but then I realize I'm not entirely sure where we are.

"I think they may have brought you up to Seattle. Sebastian mentioned attending a reception. I think it's the same one Creed was talking about, but I don't know."

The door opens, and the same guy from earlier looks in. Once he notices us sitting on the floor, he enters and sets the kit on the ground.

"Hey. We need some drinking water. Big bottles, please;

the tap water is dirty. And can you bring the mattress from her room here?" I look at the kit on the ground. It's a decent size, so there should be more than enough to get us both feeling better. Suddenly, my bladder reminds me. "Can you take us to the bathroom?"

"That's what the bucket's for, princess." He snickers, pointing to the space under the sink.

Sure enough, I missed the large pail in the corner. Of course I missed it. It's covered in enough dirt that it matches the floor and the walls.

"I'll get those other things."

When he shuts the door behind him, I eat my last fry and stand, carefully lifting my arms above my head to stretch. I don't bother to push for more than we need.

I flip the latch to the kit and lift the items out, taking stock of each one. There isn't anything I can use as a weapon, but there are tweezers, so I can get to work digging out the remnants of glass from under my skin.

A bottle of painkillers makes me sit up straight. Sebastian wouldn't be so stupid that he'd give me something I could overdose on. When I rattle the bottle, it sounds like there are only a few pills in there. Just enough for one dose each. I drop it back into the kit. I'm not taking those unless I really need to.

Now that I'm feeling steady on my feet, I circle the room once more, flipping a switch I missed earlier, and a dim overhead light turns on. It's better than before.

Cora stands and stretches her back out as I return to the sink. This is the one thing I could have done without better light. The sink isn't yellow because it was made that way. Years of rust and neglect have turned this corner into the opening scene of a slasher movie.

I rattle the sink, checking where it meets the wall and paying close attention to the pipes.

"What are you doin'?" Cora joins me, groaning her displeasure when she sees the state of the sink.

"Well, the way I see it, we have about five days before Sebastian gets what he wants and kills us. We need to figure something out before that happens."

28

LENNOX

My father let me spiral for three days before he sent another text.

I lost my shit on the first day and ended up back at my own place, leaving Henry with Ryder and Amara.

I couldn't let anyone witness my spiral.

I texted again and again with offers to meet Sebastian and discuss terms.

I got no reply.

I slipped into the state my father has always wanted me in: desperate obedience.

I went through every stage of grief except acceptance. I wouldn't accept that Sloane was gone. I will never accept it.

I ended up settling into anger.

We all got played, but she was under Creed's protection when she was taken.

Mostly, though, I'm angry at myself. I never should have let her leave Eros with Creed. Rationally, I know there was no other choice, but I will still allow this turmoil to eat away at me as penance for how badly I failed Sloane.

I needed to fall. I needed to shatter apart so I could bring myself back. I needed to get every emotion and every fear out so it wouldn't poison me from the inside.

By the time Cole stopped by the next morning to bring me back to the house, my self-loathing and anguish had already begun breaking apart.

My father is an arrogant man.

If he killed Sloane during the night, or even harmed her worse than the last photo he sent, he wouldn't be able to stop himself from sending another photo to crush me and force me down to his level.

But none came.

Creed and his group haven't heard anything yet either.

When we arrived at Sloane's last known location, the fire department and paramedics were already on the scene. The vehicle she'd been in was flipped and destroyed. One of Creed's men was dead, and Darius had been knocked out on impact.

Everyone seemed to vanish as soon as they had Sloane.

Now, Sebastian's lack of communication is doing the opposite of what I'm sure he hoped it would.

The next day went by without a word, and I joined my brothers and Henry again. I carried my burner phone everywhere, the ringer turned all of the way up.

It didn't ring.

When I woke up to a second day without her, I slipped into the stages of grief not many of us are ever afforded: hope and determination.

Every minute I don't have confirmation of Sloane's death is another minute that she is alive, and we've been scouring the city for any signs of her since.

I've called in every favor and created new debts in search of her.

Amara, Harlow, and Nyla have taken to caring for our mother and spending time with her while she adjusts. We've set her up with some doctors of our own to assess her health. As far as she knew, Sebastian had taken her on an extended retirement vacation, and none of us had the heart to sit her down and tell her what's been happening.

Finally, my phone pinged with a new image.

Sloane wasn't smiling, but she was alive. The color had returned to her face, and the dried blood was gone.

The photo came with an announcement and a list of demands. Sebastian would be attending the Rossi wedding in a few days, with Sloane as his plus-one. We were all to stand down and allow him to waltz right through the front doors with her.

With everything going on, I had forgotten about the reception. I wasn't planning on attending in the first place. Ryder often handles functions like those, but I made a call and had myself added to his table. Then I contacted Creed.

Angelo Rossi does not take his rules lightly. If we try anything when he's explicitly called a neutral zone, it's considered an act of war against him and his family. While I'm ready to commit myself to burn in hell for eternity to make sure Sloane is safe, I'm not willing to take my family down with me, and the repercussions would have a far reach.

Thoughts of Sloane have been consuming my attention, so I startle when Cole knocks on the open door to the office. "We might have a problem."

"Just one?" I prop my elbows on the desk, cradling my face in my hands before combing my fingers through my hair.

"Cora hasn't shown up for her shift for the last three days, and my staff can't get a hold of her."

That woman is as reliable as they come. This is definitely a problem.

"I want to know when the last time someone saw her was."

That both Sloane and Cora are missing at the same time is too much of a coincidence. If Sebastian is behind this, then Cora is most likely already dead.

When he nods and takes a step away, I lower my head, dragging my hands down my face to try to keep my demons at bay.

"Hey. We'll get her back." Cole hovers by the door.

I thought I was alone.

I try to recover and sit up straight, but Cole just takes it as an invitation to keep talking.

"Sloane won't give up. She's smart, and she's strong even when she doesn't think she is. She won't stop fighting to get back to Henry—and to you."

I send one last text and hate myself immediately.

Lennox: Tell me what you want.

**Unknown: I have special plans for you, boy.
See you soon.**

The days after my father's ominous reply moved slowly.

I never texted again. Doing so would only show Sebastian how desperate I was becoming.

By the time we were ready to leave for the reception, I had cycled through every emotion there was. I had to mentally prepare myself to face my own father. I played scenarios through my head so I was prepared to stay in control through anything he might throw at me.

I would be strong for Sloane.

The plan was to split up everyone in our group according to strengths.

In the end, we agreed that I would attend with Ryder and

Nyla since Cole and Dagen would be working the grounds, searching for a way to extract Sloane from the event without causing problems.

We had to narrow our priorities, so Amara and Harlow left early this morning with Yuri and a full security detail. They escorted our mother and Henry out of range to a safe house Cole set up. They made contact an hour ago to let us know they are settled in and secure.

Amara fought to stay with us, which is exactly why she was sent away. She attempted to go toe to toe with Sebastian once before, and she came dangerously close to being added to his hit list. It got to the point where I had to make an appearance to warn her to back off.

This makes Amara a loose cannon.

There's no telling what she'll do if she sees something she doesn't like. I'm not saying I'm much better, but I can't be worried about holding myself together and keeping her in check at the same time.

"Jesus. You look delicious." When I look over my shoulder at Dagen, I find him staring up the stairs. Nyla smiles shyly as she descends, waving her hand at him as if telling him to stop.

Meeting her at the bottom step, he holds out his hand for her and twirls her into his arms when she reaches the main floor.

She steps back with a smile on her face. "Look at the best part." She reaches into the slit of her full-length gown, and Cole and I turn our attention to the show.

Dagen jumps in front of her, blocking our view. "Woah, woah—WOAH! We don't need to show *everyone* the best part."

Confusion creases her forehead before she realizes how it sounds, then she laughs. "Not that! This." She unhooks the lower part of her dress at the waist, leaving her with tights underneath. She smiles up at Dagen. "It's very spy-like. If I need to, I can tear it off."

"What kind of dinner do you think you're going to?" Cole asks with wide eyes.

"All I'm saying is it's cool, and at some point tonight I'm tearing it off in a grand gesture."

"Just keep it in your pants, Blanche. I'll tear it off you later." Dagen winks as Nyla blushes.

Ryder approaches the top of the stairs in his tux, and the demeanor in the room shifts.

It's time to go.

"Do we all understand our roles?" I ask, adjusting my cuffs.

Cole raises his hand to go first. "Dag and I are circling the grounds, looking for any of Sebastian's men or an opening to Sloane. We're outside unless something goes wrong."

"I'm with you both." Nyla meets Ryder at the bottom of the steps, and he holds out his arm for her to hook hers into. "I'll fade into the background once we're in. If I can get close enough to pull Sloane away, I will."

Ryder nods at me in agreement. Our roles are the same. We are to show up and try to figure out what our father's plan is. Ryder is also there to make sure I don't publicly lose my shit and murder my father in front of over four hundred wedding guests.

As for me, I just want to see Sloane.

I want to figure this out and bring her home to her son.

Then I want to put a bullet in my father and finish this. It's what I should have done twenty years ago, when he first put that gun in my hand, and it's what I wished I could have done every day since, but there was always something stopping me.

There's nothing stopping me this time, and he knows it.

He's going to come at us with his best play.

I just hope we're ready for it.

29

SLOANE

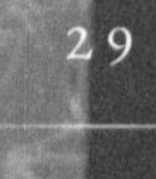

Cora and I stand side by side, staring at the mirror over the sink before exchanging a glance with each other.

Today is the day of the reception.

I know this because I was finally allowed to shower. Cora still hasn't been given that kindness.

When I got out of the shower, a woman was waiting for me in another room. My hair was curled, and I was slathered in enough layers of makeup to hide the welt on my cheek.

Then I was fitted into a purple, knee-length taffeta dress that looked so hideous, I wish I could have worn one of the tacky options the salesgirl picked out for me earlier this week. At least it had long sleeves to cover the thin scabs under my forearms from my wrists to my elbows.

I wanted Lennox to see me in the gown I had chosen, and now this is how I'm going to be presented: like Sebastian's dressed-up doll.

Before he returned me to my room, he spun me to face him, shoving my back into the wall behind me. "Don't get any thoughts in that pretty little head of yours tonight. You'll do well to remember that that woman"—he points to the room Cora and I are sharing—"is still alive because you are doing as you're told. Cross me, and she's dead."

Then he opened the door and told me he'd retrieve me within the hour.

Cora and I have had five days to work out a plan, and this is the only one we've got.

Sebastian's men never bothered to remove the first aid kit from the room after the first day. I used the tweezers and antiseptic to remove the rest of the glass from under my skin, then I bandaged myself up.

Once I was finished with the tweezers, I started using them on the caulking around the medicine cabinet. Each time I removed a little, we dropped it in our pee bucket. We had to make sure we kept the debris to a minimum so no one would notice it when they took the bucket out to empty it. It didn't take long to get enough cleared away that we could pull the mirror off of the wall when the time came.

We've been practicing removing it and putting it back quietly for the last day.

"I don't feel good about this." Cora looks from me to the mirror on the wall. "I think I saw this in a horror movie once, and it did not end well for the broad who went through the hole."

"Nothing is going to end well for us if we don't try." I stare at her in the mirror, and she nods.

"Why don't we both just go now?" She reaches out for my hand, tangling her fingers in mine, and tugs.

"You know why," I say for what feels like the hundredth time.

We've been over this many times before.

If we try to run early, they will for sure catch us since I'm the one they really need. Sebastian will kill her if I defy him.

Our plan is to wait until I'm gone. Cora will remove the medicine cabinet and get to work on the one behind it that faces into another room.

Today was the first day I was allowed out. When Sebastian led me back from my wardrobe fitting, we passed the room beside ours, and the door was left open a crack. It doesn't look like it's being used, so that is one less worry.

"From what I could see, there are two staircases that lead out of the basement to the main level." Cora let me climb up on her shoulders to look out the little window. We face an alley, so I couldn't see much else, but it confirmed we're below ground level. "Go left when you get out of the room, and you should see both."

Cora takes a deep breath, bowing her head as she releases it. Uncertainty creases her features. It's an expression I feel in my gut.

I'm so terrified that I think I've turned myself off.

I have nothing left but a will to do whatever it takes to stay alive. "I mean it, Cora. Fifteen minutes after we leave, you need to get out. If you stay here, they're going to kill you." I pause to make sure she understands my next words. "We don't go down like this."

She locks her gaze with mine, repeating, "We don't go down like this."

The corners of my eyes sting, and I blink rapidly to whisk away the tears threatening to form as the door creaks open. We both spin around and step away from the sink.

"It's time to go." Sebastian looks at me before continuing on to Cora, and I take a step in front of her, drawing his attention back to me.

"I wish to speak to Cora once, at the end of the event, before we leave to come back here." As soon as he cocks his head to the side, I know I'm in danger of pushing too far, so I try to adjust my request. "I want to make sure no harm comes to her when I'm with you, and I'll do as you say."

When he takes another calculated look in Cora's direction, a chill rolls across my skin. A little voice inside my head tells me he was planning on having her killed as soon as we left.

She never would have had a chance to escape.

Sebastian speaks to the man at the door behind him without taking his eyes off us. "You heard her. I'll be calling for this one in a couple of hours. She is to remain unharmed." Then he steps aside so I can walk out of the room.

Another man leads me down the long hallway, but Sebastian isn't behind us. I try to slow my pace as we near the steps, but he pushes me forward. Then Sebastian enters the hall, walking toward us with the other man from the room, and I release a breath I hadn't realized I suppressed.

The timer starts now.

I climb the stairs, trying to track how many minutes pass, and worry settles into me as doubt creeps in.

What if we don't leave right away? I should have told Cora to wait twenty minutes.

It's late in the day. Menacing clouds cross overhead, carrying the threat of rain.

"Smile. We're going to a party." Sebastian stares at me wickedly with one hand on the car's open back door. As if he's a gentleman.

I ignore his comment and tuck my head down to get in, savoring the few seconds when I'm alone in the car. I think a couple of minutes have passed since I left the room. While I don't want Sebastian to get in the car with me, we need to start driving away soon.

I stiffen when the back door opens and he slides into the seat beside me. Two men get into the front seat, and we're driving before another minute is up.

That should give Cora enough time to wait for everything to settle down.

When we were in the basement together, Sebastian's men left us alone. Unless it was time for a meal, which happened twice a day, they would only come by every couple of hours to make sure we were breathing.

Still, my nerves are shot thinking about Cora trying to get out of that place.

"I have some rules you will follow tonight. They are not up for discussion. You know what will happen if you disobey me."

I stare vacantly at the back of the seat in front of me.

Sebastian doesn't wait for me to acknowledge him.

"You will not speak to any of my boys or to anyone in Creed's group. No matter what. Even if I give you the opportunity to speak to them in front of me, you will decline. You will not disrespect me in any way, and you will wholeheartedly agree to anything I say. You do those things for me, and Cora will be alive when you call for her tonight. Do I make myself clear?"

"Yes."

"You will address me as *sir*."

"Yes, sir."

"Very good."

I've lost track of time, but I think I left Cora in the room around ten minutes ago.

The first fat raindrops patter on the window, and I wrap my arms around myself to control a shiver as a cold chill works its way into my bones.

"Do you want to know how your mother died, Sloane?"

It's the way he asks the question that sends a debilitating wave of dread through me. He very much wants to tell me, and I know it's going to break me, but I can't stop myself.

I have to know.

My voice falters when I answer. "Yes—sir."

I don't bother to look at him. I can practically feel the heat from his disgusting sneer from here.

"I have to admit: I was surprised to hear your mother was Valentina, but now I see the resemblance. You both have a... rebellious streak." Derision coats his words.

This is not meant as a compliment.

Suddenly, the car around me feels like it's closing in.

"I knew she was one of Elia's whores, but I didn't know he enjoyed her himself."

I make the mistake of glancing over at him. My skin prickles in disgust when I catch him leering at me.

"Valentina was part of my first shipment of girls to Thailand. Once she realized what was happening, she tried to stir up dissent among our exports on the docks as we were loading them onboard. She tried to organize an escape. Now, I'm sure she probably could have gotten away on her own, but she had a heart. She wanted to save people she didn't even know, people who didn't save her. When I found out what was happening, I had her dragged in front of everyone and I shot her in the head."

He scans my face, searching for confirmation he's getting under my skin as he speaks about her like she was a rabid animal he needed to put down.

"Everyone fell into line after that. Since then, if we have any resistance among our shipments, I tell my men to look for a Valentina, or someone they can use to force obedience, should they need to."

Sucking my cheek between my teeth, I bite down—hard—to stop from showing how badly this is breaking me.

"Your mother died because she defied me, and I made an example of her." Then he looks out the window. "Do not defy me, Sloane."

The car is quiet after that.

Not even the men in the front seat speak among themselves.

When I thought of my mother, I pictured her smiling in the photos Cora showed me. She was happy there.

Now I can't get the image of her dying out of my mind, her body lying limp on the ground. She was all alone.

As the car slows to a stop, I pull myself out of my misery.

Fifteen minutes had to have passed by now.

Cora should have the medicine cabinet out of the wall.

Did I just make the same mistake my mother did? Am I sending Cora to her death? Sebastian will have her murdered on the spot if she's caught.

The elegant five-star hotel we've pulled up to couldn't be further from the dingy building I've spent the last five days in, yet I still feel like I'm locked away in a prison.

Sebastian gets out of the car, circles around the trunk, and opens my door, holding out his hand with a tight smile. "I won't tell you a third time. Smile. We're going to a party." He speaks through clenched teeth.

Looking up at him, my lips tremble as I force a grin on my face. He snaps his fingers then holds out his hand again. Accepting his gesture isn't an option, so I reach up and set the tips of my fingers in his palm, and he pinches them tight.

As we ascend the stairs to the lobby, a man approaches us, speaking only to Sebastian. "Everyone you've asked about is inside, but only two of your boys are here."

"I have no doubt they're all close by." Sebastian dismisses the guy, who returns to the hotel.

Tilting his head to draw my attention to him, Sebastian looks through me with dead eyes. "It's time."

30

LENNOX

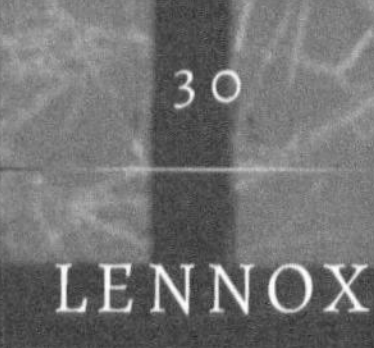

When we arrived at the reception, we were met with security, which consisted of emptying our pockets and walking through a metal detector. The Rossis mean business.

Nyla had suggested trying to tag Sloane with a tracker, but I'm glad we decided against it, as we would never have gotten it through this group.

Once we were cleared, Ryder and I approached Angelo Rossi to offer our congratulations on his daughter's wedding while Nyla broke away from us to look around. Ryder stayed to talk with him longer than I did since he's better at appearances than I am.

I've circled the ballroom twice, and there is no sign of Sloane or Sebastian. I noticed a couple of men who I've seen with my father before, and they both stiffened when we made eye contact.

Security is tight. Even if I had decided to conceal a gun, it would have been taken from me before I entered the front doors. Showing up without a weapon is a sign of respect for Angelo and his family.

When Creed's entourage files in, Darius breaks away from their group and stalks toward me as soon as we lock eyes. Creed glances over at him, then me, before turning his attention to Rossi's group for his own greetings.

"Lennox." He stops beside me, turning to face the room.

"Darius." I take a sip of my soda.

"Are they here yet?"

I shake my head even though he isn't looking at me. "Not yet. Some of his men are scattered around the room."

"Yeah. I see them." We people-watch for a minute before he breaks the silence. "Listen—about Sloane—I'm—"

When Darius chokes on his words, I glance over at him.

The guy is visibly bothered by what happened.

Darius was knocked out cold when their vehicle rolled. He's lucky he was, or he'd be as dead as the guy in the passenger's seat, and Sloane would have still been taken.

Regardless, I understand him feeling responsible for what happened. I feel it too. Even Creed seems more focused on helping her than winning his bid for Elia's successor.

Sloane has that effect on the people around her.

"Stay focused on what we do now." I take another sip.

Darius nods once then steps away from me, returning to Creed's side. He speaks to him before they head into the sea of tables.

"Everything okay?" Ryder asks as he and Nyla take the spot Darius just left.

"Yeah. Creed's group is taking their seats. Have you spotted anyone I should know about?"

"There are a couple of groups here that have done business with our father in the past, but I'm not sure where they stand with him. Rossi asked about Dad. He was curious as to why we were at different tables. I told him we were in the process of reorganizing, but it's nothing to worry about."

The hairs at the back of my neck bristle before I see her walking into the room.

"They're here." Ryder and Nyla follow my line of sight.

The moment I take her in, I'm angry.

I know Sloane; I've watched her for years.

She would never have done her hair like that, and the dress is something gaudy that I'm sure Sebastian has chosen to make her stand out.

She looks lost and embarrassed, crossing her arms over her front in an attempt to hide her flashy self from the room.

Ryder huddles in. "Is that—is she tanned?"

I clench my glass so tight, my drink shakes and spills over my fist before I catch myself.

I recall the first photo Sebastian sent of her. "Considering she should be sporting a shiner on the right side of her face, I'd say he put layers of makeup on her."

Sloane's eyes widen when she glances in our direction, then she looks away.

I turn my attention to Nyla. "She's seen you with us. Now go."

Nyla doesn't skip a beat. Raising her hand, she catches the attention of a waiter and steps toward him, taking a flute of champagne off his tray. Then she slips in between some tables.

Our father's attention will be on us all evening. If anyone has a chance of getting near Sloane, it's going to be Nyla. I follow her as she weaves through the crowd.

I always wondered what Dagen looked like when he was working a job. He would tell some funny stories, but he'd stay away from the more technical aspects of his work. Watching Nyla case the room is impressive. She's focused and aware of everything around her.

The moment Creed sees Nyla, disappointment shadows his expression. He glances over at us before he looks back to her and points to an empty seat at his table.

He's trying to make sure his little sister is safe. His actions are admirable, but Nyla declines and moves on with a smile.

Nyla has a specific job to do tonight, and she can't do it if she's seen with either of our groups.

Ryder swears under his breath a second before my skin crawls at the sound of my father's voice. "Lovely day for a wedding."

I mean to offer my father an impassive glare, but when my eyes land on Sloane standing dejectedly behind him, I can't hide the snarl on my lips.

This makes Sebastian smile.

"Sloane, are you okay?" Ryder draws our father's attention off me, and I take the moment to look her over.

She lowers her gaze to the floor, and the room slips away as I watch her fight to keep it there.

Sebastian turns to her. "You have my permission to answer my son—if you wish to." He stares at her as if his words are a challenge. She keeps her eyes cast down and shakes her head ever so gently. "Well, there you have it. I guess she doesn't want anything to do with either of you." He turns to the men standing behind him. "Please take Lucciano's heir to her seat. I'll join you shortly."

One of my father's men steps forward, leading Sloane away from us as another man remains behind him.

I want to break away from our plan and choke my father to death. I want to go after her. I want to walk her out the front door and take her home, but I know Sebastian has already prepared for every possibility.

"Leave us." I turn my attention to Ryder, and he does a double take at my gruff order.

This isn't part of the plan either.

I rephrase my request. "Find our seats. I'll join you shortly."

Ryder hesitates, then exhales sharply as he walks away from our group.

When he's out of earshot, I scowl at my father. "Tell me what you want."

Sebastian scans the room before answering. "Where's the fun in that?" He smirks. I don't return his sentiment, and he continues, "Now that I have Elia's heir, the opportunities are endless. Look over there." He points to a table filled with suits. "I could trade her for their shipping routes. Or there." Another table. "Their political connections. Or I could just use her myself, then gift her to the cartel to use however they please."

His expression darkens when he doesn't get the reaction he obviously wants, and he pushes for more.

"Or I could kill her. Just put a fucking bullet in her head and take Henry from you too. Raise him like I should have raised you boys." He sighs. "Those are all good options, but now there's something I want more than just Elia's empire."

"And what's that?"

"I want everything. Your shares, the companies you boys run, and you, my oldest son—the one who should have been my golden child—on your fucking knees and ready to do my bidding."

There it is.

After all of these years, he hates that he can't control me. He can't stand that his sons have wills of their own, that none of us wants anything to do with the abhorrent legacy he envisions for all of us.

He doesn't know how to earn the respect of our family.

He's failed to claim the patriarchal role among my brothers, and it's eating him alive.

I change the subject.

"Mom is fine, by the way." I sip my soda.

"Ah, yes. I have been meaning to thank you for moving her back into the house. I'll be taking her back from you too."

The lights flicker once, indicating dinner is about to be served.

We aren't done here, not by a long shot, but this conversation can't happen now.

I spot Ryder at a table, watching us closely.

My father steps into my line of sight, blocking my brother from my view with parting words: "Pay attention, boy. This is how a real leader leads."

When he walks away, I follow him to the table he's heading toward. Sloane sits quietly with one man on either side of her, and she's looking past my father as he approaches. She's looking at me. I know because I feel her from across the room. I feel her hurt and her vulnerability.

When he gets close to her table, one of the men from beside her stands, offering Sebastian his seat. Sloane lowers her gaze to the plate in front of her and sits quietly as my father pulls the seat up beside her and talks to the men around them.

Sebastian has done something, or he's said something, to ensure her obedience, and I want to put my fist through his face at all of the possibilities.

"Do you see Nyla?" I ask Ryder as I slide out the seat beside my brother.

"She grabbed a spot at one of the singles tables. There." Ryder tilts his head at a table two over from Sloane's.

They face each other. This is good.

Ryder lowers his voice. "What did he say?"

"Same old. We've all disappointed him. Except he's most disappointed in you." I reach over to pour myself a glass of red wine.

"Seriously? What?" He catches my smirk. "Oh, fuck off."

As everyone takes their seats, I tilt my head toward Ryder. "I never thanked you for looking out for Sloane and Henry all of these years. I know you were doing it for Grayson, but I just wanted to say it means a lot to me that you have her back." I take a sip of my wine. "I just want—if anything happens to me, please keep them safe."

The color fades from Ryder's face. "Why are you saying this? What are you planning? You promised Cole we were in this together."

I stop him before he texts our brothers to organize an intervention. "I'm not planning anything. I wanted to thank you. We—um, we never got the chance to hang out a lot when you were growing up, and I regret that."

My heart weighs heavily in my chest.

I don't mean to lie to my brother, and right now, it isn't a lie. But if push comes to shove and I have no other choice, I will offer my very soul up to my father in order to get Sloane and Henry out of this alive.

31

SLOANE

Throughout dinner, I took small comfort in the fact that Sebastian only cared to show me off and no one spoke to me while we ate. I sat quietly through each course, barely touching a thing except for the soup and salad.

Eating fast food for five days straight made me crave the healthier options on my plate.

I sat in silence, my mind on Cora. The couple of times that Sebastian's phone vibrated sent me into an internal panic.

Did they catch her? Was she already dead?

He never looked my way, and whatever messages he received seemed to make him happy.

It feels like the main course flew by, but I must have zoned out for most of it.

The waitress sets a plate in front of me, and sweet vanilla fills my nose. I've been so wrapped up in Cora that my nerves are gone, and I can't stomach another bite of anything for fear that I might wretch all over the place.

With the dessert spoon at the top of my plate, I break the

crème brûlée apart and move it around in its ramekin while the men at the table with me shovel theirs into their faces.

For the first time since we sat down, I glance listlessly around the room in a trance, until I lock eyes with the woman I saw standing with Ryder and Lennox earlier.

The first thing I find odd is that she isn't seated at their table. I made a point of looking at the seating chart when we entered so I knew where they would be sitting. I wanted to make sure I wouldn't accidentally look over and see Lennox staring back at me. I didn't want Sebastian to hold anything against me.

The second thing out of place is that she's staring right at me. When our eyes meet, she perks up, cautiously lifting her hand in front of her chest and pointing to the side of the room. I follow her finger across the ballroom. It's an exit that leads into a hall. I swivel my head back to her slowly, hoping to not draw any attention, and she mouths, *Bathroom.*

I nod, lifting my own hand to my collarbone to scratch at my skin and splaying my hand out to hopefully tell her to give me five minutes. She seems to take the hint and smiles at the woman beside her, then gets up and leaves.

I focus on my dessert and force a mouthful down before counting out a few minutes with my gaze set on my plate.

When the waitress approaches our table, I get Sebastian's attention.

"I need to use the washroom."

His expression sours for a fraction of a second before he glances over my shoulder. I know without looking he's checking out Lennox and Ryder to make sure they're seated, then he looks over to Creed's table.

When he speaks, he doesn't address me. "Escort her to the ladies room. No one goes in while she's in there."

Two men from our table stand and wait. That's my cue to excuse myself.

I push my seat back from the table and walk between the chairs toward the exit. I feel most of the eyes in this room are on me as I pass, but I keep my attention plastered on my destination to avoid looking around.

I must be quite the sight, the only woman in the room who needs two grown men to escort her to take a pee. A fresh wave of humiliation fills me when I remember I'm dressed like a cross between a clown and a pageant queen.

No one dares to approach me as I enter the hall, and I proceed to follow the first sign I see toward the ladies room. An arm shoots out in front of me as I reach out to push the door open.

"What are you doing?" My tone is a little higher pitched than I would have liked, but I hope it comes off as disapproval.

"Boss said to make sure you were alone."

"I was there. He said to make sure no one comes in. Do you want to explain to any of the other bosses here why you walked in on their women in the bathroom?"

The nervous glances the two men exchange tell me I'm right to assume there are other, equally dangerous men here tonight. I keep talking. "Look, I need to pee, and this dress isn't easy to maneuver. If you don't want to clean up a mess right here, just let me go."

The guy grumbles, then opens the door. He doesn't enter, but he does crouch down, scanning under the stalls, presumably for feet, and I hold my breath.

He pulls his heavyset body off the floor, then steps back and tells me I have five minutes.

My stomach sinks when he finds it empty. I don't recall seeing any other bathrooms in this area, but there was one farther down the hall.

I open the first stall, then the second and third. They're all empty. I step out and try the last, and before it opens all of the way, a woman whispers, "I'm in here."

Relief surges through me, and I almost cry at the sound of her voice. I have no idea who she is although she looks familiar.

I suddenly feel like I'm not in this alone, but it could be my desperate nerves fraying.

I step into the stall and close the door behind me. "Who are you?"

The woman sits on the back of the toilet with her feet propped up on the seat, clutching her dress in a fist on her lap to keep it from slipping into the water.

"My name is Nyla. I'm—"

"With Dagen. You're Creed's sister."

She leans forward and lowers her voice further. "Yes. We don't have much time. I'm going to try to get you out of here."

She opens her mouth, but I stop her, placing my hand over hers. "You can't. I can't go with you. You need to get a message to Lennox. Tell him they have Cora. She's trying to get away, but if she doesn't, they'll kill her if I don't return. I can't leave until I know she's safe. Even if I could, there are two guys waiting outside."

"Where are they keeping you?"

Now I hate myself for not paying attention. I should have been looking at street signs from the car, but as soon as Sebastian started listing his rules, followed by the story of how he killed my mother, I checked out.

"I don't know. The building looked abandoned. At least, the basement and main floor was. It was a bad part of town, but I don't remember much else. They're keeping us in a basement. There are bars on the windows." As I speak, I realize how little help I am.

"Hey. It's good information." She tries to reassure me, but I know I just described every run-down building within city limits.

A loud knock, followed by a three-minute warning, startles both of us.

I reach up under my dress. "I am sorry to do this to you, but I really need to pee, and if I go out there and then ask to come back, they'll know something is wrong."

Nyla shifts off the seat and stands to the side, averting her gaze. Reaching under the sea of taffeta, I pull my underwear down and quickly do my business, saying, "Crazy first impressions." Nyla laughs under her breath, then a realization hits me. "This is way better than the bucket they gave us to go in."

I flush and meet Nyla's eyes. She heard me, and the pity in her expression tells me I probably shouldn't have said that out loud.

"Um, don't tell anyone I said that. It'll upset Lennox, and I don't want him to do something he'll regret."

She tilts her head to the side. "What do you mean? Said what?" Then she winks.

"Thank you."

There's a knock on the door, and something tells me that is my final warning. The next time, Sebastian's men will just come in.

Nyla climbs back onto the toilet seat as I reach for the stall door.

"Tell Creed I'm sorry. As soon as I know Sebastian can't hurt anyone I care about, then he has my full support. I just don't want anyone else to die because of me."

As soon as I exit the stall, the bathroom door opens, and Sebastian's man glares at me. I lean forward, straightening my dress, then take a step to the sink. I wash my hands quickly, then walk toward the guy, forcing him to step into the hall and let me pass.

I don't hesitate once I'm out of the washroom. I won't give these guys a chance to look around, so I start walking back to our table at a brisk pace without looking back to encourage them to keep up.

By the time I enter the ballroom, they are both right behind me. Out of the corner of my eye, I see Lennox speaking with Ryder. He looks up, and I force myself to keep walking toward Sebastian.

I could turn and walk toward Lennox right now, a little voice in my head suggests, but I push it down. I could do that, but the consequences would be deadly.

Sebastian watches me as I approach him, his eyes darting between me and Lennox's table. Ryder stands and walks toward the exit without looking into the room. He looks like he's in a rush, and I hope Nyla made it out of the bathroom okay.

Sebastian stands with a drink in his hand as I near his table. When I reach for my chair, he pushes it into the table, saying, "It's time to say our hellos."

Gripping my elbow tightly, he guides me around the table and toward Creed's group. Scout spots us approaching first and stands abruptly, causing the people closest to him to look over.

Creed holds out his hand, silently telling him to back down, and Scout takes his seat before he looks at Sebastian. My heart sinks when he doesn't look at me, and I worry he feels I've betrayed him.

Sebastian wastes no time. "I'll get to the point. I have Elia's heir, and I am challenging you for his place."

Creed lifts his napkin off his lap, dropping it onto the table and taking a slow sip of his wine before answering Sebastian, whose grip tightens around my arm in frustration.

"You do know it isn't as simple as that. There will still be a confidence vote." Creed's gaze settles on me as he continues, "And Elia's heir will need to be present for that."

My head is swimming. I'm trying to follow their conversation, to look for what they aren't saying.

Is this Creed's way of trying to keep me alive?

Sebastian's disgusting laugh cuts through my thoughts as I sense someone approach our group from behind. The hairs on my arms stand on end, and I'm sure without looking that it's Lennox.

"Oh, she'll be there." He rattles my arm as he speaks about me. "It won't stop me from using her to further my plans though. I'm already working out a...business deal, and I have plans for her. Her future husband is here tonight." Sebastian lifts his glass to a nearby table, and two men seated there nod. Creed doesn't look over. Judging by the angry look on his face, he already knows where all of his enemies are seated. "I hear they've been trying to expand into the Pacific Northwest but have had some problems—until now. Backing like that, as well as the cartel, should sway many in your organization to see the light."

He's going to force me to marry one of those men at the table. I glance again, and they are both watching our conversation unfold. A cold wave of despair slithers through me when one of the men winks at me. My stomach rolls, and I'm sure he's the one Sebastian is going to try to tie me to.

The heavy presence at my back is gone, and I glance over my shoulder as Creed firmly tells us to leave.

Lennox is no longer at the table.

I don't see him anywhere.

Sebastian walks me away from the group before I snap out of my thoughts, and I glance back to see both Creed and Scout looking at me with cold, impassive stares. I take a deep breath to try to convey how sorry I am, but before I can do or say anything, Sebastian tugs me hard, and a sharp pain travels up to my neck.

I think I missed a piece of glass in my arm.

Sebastian hands his drink to one of his men, then barks orders as soon as we're away from prying eyes. "Get the car."

Two of his men break away from our group, and we continue out of the ballroom.

The remaining men step in front of us as we are cut off a few steps away from the exit.

Lennox takes a step forward. "Don't do this." His eyes are set on Sebastian. "Take me." Sebastian scoffs and attempts to step around him. Lennox spins to face us as we pass. "You want my loyalty? I will do anything you ask."

"No!" I attempt to speak for Sebastian, and Lennox's gaze flicks to mine before he stares at his father.

Where the hell are his brothers? Someone needs to stop this.

Sebastian loosens his grip only to tighten it again, and I hiss, trying to breathe through the pain.

"You will start by letting us leave, boy. You'll have your chance to show your loyalty. I'll be in touch."

Then, with that, Sebastian pulls me out the doors and toward the car. Lennox makes no move to come after us, but he stays still, watching as I'm dragged away. His hands are clenched into fists at his sides.

We get into the car, and I get half a sigh out before my head snaps to the side, hitting the tinted glass window.

Covering my cheek with my hand, I pull away and look over to find Sebastian rubbing his hand and glaring at me as though I hit his hand with my face and not the other way around.

"While you were in the washroom, I got a rather disturbing

call from my men. It turns out Cora has escaped. You wouldn't know anything about that, would you?" I shake my head furiously, and it takes everything I have not to cry happy tears. "Don't worry. I'm sure we'll find her, and she'll be dead by morning. This doesn't bode well for you though."

He's baiting me. I know it, yet I can't help asking, "What do you mean?"

I glance out the back window as we pull away. Lennox's frame is a dark silhouette. I rub the sore spot on my cheek, sure this bruise will soon match the one on the other side.

"She was my bargaining chip. You did as I said because I held her over you. Now that she's gone, you have no reason to fall in line. So now *you* become my bargaining chip. I will have my son's absolute obedience. By the time I'm done with him, there will be nothing left of the man you knew."

LENNOX

As soon as Sloane stands up to walk out of the ballroom with two of Sebastian's goons right behind her, I know she's going to meet up with Nyla, who left a few minutes earlier.

I hold my glass to my lips and speak to Ryder before taking a sip. "Be ready for anything."

"Dad's taking a call." Ryder speaks into his dessert, and I glance over before returning my attention to the door Sloane left through.

It would have to be an important call to answer in the middle of a Rossi event, and the flash of anger on his face concerns me.

Our father has a history of becoming unstable when he's mad.

He disconnects quickly, shoving the phone in his pocket and taking a drink before schooling his features.

My phone buzzes in my pocket.

Cole: Found Cora. Said she was held with

**Sloane, and she has info. She overheard Dad
tell one of his guys to go to his office to
gather some files and destroy evidence
while we're busy here.**

**Lennox: I'm sending Ryder to you. Send him
and some guys for Cora. Take a team with
you. Retrieve Dad's guy and bring them all
to the house.**

When I look up from my phone, I catch sight of a bright patch of purple as Sloane strides into the room at a determined pace.

"Head outside and meet up with Cole. He has a job for you."

Ryder tenses beside me.

I know I worried him earlier with my heart-to-heart, but we can't let a chance like this slip through our fingers.

"I need you out there now, Ryder. I'll get Nyla, and we'll be right behind you."

Without further argument, he stands and walks away as the waiter clears our table's plates.

We're done with dinner, and the toasts should begin soon. People will mingle for a bit, and I want to get to Nyla to find out how it went.

I scan the room for her, and Sebastian catches my attention when he stands with a drink in his hand as Sloane approaches him. He doesn't let her sit down. Instead, he manhandles her and drags her away from their table and over toward Creed.

Darius notices them first, as I don't think he's taken his eyes off them all night. He stands as Creed holds out a hand to settle him, then he sits down.

This might not end well.

They've already started talking, and Creed does not look happy.

Against my better judgment, I approach their group.

The first words I hear are Creed's. "...and Elia's heir will need to be present for that."

It sounds like my father made it official.

Like the weasel he is, Sebastian challenges Creed where he knows no one can touch him.

I come to a stop a few feet behind Sloane when my father laughs. As he speaks, he shakes Sloane in his grip like she's a ragdoll, and my face heats with rage.

"Oh, she'll be there. It won't stop me from using her to further my plans though. I'm already working out a...business deal, and I have plans for her. Her future husband is here tonight."

I follow Sebastian's line of sight to a small group of men sitting a couple of tables away.

They acknowledge him.

Shit.

Our father is trying to get into bed with the Nostra Syndicate.

My vision goes dark.

If anyone approaches Sloane to claim her right now, I will break my agreement with the Rossis, and I will kill all of them where they stand.

The ringing in my ears is so loud that I miss the rest of what Sebastian says.

I catch sight of Nyla, who is back at her table and watching me closely. The concern on her face snaps me out of my haze, and I step away from everyone before I do something I'll regret.

The room has become stuffy, and I need to calm my

demons. I'm in no mood to talk to anyone, so I head to the front and wait in the shadows.

I'm close enough to the doors that the night air cools my skin each time the front doors open. One of the men who was with Sebastian passes by in a rush, heading out.

Then they appear.

Sebastian has a firm hold on Sloane, and they are flanked by a man on each side who move in between us when they see me step out.

"Don't do this. Take me," I challenge him. This is a gamble, but Sebastian pretty much told me what he wants when we spoke earlier tonight. "You want my loyalty? I will do anything you ask."

"No!" Sloane's panic catches me by surprise for a moment, but I hold firm in my spot and stare my father down.

Sebastian Saint does not like to be challenged.

Sloane winces, and I glare at the spot on her arm where he holds her.

My father tips his chin, looking down his nose at me with his smug arrogance on full display.

"You will start by letting us leave, boy. You'll have your chance to show your loyalty. I'll be in touch."

Sebastian drags Sloane past me, and I follow them out to the steps, clenching my teeth and my fists to hold myself firmly in place as I watch him load her into the car.

I have a better chance of getting Sloane back if I appear cowed and helpless against him.

A thud from the car startles me, and I brace myself to listen for a repeat. It doesn't come. Instead, the car pulls out, taking Sloane away from me.

As soon as they are out of sight, I return to the ballroom to find Nyla circling the room looking for us.

Creed and Darius watch as I approach Nyla, but I don't

acknowledge them. I'm not sure if Sebastian left any men behind to see what we'll do.

When Nyla nears me, I hook my elbow, and she slides her arm through it so I can escort her out of the ballroom.

"Did you talk to her?" I ask as we walk.

"Yes. I tried to get her to leave with me. She said they're holding someone named Cora, and she couldn't leave her behind."

I wish I had that information five minutes ago.

This must be why my father didn't shut me down as quickly as he did before. He must know he's lost his leverage over Sloane.

"Cora got away, and we have her. Ryder is on his way to retrieve her, then I need you and Dagen to use your connections to help get her ready. You'll be setting her up and hiding her off grid until we can sort this out." When we leave the hotel, I point at an SUV with tinted windows at the far end of the lot. "Dagen is over there. Let's go."

We descend the stairs, and Nyla asks, "Where's Cole?"

"He's doing something for me."

When we reach the SUV, I usher Nyla to the passenger seat and send off a final text to Cole before hopping in the back.

Lennox: URGENT: I want everything you can find on the Nostra Syndicate.

Dagen looks back at me through the rearview mirror as he heads toward the house, but he doesn't say anything.

I use the driving time to replay tonight's conversations. Right now, all I have are a lot of moving parts, but eventually something has to fall into place. If it doesn't, I'll blow the whole thing up and start again.

When we arrive at the house, I send Dagen and Nyla out to

the pool house to meet up with Ryder and Cora, who should be arriving shortly.

Ryder texted me earlier to tell me what he knew so far from Cora. My skin felt too tight for my body when he told me they ate two fast food meals a day, weren't allowed to shower, and had to shit in a bucket.

With that vision firmly rooted in my head, I make my way into the main house, then head for the basement to get the room ready for my next guest.

I'm halfway through setting up my table when Cole opens the door with an angry look on his face. I turn my attention back to the table in front of me as he speaks.

"Fucker made me chase him. You know I hate running." The thing that makes me smile to myself as my back is turned is Cole's irritation.

He really hates running.

The chair clatters behind me as Cole tosses the guy into it saying, "Sit down," a little too late.

When I lock eyes with Sebastian's guy, my cheeks stretch wide in a shit-eating grin. I have been wanting to get my hands on my father's lawyer for years.

He stares at me in horror, his pupils shrinking to pinpoints in a sea of white.

"Good evening, William."

"I-I-I don't know anything."

I open my mouth to speak when a pungent odor fills my nose. The growing wet stain spreading outward through his pants at his crotch tells me all I need to know.

This isn't the first time someone has relieved themselves at the thought of what I will do to them.

Cole steps close to his other side to cage him in.

"Now that's a lie, isn't it, Willy?" I tsk him. "Here's your offer. You answer every question, then you flip, and you're my bitch until Sebastian is in the ground and I'm done with your... services. Then I'll let you catch a plane to live out the rest of your pathetic life somewhere far away."

He hesitates.

I don't.

I reach for the cloth on the table, slowly unwrap it, and hold its contents between us.

He leans forward, his eyebrows scrunched together as he tries to make out what I'm showing him.

"You should know, Ratchet didn't get this offer. Neither did Paulie—and I liked Paulie." I jiggle the cloth in my hands, and the pieces of Ratchet's finger roll over, clearly showing a nail that's hanging off the tip of one of the pieces.

William's back goes ramrod straight as he pales, then dry heaves. His body timbers to the side, but Cole catches him, slamming him back into the chair. "He's gonna yack. Hey!" Cole snaps his fingers in front of William's face. "I'm not cleaning up puke tonight. Swallow it down."

I ignore his distress.

Leaving the cloth open, I set it on the table. William watches closely as my hand continues across my tools before I pick up a pair of heavy-duty pruning shears and hold them between us.

He makes a sick dry-heaving sound.

"Do we have a deal? Or do I start cutting?"

He fists his hands into his chest and nods furiously before agreeing to my terms. I set the shears down as Cole slides a chair over from the side of the room and gets comfortable. I stay where I am, looking down on William from above. A big part of me still wishes he had refused my offer so I could destroy him, but I'm sure his day will come.

I cross my arms and start with the most important question: "Where is he keeping her?"

William flattens his hand and makes a writing motion across it as he asks for a pen. "I can give you the exact address, but they'll be gone before you get there. I was supposed to be back by now." When he's finished writing, he hands both the pen and paper to Cole, who passes it on to me.

I know the area. It's run-down and filled with squatters and transients.

I move on. "What were you doing at his office?"

He looks at Cole. "I was picking up some files and destroying evidence that your father was holding onto."

Cole follows up that answer with, "What kind of evidence?"

"Bribery, murder for hire...there was documentation of some trafficking: locations, names. He wanted to get rid of anything that would incriminate him and keep the stuff he could hold over you boys."

"What could he hold over us?" My patience is running out.

We haven't done anything wrong in any of this.

"He put various properties in your names. They are all tied to different crimes. Once he took over Elia's empire, he was going to set you boys up to take the fall."

I take a step back from the conversation, and Cole looks up at me.

Now everything makes sense.

Sebastian was slowly adding traceable properties in our names and cutting himself loose from his sins. If he distanced himself from our family business, he could reclaim it when we went down for his crimes, as long as he had Elia's money to fall back on.

"Were you able to destroy those files?" I notice William can no longer look me in the eyes when he answers.

"Your men." William turns his face toward Cole to answer him instead. "They took some files and a few memory sticks off me when you—um, caught me." Cole frowns at the memory of him running all over again. "Everything is on there."

It's getting late, and I need a break, or I'm going to lose what little control I have left and snap William's neck.

I point at the couch. "We'll revisit this in the morning. The door is locked from the outside."

I turn to pack my tools into a small leather case, then head for the door with Cole.

"Wait." William stops us. "There's no bathroom in here." He looks at the room around him.

I hand Cole my leather case and step out the door before returning with a bucket.

"Here. It was good enough for Sloane for all of those days. Surely you'll get the hang of it overnight."

I stare him down, and he backs away, timorously muttering that it's more than adequate, which just saved him a beating before bedtime.

When we get back to the main floor, I cross the room silently into the office and head for the bourbon. Cole drops my satchel on the desk and joins me.

"Damn." He raises his glass to me. "It feels really fucking good to work with you, brother."

I nod and drink everything down in one gulp because I don't have the words to describe how great it feels to have my brothers in my corner.

Cole pours a splash in both of our glasses and walks to the desk. "You and Ryder are so similar it hurts. Well, except for the part where you're batshit crazy, but give him time." He reclines into his seat and kicks his feet up on the desk. "Are we going after Sloane?"

I shake my head, take the other seat in front of the desk, and put my own feet up. "His lawyer is right. They won't be there. Have your guy look the place up. I want to know who it's registered to. Maybe that will give us a clue to where they are going next."

"So what do we do now?"

"I'll question William again in the morning, and he'll start undoing all of those properties with our names on them and distancing us from Sebastian's crimes. Then I'll get him to show us all of the stuff we have on Dad." I finish my drink and lean my head back, looking up at the ceiling. "And I still need everything you've got on Nostra. They have a weakness, and I'll use it to sever whatever loyalty they think they have to Sebastian. Then we've got him."

I close my eyes, letting the start of our plan take root. It will grow into something we can use.

I know it will.

It has to.

I just hope we put everything together in time to find Sloane.

33

SLOANE

I didn't realize how badly I stunk until I was unceremoniously tossed into a different room in the same building and told to change out of my dress and into my old clothes.

Sebastian threatened my life more than once on the ride home, but he didn't hit me again. If he's telling the truth and he's planning on giving me to another man, I probably lose my value if I'm covered in bruises.

No one wants to play with a broken doll.

The new room had even less than the first one I was in. There was no sink or fixtures on the wall, and there was no mattress. We're down a different hall, and it would have been easy to drag the old one over, but I didn't ask for it.

The one thing this room had was a bucket.

As bad as my old clothes smelled, they were better than the dress. I wasted no time peeling it off. I kept the new underwear and bra though. Then I pulled on my pants and top.

I sat cross-legged in the corner of the room, pulling the bobby pins out of my hair and trying to uncurl the monstrosity on top of my head. I thought about picking the lock, but there wasn't one on the inside of the room, which led me to notice there was no window either.

The cuts on my arms are healing. Some of my scabs came off when I removed the sleeves of the dress, leaving little slivers of newly healed flesh underneath.

One exposed lightbulb flickered from the middle of the room, and exhaustion crept in. I bit the tip of a bobby pin until the hard plastic nub came off, then slowly felt around the spot on my arm where Sebastian grabbed me earlier. Sure enough, a scab marked the spot where I must have missed a piece of glass.

Using the metal, I slowly worked the skin until my scar opened. I had to stop more than once until the urge to scream passed and my hands stopped shaking, but eventually I worked the broken piece to the surface.

Once my adrenaline faded, I cried in my corner.

Survival is a funny thing.

I cried in despair for a long time. I cried because I was sad for myself, I wanted to stay here, I wasn't ready to leave. It wasn't until I thought about leaving Henry and Lennox that my despair evolved into something stronger. It grew into a weapon, and I used my new fire to push myself out of my worst nightmare. I started fighting against it.

What could I do? Not much, but not nothing.

I began bending and molding the bobby pin until it had a curve that allowed me to conceal it between my cheek and the outside of my lower teeth. Then I did the same thing to one more pin and hid it on the other side. I left the rest of the pins scattered on the floor in case they remembered I had them.

Then I braced myself in the corner, tipped my head back, and closed my eyes.

A sharp pain in my thigh startles me awake.

It's followed by a shiver that seems to seep deep into my bones.

"We're leaving. Get up."

It's the cranky one who followed me into the bathroom at the reception.

He groans his displeasure when I stretch and rub my eyes. Then he bends over, grabs my arm, and stands me up. "What did you do?"

I follow his finger. He's pointing at the dried blood on my arm. "I had a piece of glass I needed to get out."

As I hold up my arms and answer, the bobby pin digs into the gums below my teeth, and I snap my mouth shut and hastily stand without another word.

There's a lot of commotion in the building around me, but when I'm led through the hallway, the men halt their conversations, then resume their tasks after I've gotten far enough away.

Being in a basement room with no windows is disorienting, and I'm surprised it's still dark when I pass by the first room with a window.

I'm being moved in the middle of the night.

Something has changed.

Sebastian is getting into a car as I step into the alley, and he glares at me in disgust before my head and face are covered with a coarse fabric that scratches my skin. My arms are jerked together in front of me, and my bones ache as my wrists are bound. Then I'm pushed forward a few steps before I'm loaded into a van, the telltale sliding door behind me sealing my fate.

I stay where I land and don't bother moving for the entire drive. I can't tell if I'm just trying to appease my captors or if I'm paralyzed with fear, but all I see behind the sack on my head is Henry's beautiful face.

I wonder if my mom pictured my face when she was scared.

Delirium sets in, and I imagine I must have fallen asleep from the gentle rocking motion of the vehicle, because I startle when I'm hauled out of the van. I stumble two steps to the side before someone grabs me by my upper arms and sets me upright.

Then the men around me start walking, and I'm dragged along with the sounds of their footsteps as I'm led somewhere else.

I tell myself over and over again: as long as I'm moving, I'm still alive.

Then we stop walking, and I'm shoved to a kneeling position.

The sack is still over my head, and it makes no difference, but I blink my eyes shut and pinch my lids as hard as I can as the sound of my heartbeat rushes through my ears. If this is it, then—

I shiver and clutch my chest as the fabric is pulled off my head. The light in the room is entirely too bright to focus. Blinking rapidly, I look down at the designer shoes two feet in front of me.

Once my eyes adjust, I look up to find Sebastian glaring down at me, taking satisfaction in my suffering.

"One of my men didn't check in, so you have a new home for a while." He averts his gaze over my shoulder and lifts his hand in a subtle wave to whoever is behind me.

The guy steps in front of me with a pocketknife, and I flinch, making the smile on Sebastian's face widen. He slices the zip tie binding my wrists, taking a little piece of skin with it, and I growl to suppress the scream in my throat.

"If I'd known how much of a problem you would cause for me, I would have killed you a long time ago, and—like your mother—they would never have found your body." Sebastian brushes a speck of dust off his jacket in annoyance as his man pulls my arms tight behind me, replacing the zip tie with handcuffs.

The metal is cool against my sore wrists.

Once I'm secure, he pulls my arms up and back, attaching the cuffs to a chain on the wall. He allows the heavy metal some slack so I can remain seated and possibly lie down.

"Get some rest, Sloane. You're going to need it." Sebastian waves to his man, who heads over to a chair near the door and takes a seat.

He takes one last triumphant look down on me before turning and walking ten feet away. Then he stops to look over his shoulder at me.

Not once does his sneer leave his face.

"I thought you'd appreciate my choice of venue. It holds so much—family history." He points to a closed door off to the side of the room. "My boy killed a man for the first time just through those doors. Shot him in the back of the head on his sixteenth birthday." He points his forefinger at me, pretending to shoot, and his repugnant pride makes me sick.

"You're lying."

His expression slips, and it is only for the briefest moment that I see how badly he wants to kill me. But for some reason he can't—yet, and I shrink into myself.

"That's not the best part." He braces his foot on a wooden pallet and pushes it. It skids five feet away, revealing a large brown stain. Sebastian turns to walk away. Numbness creeps into my arms as my skin prickles in an innate awareness I don't yet understand.

When I hang my head, refusing to ask, Sebastian turns to leave, saying, "I thought it fitting you should die where Henry's father took his last breath."

The room feels as though it is expanding and contracting around me as I look at the stain on the ground, matching it against the memory of the video Creed showed me.

This is where I lost him. I never asked to see where it happened. I didn't think my heart could handle seeing the place where he was taken from me.

It turns out I was right.

I can't handle it.

I wait until the door closes behind Sebastian, then I sob myself to sleep.

34

LENNOX

Dagen and Nyla left town last night. They took Cora to a place Cole owns in the middle of nowhere until we can sort this out.

If this keeps up, Cole is going to run out of properties to hide people in.

I wait until Cole and Ryder are asleep upstairs before I slip away early in the morning, telling the guards at the front gate to look the other way for a couple of hours.

The old building is abandoned, as I knew it would be.

I follow Cora's description down the stairs into the dank basement and find the room she and Sloane were kept in for the past five days. The area is littered with discarded fast-food bags, and the pail they were forced to use is right where she said it would be. The medicine cabinet rests on the floor beside the sink.

There's no one here.

I walk the halls, peeking into each room as I pass it until I find a pile of purple fabric.

It's the dress Sloane wore only hours ago.

"So why are we meeting here?" Creed asks from the doorway. Then his eyes settle on the bright purple fabric. He answers his own question with a solemn "Oh."

Behind him, Darius steps into the room a little too quickly. The sight of Sloane's dress catches him off guard, and he backs into the wall at the sight as though it'll attack him.

I waste no time. "You know who Sebastian is pulling to his side?"

"Nostra."

I nod. "We're waiting on information we can use against them."

"Already have it." When my expression morphs into impatient frustration, Creed explains. "It turns out the head of the family has a fiancée who ran away years ago, and they haven't been able to find her."

"But you can?"

"But we *did*," Creed corrects me. "Darius is catching a flight in a few hours to secure the package. We'll have her by lunchtime. Do you know where he has Sloane?"

I shake my head.

I'm not sure what Sebastian will do once he realizes he's lost Nostra, so we have to find her fast.

Darius crouches over Sloane's dress, pulling at the fabric and scanning the area.

"How is Ghost doing?" I ask.

"Why don't you ask him yourself?" The answer comes from Creed's direction, but his lips don't move.

Creed stands and steps aside, and his second enters without a sound.

That's why they call him Ghost: no one hears him until it's too late.

He tips his head once in greeting and circles the room.

I address Creed, putting everything on the line. "I'm ending this, and I need your help."

Sebastian is running out of time, and that means I am too.

So by the time the sun breaks the horizon and brightens our dining room, I've got every file on my father spread out over the table and I'm on my third cup of coffee.

"Jesus. Did you get any sleep last night?" Cole rubs his eyes walking toward the coffeepot.

"An hour or so. I need to figure this out."

He breaks his stride, looking at the papers and files all over the place. They were able to grab a lot of documents when they picked William up.

Cole takes a step to the table. "What are you thinking?"

I detach myself from my real thoughts and stick to the facts. "I think things are going to get bad really fast, and we need to find out where he has Sloane."

Dagen checked in an hour ago. Nyla and Cora are settled, and he's on his way back to us.

I've sent Ryder out with our men to all of my father's hidden properties listed in the documents we recovered. The building Sebastian originally kept Sloane and Cora in was one of his, so it would make sense that he'd access another property he thought we wouldn't know about. So far, the first two on the list were dead ends, but they are still checking in.

I stand, gathering a pile of papers. "William has slept long enough. It's time he earns the air he breathes."

"Give me a sec. I'm coming with you." Cole grabs two mugs and fills them, putting cream and sugar in only one of them.

William sits up as soon as we enter the room. I can't tell if the urine stench is from his accident last night or him using the bucket.

Ignoring the smell, Cole crosses the room and hands the guy a black coffee. He lifts his own mug to his nose and inhales deeply before setting it on the table and taking the bucket out of the room.

"Your life is tied to Sloane's life, and I'm running out of people to kill to find her."

William chokes on his first gulp. "I don't know where she is. Sebastian never shared his next move until we were ready to make it."

I already know all of this.

Cole returns to his coffee and leans against the table while I toss the papers on the couch beside William. "These are properties in his name we knew nothing about. Do any of these stand out to you?"

William is wise not to waste any time. He sets his coffee on the floor in front of him and picks up the papers, flipping through each page, muttering, "It'll be somewhere he wouldn't be noticed, an out-of-commission building. Most of these are legitimate businesses that operate during the day to conceal what he does at night." He pulls two sheets to the top, then holds them out to me. "Check these first."

Disappointment sets in when I check the addresses. These two have already been cleared.

I check the time on my phone. Darius is already on a plane.

"I'm going to have breakfast brought to you, then you'll be working with my men to fix everything in here that ties any of my brothers or me to what Sebastian has done. Then you'll create a nice little package that points the authorities right to Sebastian."

"But everything that implicates him implicates me."

"Then you better choose a final destination that doesn't

allow extradition." I shut him down and turn to Cole. "We have some things to take care of."

It took most of the day, but all of Sebastian's hidden properties came up empty. Creed called to tell us Darius was on his way back in a private plane with the woman he was sent to find and they were in the process of negotiating with Nostra.

For some reason, they really want to get their hands on this woman.

As soon as he sent video confirmation that he had her, they were open to talks. It's surprising because Creed and Elia Lucciano were the reason the Nostra Syndicate never got a foothold on the Northwest coast.

Sebastian hasn't contacted me with a task to prove my loyalty, and that isn't a good sign.

As each minute passes with no new information, I inch closer to desperation.

Sloane is in imminent danger. I feel it at the core of my being.

My brothers have all returned from their tasks to rally around me from here, but until we know something we don't already know, everything is useless.

I snap.

When I step out of the office, followed closely by Dagen, Cole and Ryder stop what they're doing and approach me.

The apprehensive look on Cole's face tells me I'm not hiding my emotions.

"What's up?" he asks.

"William knows something. Even if he doesn't think he does. I'm questioning him again."

I expect them to stop me when I head for the basement

stairs, but they don't. They file in after me, and William looks like he's going to shit himself when he sees all of us.

"We're going over this once more." I point at the papers I tossed on the couch this morning. "If he isn't in a hidden property, what other options does he have?"

William stands up from the table he was hunched over and crosses the room. One of our men who was sitting with William tells Ryder they have everything they need to proceed, and Ryder sends them away, telling them to take a break.

"He—he was talking a lot with the cartel, but I'm not aware of any places where he could hide out for an extended period of time."

As Sebastian's lawyer tries to tell us something we don't know, Dagen steps over to the table and slides some papers around.

He speaks over his shoulder. "What was Paulie taking care of?"

I don't immediately follow Dagen's question, so he elaborates. "You said Paulie was Dad's proxy at a meeting when you picked him up. What was he doing for him?"

William looks ill all over again. He knows Paulie didn't make it back.

When he notices me shift my attention to him, he averts his eyes, flipping furiously through his pile of papers.

"They were transfer docs for Saint's Wharf. Your father was finalizing ownership to make sure he had complete control of the waterfront—well, everything except one building for some reason."

A strange sense ripples along the skin at the back of my neck. "Which building?"

He continues to thumb through the papers, licking his finger every few sheets until—

"This one." He passes me the sheet, and I scan the information for something that stands out.

It was in front of my face all along.

My father tried to bury it until it was too late.

"Sebastian is keeping her here." I turn to face my brothers.

Ryder speaks up first. "How do you know?"

"Dad always makes an example out of those who challenge him. This is about me." I hold the paper up. "This is where he had me shoot a man for the first time—on my sixteenth birthday."

I never told them any of this.

Dagen looks like he's going to pass out. He's old enough to remember what we thought that night meant to us. Cole drags his hand through his hair, swearing under his breath.

"That's not all."

"It never is," Cole mutters.

"This is where I found Grayson's body. He's going to kill Sloane where Grayson died, and he left the building in my name to punish me for my disloyalty. He knows this will eviscerate me. I won't be able to part with the property, but I'll never be able to look at it. It will forever be a shrine to what he sees as his retribution."

I know without a doubt that this is where Sebastian has Sloane, and I run out of the room, taking the stairs two at a time on my way to the office. Grabbing my phone off the desk, I dial Creed's number, and he answers on the first ring.

"I'm texting you an address. I'm positive they're there. I need your men because he won't be alone. And Creed—it goes down like we discussed."

There's a pause on the phone before he answers me. "Agreed."

The line goes dead.

When I reach for my keys, I lock eyes with all of my brothers.

Cole steps forward. "Tell us where you want us."

This is the end, and it's all too real.

I hesitate, and Dagen catches on. "I know that look, Lennox. We are all doing this—together."

When I try to explain, Ryder cuts me off. "Lennox! You have literally"—he points to his mouth as he repeats and enunciates the word—"lit-er-al-ly saved all of the women we love. You sacrificed everything for us, and it's noble. Any of us would have done the same thing, but it ends here. WE"—he points between himself and my brothers—"are in this with you. We are doing this as brothers. Now, tell us where you want us, and let's finish this—together."

By the time we reach the wharf, we have all of the intel we need thanks to Creed and his group.

It turns out, Sebastian had brought in the cartel for a full-on ambush, but things began to fall apart for him when Nostra backed out.

This was all thanks to the leverage we're holding over them.

The cartel is still in place, waiting for a signal to start fighting, and they are Sebastian's only hope of getting out of here alive.

Cole and Dagen broke away from our group to support Creed in finding and capturing the cartel's ringleader. Once we have him, we'll be able to force their surrender, and Sebastian will have nowhere else to turn.

The roads around the block of warehouses are deserted, eerily so. There is no easy way to pull up to the warehouse I need without exposing ourselves from all directions.

Ryder parks the car close to a side wall. I get out and point to the building where I'm going to start searching for Sloane.

Close to ten of our men join us, waiting for their orders. The rest of our guys are positioned all over the wharf in an effort to cut off Sebastian's ways of escape.

Ryder follows my finger. "We can't just walk in there. You'll be shot before you reach the front door." He points to the tops of the buildings surrounding us, and we all look up. Turning his attention to the men around us, he quickly breaks them into groups.

Some are tasked with searching nearby buildings in case Sloane is being held somewhere else, and others are to find a good spot and provide cover.

Then Ryder looks at me.

"Give me a second. I'm going to create a distraction."

"What are you going to do?"

Ryder doesn't answer my question, and I follow him as he walks to the back of the car and opens the trunk. Holstering his gun, he reaches in and pulls out a grenade launcher, looking at me with a grin that eats up his entire face.

"I have no fucking idea, but I've been dying to use this. When you hear the signal, run flat out to the front of the building. We've got you."

I nod, asking, "What's the signal?"

Ryder's laugh is sinister. "You'll know it."

He sends everyone away with their roles before slipping into the shadows himself.

I look at the warehouse across from where I'm standing.

Sloane has to be in there. It's the only place that makes sense, especially now that we have confirmation that the cartel is here.

I hang back in the shadows and wait, my sight focused on my goal.

It only takes a couple of minutes before a soft *thwup* catches my attention. Less than two seconds later, a delivery truck explodes in the middle of the road, and it goes flying into the air.

I take off running.

A couple of gunshots cut into the sound of the explosion, but I'm not hit, so I keep moving until I reach the front door.

The sight in the room sends a raging inferno through my veins.

Sebastian.

I pull out my gun, shielding myself behind the first thing I see as the fighting starts in the streets outside and Sebastian dives behind a counter. The man with Sebastian isn't so lucky, and I catch him with my second bullet. He doesn't get back up.

"It's over!" I holler.

"You—"

I don't hear the rest of Sebastian's response. I'm pretty sure I hear Sloane yelling, and I block out the rest of the world, trying to focus on her words. I can't make anything out, but the emotion behind it is loud and clear.

Distress.

"YOU CAN CATCH ME OR YOU CAN SAVE HER." When I look back to where Sebastian is hiding, I find him pointing a gun at the wall. It's only when he fires that I realize it's a flare gun, and the weathered walls of the warehouse light up in an instant.

I try to run into the warehouse, but I'm halted when a bullet tears apart a piece of the wall near my head. Sebastian is holding me back until the fire has spread too far to contain.

He is right: I can't get them both.

Not when he opens a door behind him. It's a side exit, and the door I need is at the opposite end of the room.

A blood-curdling wail grips my soul and seals my fate.

I wait until the door flaps shut behind my father before exposing my location, then I run in the direction of the scream.

By the time I reach the place where I found Grayson, the fire has fanned out. The air is thick with smoke, and breathing is difficult. The cracking and popping of the heavier beams chills me as I burst through the doors.

I shatter at the sight of Sloane kneeling and hunched over. The tips of her hair touch the floor in front of her.

She doesn't stir when I reach her and cup her face, desperately trying to wake her before she leaves me for good.

"Wake up. Open your eyes."

A small murmur gives me hope, and I reach behind her to look at her hands. She's cuffed, and it's fastened as tight as it can be. Red lines wrap around her wrists. She's been fighting to get out.

The chain attached to the wall is a beast. Thick metal secures her tightly to a wrought-iron ring on the wall, and the fire is nowhere near this wall yet. I grip the chain and pull as hard as I can, but it doesn't give in the least.

I only have my gun with me. I scan the room, but there is nothing in here I can use to get her out of these chains. This place has been cleaned out.

I could leave to find something, but I'll never make it back in time.

My world slips away.

I'm where I want to be.

I'm with Sloane.

I won't let her go again.

Kneeling in front of her, I cup her beautiful face in my hands once more and lean in, kissing her lips softly as I let myself feel everything I've ever felt for her.

"Baby, don't leave me."

SLOANE

I knew when I didn't get breakfast—or lunch—that something was wrong.

It took me begging not to wet myself before one of Sebastian's men dragged a bucket over and pulled my pants down so I could crouch and go. By then, I didn't care. I peed then stood stiff while he pulled my pants back up like I was a child.

He never did release my hands from the cuffs behind my back. I'm convinced it's because he doesn't have the keys.

Sebastian would only treat me this way if I've lost my value.

My shoulders and wrists ache from the strain of being fastened to the wall. I'm tired and broken to the point where I'm kneeling, hunched over myself in the middle of the room.

I can't stop looking over at the stained spot on the floor.

I miss him every day.

Grayson was my rock, and he would have been a wonderful father.

Henry.

I take a deep breath and imagine the smell of his clothes, but it just isn't the same.

The door creaks, but I don't look up. I'm too exhausted to stand and face Sebastian, and I can't bear to look at him.

The door opens and closes again without the sound of footsteps approaching, so I sneak a glance at the exit.

No one is there.

No one.

Even the man who was guarding me is gone.

This is the first time they've left me alone since we've arrived.

I strain to listen for voices—anything. I should feel relieved to be left alone, but worry prickles along every nerve ending.

An explosion booms from outside, rattling the walls around me and reverberating into my bones.

"H-hello?" When no one comes in to shut me up, I try again, raising my voice a little more. "I—I'm in here."

Two loud pops: gunshots.

I jump to my feet in spite of the pain in my back and limbs.

"Help! I'm in here!" I yell in the direction of the only door.

I have no idea who's out there, but I'm dead if I stay quiet.

I thread my fingers around the thick chain attaching me to the wall and start tugging, fully aware that I've lost most of my strength.

I raise my voice, trying again, and I hear yelling from all around the building as shots continue to blast outside.

Adrenaline sends shockwaves through my body as my nerves fray, and I pull frantically as tears roll down my dirty face.

"I'm here. Help me. Please."

Vertigo sends me to the side. I've barely slept, I haven't eaten, and I'm at my limit. I land hard on my knee. The impact sends a sharp pain into my hip, and I fall over, wrenching my arms behind me.

I try to stand again, but my knee won't support me, so I grab the chain from my position on the ground and try to pull when a terrifying smell fills my nose.

Smoke.

I freeze for a fraction of a second. Then the possibility of burning to death registers, and I scramble up, standing through the pain.

"Help." My voice is barely there, and I yell again as I pull at the chain, planting my feet into the ground, trying to wrench myself out of my cuffs.

My feet slide along the dirty floor, failing to gain purchase over and over again.

The skin around my wrists burns, but nothing gives.

Stopping to catch my breath is a mistake because my body mutinies against my heart, shutting down my will, and I break.

My eyes sting, a combination of smoke and tears, as I tuck my legs under my body and rise to my knees. I pull once more, but all I manage to do is hunch myself over into a bowed position, held up by my hands tied to the wall behind me.

A pained scream fills my ears before I realize it came from me.

I'm so tired.

Remember Henry's smile. I screw my eyes tight to picture him, then I feel nothing as darkness wraps itself around me.

I've had this dream before.

Grayson always tells me it's a shame to hear a slow song and not spend it with me in his arms.

My dream always starts the same way. We're at the club

above Eros, and the first chords of a slow song start, parting the crowd on the dance floor.

Grayson steps to my side. He tickles his fingers down my arm before tangling them in my own. Then he asks me to dance.

I always say yes.

Stepping in front of me, he leads me through the crowd and onto the floor.

We look each other in the eyes as we start to sway, and I imagine it's Grayson's way of silently telling me we are in this together.

He searches my face and waits for me to smile at him before pulling me close and holding me tight, drawing swirls on my skin with the tips of his fingers.

Every now and then, he kisses the top of my head. Sometimes he combs his fingers through my hair.

It's the way we move, like one, as the music plays that comforts me the most.

To everyone standing around the dance floor, it's a simple dance, but it is so much more. It's a connection that makes my heart sing.

When I am out here with him, I am safe, and I am home.

A few couples join us on the dance floor, and we continue turning, swaying, and moving together.

Grayson tips my head, looking down at me with his crooked smile.

"Wake up. Open your eyes."

His words are odd, but we keep dancing because I don't want this song to end.

I want to stay here with him.

The music isn't over yet, but the other people on the dance floor have left.

This is new.

Then I see him, standing off to the side, watching us.

Lennox.

He's never been here before.

Grayson stops moving but holds me tight as Lennox approaches us, but he doesn't look mad. Lennox looks regretful when he puts his hand on Grayson's shoulder and asks if he can cut in.

Grayson looks at me, then smiles at Lennox and takes half a step away from me. He kisses the back of my hand before answering him. "I've been waiting for you to ask. Take care of her." Then he lets my hand go and backs away.

Grayson vanishes before I can call him back, but Lennox is here now, rocking me in place, and he kisses me.

Suddenly, he speaks, and his tone sounds urgent.

"Baby, don't leave me."

My eyes snap open.

Lennox kneels in front of me, cupping my face between his hands.

The noise in the room around us is terrifying as wood crackles apart and a thunderous roar fills my ears.

I try to suck in a deep breath, but only heated air fills my lungs.

"Nox?" I choke on his name.

"Peach." Tears fill his eyes. "I thought I lost you." He reaches around to tug on the chain behind me, reminding me of my situation as my eyes rise to the ceiling. Flashes of bright orange and yellow appear through the rafters, and it's now I realize how hot it's become.

"The building is on fire. I'm trying to get you out, but I can't. Baby, I love you. I won't leave without you."

Lennox wraps his legs around my body as if to settle

himself in with me while we burn to death, and everything comes crashing into me.

I jerk myself back from him hard, and he watches me in surprise as I work my tongue around the outside edges of my gums. The bobby pins are hard to access at first, but I manage to pry them loose. With wide eyes, I spit them out between us. Then I lose my shit and wail, "I LOVE YOU TOO!"

He stares between the pins and me in utter shock before he jolts up.

"What—how did you—never mind."

Picking the bobby pins off the floor, he works them open then disappears behind me. Every little move hurts my arms, but I don't make a sound as he picks the handcuffs.

I cry once the tension in my arms goes slack and the blood rushes to fill the spots that had been cut off.

Lennox doesn't ask me if I can stand.

Scooping me into his arms, he runs toward the exit, and I watch in horror over his shoulder.

The whole room looks like it's going to collapse any minute.

Sirens wail in the distance as Lennox bursts out of the building and into the evening air. I suck in a deep breath. It feels shockingly cold as it fills my lungs, and I start coughing to clear the sludge sitting in my airways.

The warehouse is an inferno on the outside. Flames lick up the sides and look as though they reach the sky from my point of view.

I rest my head against Lennox's shoulder and close my eyes.

I have no strength left to fight, but I don't have to. Lennox is here, and he's got me, and my body responds by surrendering to him and allowing him to take control.

"Holy shit, Sloane." I vaguely place Cole's voice as a vehicle pulls up beside us.

Lennox's chest vibrates as he speaks. "We're taking her to the house. Have the doctor meet us there."

A door opens, and Lennox climbs in, holding me in his arms. He doesn't let go for the whole ride home, and I drift in and out as I finally allow myself to let go.

The next time I open my eyes, I'm cradled in Lennox's arms, and he's sitting on the couch in the pool house while he combs his fingers through my hair.

I cough some more when I come to.

"Hey. There's someone here who's going to take a look at you."

I lift my head, looking around at all of the Saint brothers seated around me before my gaze lands on Cole. He's sitting on the coffee table in front of us, watching me closely and holding out a glass of water.

I take it, then smell the air, looking wearily at Cole. "You smell like a dumpster fire."

He chuckles. "Actually, that's you, Sunshine."

I glance down at my old clothes and sniff myself. "Oh, right." When I notice Ryder, I ask, "Where's Henry?" I sound panicked not because I'm worried about him, but because I don't want him to see me like this.

Ryder leans over, placing his hand on mine. "He's safe. He's out at Cole's place on Bainbridge Island with our mom. Amara and Harlow are with them."

"Cora, she—"

Dagen leans in. "She's safe too. Nyla—the woman from the bathroom—they're hiding out together."

Cole snickers again. "Yeah, man. I don't think you thought

that one through. You know Cora is going to talk shit about you the whole time they're out there, right?"

A flash of worry crosses Dagen's face before he tells Cole off, and I glance over to find Lennox smiling at their banter. He's never had an adult relationship with his brothers like this.

The look on his face is relaxed, like everything is right in his world.

Lennox smiles at me, then tells his brothers to give me some space as he shifts and sets me on the couch beside him. Waving over an older man standing off to the side of the room, he introduces him to me as a doctor before looking up at the guy. "Just give me an all clear for now because I'm putting her to bed."

The doctor begins by saying he'll need to run some tests, but Lennox stops him and says he can run all of the tests he wants when I wake up in the morning.

The moment the doctor relents, Lennox is on his feet and herding everyone out the door.

He's so stealth, I don't notice his approach until he speaks. "Can you stand?" He takes the cup of water away from me, then holds his hand between us to help me up.

When I reach out to take it, a pain stops me, and I rub at the pulled muscles in my shoulder. My arms weigh a ton.

Bending over me, he hooks an arm under my knees and another around my back to carry me into the bathroom.

My stench follows us in. So when Lennox helps me to stand on my own and tells me to get undressed, I don't hesitate. I go for my top first, but I'm unable to lift my arms all of the way up, so I turn my attention to my lower half.

I step out of my shoes and kick them to the far side of the room, then step on each sock to slide my feet out of them.

Lennox hovers nearby, looking ready to jump into action if I start tipping over.

I smell so bad.

"I must look awful." I take a tentative step toward the mirror above the sink, but Lennox stops me and walks me back to the toilet, putting the seat down.

"You're beautiful, Sloane," he whispers, grabbing a bath towel off the rack. "You're so fucking beautiful."

Unfolding the towel, he hands the edges of it to me, as if creating a wall between us. When I take it and hold it there, he asks if he can help me take off my clothes. His voice is low and restrained.

I nod.

Reaching behind the towel, his eyes stay on mine as he pulls my pants down, leaving my panties, then guides me back to sit on the toilet.

I drape the towel over my lap and let my arms sit limp on my thighs.

One by one, he guides each arm out of my sleeves, pausing each time I wince. Then he pulls it over my head, leaving me in my bra.

"Stay there. I'll be right back." He picks up all of my clothes, then leaves the room. When he returns, they're gone.

Sitting on the ledge of the oversized tub, he turns the water on and reaches for a bottle of bubble bath, adding a little to the water. When the scent of eucalyptus with a hint of citrus fills my nose, I take a second look at the bottle in his hands.

It smells like him.

But that isn't my bodywash. Then I remember Amara telling me it was Lennox who was staying here with Henry.

"You've been sleeping here."

He looks at me guiltily.

"I wanted to be close to you." Lennox stands, unbuttoning his pants and taking them off, along with his socks and shoes. Testing the water as the tub fills once more, he closes the distance between us and helps me up. "Let's get in."

He pulls me toward the bathtub, sucking in a sharp breath when the towel falls off my lap. Then he clears his throat and forces his attention away from my body.

I tug my hand back until he meets my eyes. "If you're getting in with me, I want you to take your shirt off."

He keeps one hand on me at all times while he undresses himself. He keeps his boxer briefs on, and I don't push it since he's made sure I'm wearing my underwear.

This isn't about anything more than care.

Coaxing me to the tub, he steps in first. Then he turns me so my back is to his front as he helps me sit.

His muscular legs wrap around each side of my body, and I release a sigh when the hot water works its way into my muscles.

Lennox waits until the tub is full before turning off the tap and reaching for my shampoo and a washcloth, handing me the cloth. "Here. I know you have some bruises, and I don't want to hurt you. I'll let you wash your face."

I plunge the cloth into the soapy water and wring it out before I take the first few swipes along my cheeks, forehead, and mouth. I move slowly, lowering my head to meet my hands instead of the other way around.

A combination of dirt and the wrong shade of foundation cake the cloth, and I plunge it into the water a second time.

Reclining his body, Lennox leans me back with him, and I briefly abandon my task when he pours a cup of water over my hair.

I moan out loud, and his chest reverberates with humor as he does it four more times, and I relax further into him. Then he works the shampoo into my hair, massaging my scalp, and it is the best thing I've felt in a while.

When he rinses my hair, he runs a small amount of conditioner through my strands. Then he surprises me when he takes extra care to comb my hair with his fingers. It takes me back to the times we spent together at Eros. Lennox was fierce, demanding, and possessive when he had me, but after, when he took care of me, it felt like I was his most treasured possession.

He doesn't say anything, and I sit in silence listening to the sounds of his breathing and the occasional splash of water.

When he finishes rinsing my hair, I prop my back against his front and slip my wet panties down my legs, tossing them onto the floor.

I sit up as Lennox freezes. Glancing at him over my shoulder, I ask, "Can you—um, undo my bra?"

There's no way I'm getting my hands all of the way back there.

He draws his fingers up my back and unhooks the clasp on the first try. I hunch forward, letting my straps slip down my arms, then I push the bra out of the tub. I won't be wearing that thing ever again.

Lifting the cloth, I twist the water out and start cleaning along my stomach. The water is turning dirty around us, and I steal nervous glances at Lennox over my shoulder. I would rather he do this, but I've turned into a giant chicken all of a sudden, and I don't ask.

He sits still behind me, allowing me to clean myself for a few seconds longer before the depth of the water drops as Lennox sits up, reaching for the cloth in my hands. He pulls me against him and settles us back in the tub with my breasts poking through what is left of the bubbles like two islands.

His hands work the cloth around my chest and over my abdomen, then between my legs. He shushes me when I attempt to finish cleaning myself and settles me when my body responds to his touch.

He pinches my nipple gently, and his deep voice in my ear sends shivers through me. "There will be time for this when you are healed, Peach."

Once he's satisfied I'm clean, he drops the cloth on the floor and pulls my head to his chest, languidly brushing his fingers along the curve of my breasts.

"I noticed the marks I gave you are gone." He kisses the top of my head.

I lift myself off him and turn over so I am facing him. The move sends a stabbing pain along my arms, but I fight through it.

Settling my front to his, I meet his eyes. "They're not gone." I point to my head. "They're in here"—then I point to my heart —"and here."

I've never seen Lennox cry, so I'm not sure if it's tears in his eyes or the water.

"I choose you, Peach."

I'm not prepared for the rush of emotion, and my own eyes sting as they fill with tears.

"I choose you, Nox."

He hugs me to him, and we stay with my head resting on his chest until I doze off.

It can't have been for long, as the water is still warm when he shifts again and I stir.

Lennox helps me out of the tub, then wraps me in an oversized towel before removing his wet boxer briefs and wrapping a towel around his waist.

Then I'm hoisted up and carried to my room. I stay where he sets me on the bed, too tired to adjust myself, and Lennox reaches to the nightstand for a plate.

"It's a jam sandwich and an apple. Henry told me this is your favorite breakfast. I want you to get something in your stomach before you go to sleep." He picks at the plastic wrap, then sets it on my lap and points at it. "Can I?"

I want to cry at the sight of the plate in front of me.

I did tell Henry this was my favorite once. I was trying to get him to eat his breakfast. The thing that guts me is how it looks. It's exactly the way I made it for him. The crusts have been removed from the sandwich, and the apple is peeled and sliced into "fries," which is what I called them to get him to eat.

Lennox has been spending time with Henry.

I swallow the lump in my throat and nod, allowing him to pick up half the sandwich and feed it to me before he reaches for a glass of water to wash it down.

I ask him some questions while he helps me eat the rest of the sandwich, but I stay away from the one person I don't want to talk about, and Lennox doesn't bring him up.

Lennox leaves the room as I take the final two bites on my own. When he returns, my water glass has been refilled, and he sets it on the nightstand along with a bottle of painkillers

"I'll get you something to sleep in."

Lennox doesn't falter, he doesn't look around. He walks over to my dresser and opens the second drawer from the bottom. He knows where everything is. My face warms as I glance over at the nightstand beside my bed, imagining my vibrator tucked neatly away.

He had to have seen *everything*.

That's how he found the letter I kept.

When I look up to him from the nightstand, he's watching me closely with a smirk on his face. His expression falls away when I clear my throat, asking, "Can I—um, sleep against your skin?"

Tossing my pajamas onto a chair, he circles to the other side of the bed, removes his towel, turns off the last light, and climbs in.

He pulls me into the middle of the bed with him, and I climb partially on top of his body.

There was a point tonight when I felt this was all slipping away.

There was a point when I gave up.

But Lennox never gave up on me, and that's the only reason I'm still here.

I close my eyes to try to settle my mind, but images of my last week flash through my head. Reminders of Sebastian and everything he said and did.

"He told me he killed my mom." The room is quiet, so my whisper is definitely heard.

Lennox tenses under me.

"I'm so sorry, Sloane."

I don't feel safe.

I will never feel safe until Sebastian is dead.

"I need to know what happened to him."

My body rises as Lennox takes a deep breath in the dark. "I was faced with a choice to stop him or save you, and I chose you. Sebastian will pay for what he's done."

I rest my hand near my head. The sound and feel of his heartbeat is soothing.

"So he's still out there?" My heart sinks knowing none of us are safe.

Lennox combs his fingers through the strands in my hair before cupping his free hand over my bottom to hug me closer to his body.

Pressing his lips to the top of my head, he takes a deep breath, smelling my hair.

"I didn't say he got away."

36

LENNOX

Once we finally closed our eyes, we managed to sleep for a few hours. Then Sloane woke up coughing in the middle of the night, and neither of us could doze off again.

We stayed in bed, naked and holding each other while she told me what she learned about her mother from Cora, along with how Sebastian told her he killed her. She told me a little more about when she was locked up for the week and about her time with Creed and his men.

I owe Creed a debt for doing everything he could for her, but I know he didn't do it for me. She grew on him just like she grows on everyone.

Sloane asked about Henry again.

His group on Bainbridge Island will stay out there for a few more days so Sloane can get accustomed to being at home before seeing her son. It was a decision I made, and she fought me on it at first. She held firm until she used the washroom and caught a glimpse of the bruises on her face in the mirror.

Then Sloane shut down and I recognized her withdrawal

immediately. It's the same thing I did twenty years ago, the night I got home from shooting a man for the first time.

I still don't know his name.

The moment I pulled the trigger, I shut myself away. I built up my defenses, and I pushed everything good to a comfortable distance so I wouldn't drag anyone I loved down with me. I told myself I was doing it to protect them, but it isn't entirely true. I did it so they couldn't get close enough to see how broken I was.

How could anyone love a monster?

Only, looking at Sloane now, I realize I wasn't damaged.

Sloane loved me through my worst; she believed in me when there was nothing good to see, and she sensed me with her soul. Her fierce heart destroyed my walls, and she dug through the wreckage looking for the man she knew, without a doubt, was lost inside.

So when I saw her start to shut down, that little boy inside of me fractured.

I broke her down before she could firmly close herself off to the reality of our situation. I challenged her to stay here with me in our hell, because we are so close to breaking free from it. I told her there was no shame in crying, there was no shame in being scared or scarred. There was no shame in falling apart. I told her I would let her break, but I would always be here to hold on to every single piece of her, because she was mine, and I would never let her stay broken.

Then I held her while she cried.

Sloane is a fighter.

We will heal, and we will all grow stronger together.

Nyla and Cora arrived at the house in the middle of the night. They weren't supposed to be here until later in the day, but as soon as Cora heard Sloane was safe, she insisted they drive back immediately.

Now they are sitting in the dining room. Our cook and

serving staff won't arrive for a few more hours, but Cora managed to take over the kitchen and whip up some coffee and breakfast.

The smells woke the rest of the house, and my brothers joined us one by one until we had a full table at four in the morning.

Cole takes a bite and groans, rubbing his stomach. "Damn, Cora, this is delicious. Maybe you should just move in here."

Everyone around the table agrees as knives and forks clatter against plates. Cora waves them off, but I catch her little grin when everyone looks away.

When Cora first approached me asking to leave Seattle, I knew it was my father she wanted to get away from. She doesn't have any family, and she seemed to enjoy her position in Cole's restaurant, but watching her here with Sloane and my brothers makes me realize that she considers them her family.

"Maybe you should." I take a sip of my coffee as everyone stills and looks at me. I shrug my shoulders. "Why not? It would be a full-time position—live-in." I glance around the table at my brothers. "It's more than just us now." I raise my hand and gesture toward Sloane and Nyla. "There are others, and kids to think about. We need someone to help our mother manage this household. Someone who doesn't take shit when they shouldn't."

My brothers look back to Cora, who is staring at me with her mouth hanging open.

We might not have always seen eye to eye, but Cora has always been there for us. She's the one who came to me when she heard that Cole was going to be killed, and she put her life on the line when she escaped Sebastian to tell us where Sloane was being held.

There is no one better qualified to look after our growing family than her.

One by one, my brothers look back at me and nod, but Dagen adds, "I'm in, but she's not allowed to mess with my food." They exchange a look with each other as he takes a sip of his coffee.

She smiles. "I've never done anything—to your food." She glances at the cup in his hand, and Dagen follows her unspoken threat as he sets his coffee down and slides it away from him, muttering, "Old bat."

To which she mutters right back, "Little shit," and Cole snorts into his coffee mug.

When Cora looks at me curiously, I end the conversation. "It's settled, Cora. You belong with us." She opens her mouth to say something but chokes on her words before nodding. Then she clears some plates, taking them into the kitchen.

She'll tell me later if she truly does not wish to be here, but in my life, I've never seen her tear up, so I imagine this is exactly where she wants to be.

Sloane sat quietly through the whole meal. I watched her out of the corner of my eye as she simply absorbed the room around her, smiling now and then. It will take some time for her to settle into her life and to trust that it will always be here for her, but I'll be there with her every step of the way.

My phone vibrates in my pocket. I lean back in my seat and hold it under the table, checking the message.

It's the one I've been waiting for.

Creed: We've got him.

When I met with Creed in the building where Sloane was held, I created a debt when I asked for his help. It's an open ticket for him to hold on to if he should ever need something from me.

Even though the results of this debt will ultimately ensure

his rise to the head of his syndicate, it is still asking a lot of the man who wanted to be the one to end Sebastian's life.

When we surrounded the warehouse last night, I sent Cole and Dagen to help Creed in exchange for Ghost shadowing me with one goal: as soon as he had eyes on Sebastian, he was to make sure he was captured and brought to me.

I knew Sebastian wouldn't give me the chance to get near him, and he didn't.

Ghost works in the shadows.

I was always going to choose Sloane, but knowing that Ghost was out there somewhere made it an easier pill to swallow. I had to trust him to pick up Sebastian, then I had to trust Creed to deliver him to me alive.

Sloane and Nyla are sitting together talking when I look up. Ryder is immersed in something on his phone, and Dagen is eating his second helping of food. Cole is the only one who is watching me closely while he drinks his coffee.

I push my chair back and drag my hand over the scruff of hair at my jawline. "I just heard from Creed. We have some business to finish."

The room slips into a brief moment of silence before more chairs are pushed out and my brothers rise.

I circle the table to Sloane. She looks up at me warily but doesn't ask.

Cupping the back of her head, I lean over and kiss her. She tastes like the berry muffin she's been picking at. "I'll be back soon. Nyla and Cora are with you."

Nyla stands, pulls Dagen into her for a kiss, then tells him to be safe.

We've all been stuck in limbo because of our father. Ryder and Amara haven't been able to officially announce or publicly enjoy their marriage. Cole and Harlow have been hiding away, and Dagen hasn't met his own daughter yet, and it's all because of one man.

This ends today.

The early hours of the morning have always been my favorite time of day. The air outside is crisp, and the streets are quiet as we casually get into my car. We drive in silence as we all contemplate what this moment means for each of us.

Retribution, freedom, vengeance, peace. It means all of those things to me and more. With this, I'll close this chapter of my life. I want to think that I'd burn my whole damn book, but there are lessons and outcomes that came from every single word in my story that I wouldn't sacrifice, even for the chance at an easier go of it.

I am who I am for a reason.

***

The sun won't rise for another hour.

The smell of smoke hangs heavily in the air around the docks hours after the fires have been extinguished. Even from the far side of the wharf, the combined scent of sea air and bonfire wafts in when the wind blows in the right direction.

Dagen takes a deep breath, glancing over his shoulder in the direction where it all went down. He smells it too.

Ghost steps out of the shadows along the side of a building, and I meet him halfway, my brothers falling in behind me.

Ghost makes eye contact. "Weapons?" Then he looks at each of my brothers, and we all shake our heads.

I may have requested to be the one to kill Sebastian, but I have to do it on Creed's terms and with Elia's gun.

"Were there any problems?"

Ghost tips his chin to all of us then shakes his head.

"Sebastian thought he'd made it. Had one foot on a boat when I grabbed him."

"And Nostra?"

"They've been agreeable since we picked up their property. Darius says he's looking forward to giving her back to them. Pretty boy is sporting a nice shiner because of her." He taps his cheek below his left eye. "Personally, I think he's found his new kink." It's rare to see Creed's second crack a joke, much less a smile.

Ghost doesn't continue the conversation. Instead, he turns and walks toward a building. I trail close behind with my brothers following.

The stench in the room turns my stomach on the first inhale.

Creed stands off to the side of the room, while Sebastian kneels in the middle with a sack over his head and his hands bound behind his back, the way he made so many men kneel for him.

It's fitting, really.

So is the location.

"It reeks in here." When Ryder speaks, Sebastian perks up, tilting his head to try to listen better.

I've never seen my father with a speck of dirt on him, yet here he is kneeling and covered in it.

I don't prolong the suspense.

Crossing to stand in front of Sebastian, I pull the fabric off his face, and he blinks a few times before looking around to see if our choice of venue is suitable for him.

His soured look tells me it isn't.

Sebastian has always had an inflated sense of himself, and his lips thin into a grimace before he bares his teeth at me like an animal when he realizes that it is only us and Creed's little group. Not only that, but we're standing in the middle of our dumping ground. This is the central building for all of the trash that leaves the wharf.

Fitting.

"It looks like your alliance with the cartel broke down." My father's head snaps back toward me as I start talking. "Granted, Cole and Dagen did capture their leader, so it's hard to wave your big dick energy around when someone's got you by the balls."

Sebastian glares at my brothers before I step into his line of sight.

Reaching one arm behind me, I glance at Ryder, who steps forward and hands me a bottle. I hold it between us as I open it, and he scoffs at me.

"That's not my thing, boy."

Without looking up, I say, "I'm not you."

The top comes off with a *pop*.

Grabbing a fistful of his hair, I wrench his head back. When he opens his mouth to argue, I shove the bottle of rye in. Sebastian gurgles around the glass neck and splutters all over himself when I pull it out.

Then I take two steps back and pour it all over the floor in front of him with my three brothers standing a couple of steps behind me.

He understands the meaning.

It's bad luck to drink a dead man's drink.

"All of this for a whore, and she's not even your whore." Now he's taking cheap shots, trying to rub the lie that she chose Grayson in my face. "Look at you. You're pathetic." Sebastian spits.

I find my peace.

No matter what he says on his way out, his sentiment will never be accepted by anyone in this room, and wasting my anger reacting recklessly doesn't serve me at all.

Slipping an automatic knife out of my pocket, I crouch in front of Sebastian. Gripping his jaw in the palm of my hand, I dig my fingers into the sockets of his cheeks, forcing his pliable flesh through his teeth so his mouth opens, and the disgusting scent of his liquor makes me more nauseous than the garbage around us.

Holding the knife in front of his face, I flip the little tab, and the blade snaps open. His eyes go wide when he sees its full length, and I speak with a calm I haven't felt in a long time.

"Speak about her again, and I'll cut out your tongue while you're still alive and send you to the afterlife without a voice to beg for your soul."

For the first time in his miserable life, Sebastian flinches, but he recovers quickly.

I close my knife, secure it in my pocket, and stand.

"Not many of us have the luxury of knowing how our life will end. This is our gift to you." I extend an arm to my brothers, who are still standing around me.

We are in this together.

I circle him as I speak. "Later today, your lawyer will board a private plane under your name. As we speak, we have someone working on doctoring footage to show you leaving the country. Which is wise, by the way, because you will be wanted for questioning since William has effectively linked you to all of the crimes you tried to pin on us, and let me just tell you"—I pause, pointing to my three brothers, then I clutch at my chest—"we are shocked!"

He snarls at me when I mock outrage.

I'm not done.

Taking a threatening step toward him, I wait for him to look me in the eyes before I continue, "You'll die here—alone. No one will miss you. No one will mourn you. You will be forgotten. Nostra made a mistake by trying to align with you, but they've offered to make it up to us. They'll be by shortly to retrieve your body, and we've arranged to have you dumped in the middle of the ocean."

That is my gift to Sloane.

Creed and Ghost bear witness in silence.

"You won't kill me. You're weak." Spitting his words, Sebastian glares past me at each of my brothers. "None of you have it in you."

I don't respond.

My father devoted his life to pushing me and my brothers apart, and now I know why. It's because he knew, deep in his soul, that together we were stronger than he was.

I circle wide, and when I near Creed, he holds out the butt end of a gun. I take it as I casually walk around and stop behind my father's kneeling body.

I look at each of my brothers one last time.

When I look at Ryder, he crosses his arms and shakes his head.

When I look at Cole, he rubs his palms together in front of his chest and shakes his head.

When I lock eyes with Dagen, he takes a half step to Cole, puts a hand on his shoulder, and shakes his head.

We are in agreement.

There is nothing left to say, except—

I crouch behind him and get close to his ear, lowering my voice so only he can hear me. When I'm sure I have his attention, I let my demons loose.

"You should be proud—you created a monster. I'm just not your monster. I belong to Sloane and Henry."

His body goes rigid as I stand.

He knows the repercussions of his choices have returned to claim their pound of flesh.

Then I raise the gun to the back of Sebastian's head, and I pull the trigger.

Click.

The anticlimactic snick of the gun is overshadowed by my father breaking down into panicked sobs as he hunches over.

My surprise matches the expressions on all of my brothers' faces as we stand in silence, witnessing the man we've all come to fear losing his shit in front of us.

Granted, he thought he only had to hold on to his arrogance until the gun went off, and he was betting he wouldn't be alive for this part.

He shouldn't be alive for this part.

I scowl at Creed.

He knew the gun he handed me wasn't loaded.

I should have noticed, but my heightened emotions have blurred my senses.

Creed steps to Sebastian's body, which is now curled up in the fetal position, and wedges his boot under his body, silently telling him to get back in position. Sebastian rolls his weight over his knees and lifts himself up, which isn't an easy task with his hands still bound behind him.

His pride gone, Sebastian refuses to look up at any of us.

I glance at the empty gun in my hand. "What's this about?"

Creed pulls his phone out and taps at the screen before squaring himself on the four of us.

"I was fine to let you kill him, I really was, but—"

"But what? We had a deal." I kill our father in exchange for Sloane.

Creed nods remorsefully. "We did—but I got an offer I'm bound to honor."

I open my mouth to ask who could possibly offer him more than I could. Then the door creaks open, drawing all of our attention to the front of the room.

Darius pokes his head in, scanning the room before nodding at Creed. He enters, then steps aside, allowing room for another person to join us.

The name is spoken in unison as my brothers see her at the same time I do.

"Sloane?"

37

SLOANE

Lennox turns to leave, and his brothers file out after him with Nyla and Dagen bringing up the rear.

"I'm going to get some sleep," Nyla says. She glances back at us, and Cora and I nod in unison.

Sleep is one thing we all desperately need right now.

As soon as everyone clears the room, I meet Cora's eyes as I pull the temporary phone out of my pocket and cradle it in my hands. "Can you get me in touch with Creed?" I don't have my phone with his number programmed into it.

Cora glances at the door before tensely dragging her palms down the apron she put on earlier. She levels me with a glare as she steps to the table, holding out her hand, and I set the smartphone in her palm.

She knows I'm up to something, and I can tell by the way her fingers hesitate over the phone that she isn't sure if she should support me or try to interfere.

As she taps the screen, I stretch out my arms. The tendons in my shoulders and back ache, bringing the memory of my captivity to the forefront with each jolt of pain.

I can't get the stain on the warehouse floor out of my head. Sebastian left me there to stare at the spot where Grayson died, and I painstakingly committed every inch of it to memory before he tried to burn me alive.

"I'm with Sloane—she wishes to speak to Creed. No, now. Put her through." Cora doesn't wait for any objections; she hands me the phone, and I put it to my ear.

There's silence on the line, and I look up at Cora, wondering if the person on the other end of the line hung up. But then the phone clicks, and Creed answers.

"Sloane?"

"I—yes, um. Lennox just left. Is he coming to you?"

There's a pause before, "He is."

"Do you have Sebastian?" The tight expression on Cora's face falls when I say his name.

Creed exhales a deep breath, and my leg starts bouncing nervously under the table as I force myself to wait for his response. "I do."

"He's mine."

"Sloane—"

"By rights, Sebastian is mine, Creed."

The line goes quiet.

This feels like a game, and I sense Creed has a good idea what my next move is going to be, so he's stalling for time to think.

Cora pulls a chair out from the table and drops her weight onto it.

"Lennox is already on his way here to finish everything. I saw where they kept you. You have nothing to prove to any of us, and anyone who says differently will answer to me."

I appreciate what Creed is trying to do for me, but that's not what this is about.

My palms turn sweaty as I remember the reverence in

Creed's words when he ordered his men to stand and show respect for Elia's blood.

I take my shot.

"Creed, I'm asking—no, I'm telling you, as Elia's heir: I'm laying claim to the death of Sebastian Saint. He's mine to end."

Creed swears on his exhale.

It goes deeper than retribution for Elia Lucciano, but none of my other reasons carry the same weight for Creed and his men.

Sebastian killed my mother, he murdered Grayson, he would have killed Cora, he took Lennox away from me, and he tried to have Henry kidnapped. He's hurt everyone I love, and we are all forever damaged by his hand.

"Can you send someone for me?"

Creed's resigned groan is the only confirmation he is still on the line until he says, "Scout asked to watch over you until this was sorted. He's about five minutes away."

His words surprise me, but I don't dwell on it.

"What's his number? I'll message him once I clear the front gate."

Yuri is still out on Bainbridge Island with Henry, so security might be easy to get around. I knew of one undetectable way off the property before, and I'm hoping it hasn't been found. Although I'm sure once I pull this stunt, Lennox is going to circle the perimeter himself to lock it all down—right after he deals with my disobedience.

The thought makes me shudder.

When I hang up, Cora leans back in her chair and crosses her arms.

"Don't say it. I'm not on the fence, Cora. There is no doubt in my heart that I am going to do this."

"You are your mother's daughter. I wasn't going to say anything except I'm coming with you. Those boys will forgive me for letting you go, but they will never forgive me for letting you go alone." Then she lowers her voice, as though admitting the next part is difficult for her. "And I really want the job Lennox just offered me."

"I won't be alone, I'll be with Creed's men. Besides, I need a distraction at the front gate. I just need their eyes off the cameras for a minute." I'm hopeful that Lennox hasn't had the time to go over every camera's footage and see the whole path I took off their property last time.

Cora pushes her chair back from the table and stands. "Well then, it's a good thing I have fresh muffins in the kitchen, now isn't it?"

The crisp morning air wakes me up as I stand along the side of the road, partially hidden by some bushes. A couple of cars have already gone by—none of them Scout, so I decide to stay put until someone comes to a complete stop.

If one of our security guys happens to drive by, they'll pull me back and message Lennox, then my chance will be gone.

I've been replaying my thoughts since the moment Lennox got the text from Creed. In the span of a few seconds, determination settled into my bones.

How easy would it be to sit back and have Lennox damn his soul further to shield me? What's one more sin to weigh you down when you've already fallen so far from grace?

I don't have the answer.

All I know in my heart is: this cross is mine to bear. It feels like nobody will heal properly if it isn't me who ends Sebastian's life. Maybe it's my broken heart making excuses. Maybe it's my rage demanding vengeance. I've been obsessed with finding justice for Grayson, and the reasons for wanting to kill Sebastian Saint just keep piling on.

I loved two men.

I still do.

Sebastian took both of them away from me.

I lived in fear of why Grayson was killed and what that would mean for Henry. Then I learned the truth, and in the end it didn't kill me. It kicked the ever-loving shit out of me, but I'm still here, and I'm not afraid anymore.

I'm pissed.

"Come out, come out, wherever you are." Scout's low, melodic taunt startles me from my thoughts, and the leaves jostle as I step out from my hiding spot and meet him under a streetlight at his car.

His smile turns to shock as he opens the driver's door, not wasting any time.

"You look like hell, Lucciano." Scout scans my face, his eyebrows pinched together in concern, and I run my fingers along my cheek.

He starts the car and pulls onto the quiet road.

"It's not as bad as it looks." Then I lean forward, examining his face. "Was that Sebastian's guys?"

Scout winces and shakes his head with a chuckle as he points to his own bruise. "No. That is from a batshit crazy housewife with too much time on her hands. She's a real hot mess—emphasis on mess." Then he murmurs, "And hot."

After a few minutes, he breaks the silence we comfortably slipped into. "You really going to do this?"

For someone who went her whole life without any siblings, it feels like I have an abundance of older brothers watching over me.

I consider his question for a minute longer.

"I didn't kill Ratchet."

He doesn't look at me when he says, "I know."

"Creed told you?"

He's already shaking his head. "No." He waits until he's stopped at the next light before turning to look at me. "That's not who you are, Sloane. Any sane person can see you aren't in your element. We're trying to help you navigate your way through our world because we are loyal to Elia, and you've earned our respect. You're doing your best with the hand you've been dealt."

That's a lot to unpack, and I will, but now is not the time. Instead, I focus on one piece of the puzzle.

"That may not be who I was, but I think it's who I am." I lower my attention from the road to my fingers in my lap as I fidget. "Not sure if that makes sense. Nothing makes sense right now."

Scout stops the car. I look up to see where we are, and I'm surprised when he turns the car off, pulls his phone out of his pocket, and sends off a message.

We're here.

"It will make sense again." He shifts in his seat and angles his body to mine. "When you feel chaotic and out of control, it just means you're growing beyond the limitations you set for yourself. You're taking these new experiences and adding them to your life story, and you're using them to evolve into something new. The uncertainty, doubt, and vulnerability that come with it suck, but I have a feeling your transformation will be legendary."

He swivels his head toward one of the buildings, then takes a deep breath and looks back at me. "You ready?"

My stomach twists when I step into the room and meet Lennox's gaze. His eyes warily scan my face, and a mixture of confusion and hurt soften his expression as he says my name.

Lennox stands over Sebastian's cowering form with a gun in his hand, and he freezes in place for a moment before snapping out of it, tucking the gun into his pants, and taking a step toward me.

"Why are you here?" Lennox's attention flits from me to Creed. His features harden as they land on him in silent accusation, and Creed takes a step back, raising his hands.

I point at Sebastian. "I'm here for him."

Sebastian snarls, showing his teeth, and glares at me. "I'm not kneeling for a Lucciano bitch."

Lennox turns on him, lifting his hand as though he's ready to strike, and I raise my voice.

"Enough!" The men watch me as I close the distance to Creed, holding out my hand as Sebastian struggles to stand up.

"This one is loaded," Creed warns with a lowered voice as he hands me the butt end of a gun. I turn, taking two steps toward Sebastian just as he gets one foot out from under him and on the ground.

I aim for his knee and shoot.

The bullet barrels into his thigh, and his high-pitched yell makes everyone flinch as he returns to the ground where he belongs.

"I beg to differ. You can try to stand up again, but you only have one good leg left." I lift my gun and wave it between us. "I have more than one bullet."

"You c—" Sebastian's words die on his tongue as Lennox takes a step toward him.

I keep my body squared on Sebastian but sneak a glance at Ryder, Cole, and Dagen as they watch everything unfold.

There isn't anyone in this room who wouldn't kill Sebastian

themselves. Ryder is my closest friend, and he looks the most concerned when he meets my eyes. I pinch my lips in a tight smile, and he nods in support.

Cole and Dagen stand side by side to witness their father's last moments, neither showing any signs of doubt for what we all know is coming.

I rack my brain to come up with some parting words, my last fuck-you to Sebastian for destroying countless lives.

I can't think of a damn thing. Not one word I want to say, because he doesn't deserve to hear the names of everyone he's taken from us.

Lennox takes advantage of the break to approach me. He leans in and whispers, "You don't have to do this."

I know I don't *have* to do this.

Any of the men standing in this room would do this for me, which is exactly why I lift the gun without warning, aim it at Sebastian, and pull the trigger.

The loud pop of the gun rattles through my rib cage, sending zaps of electricity down my arms as Sebastian tilts back and timbers over, bouncing once on the ground.

It takes Lennox a split second to react. He lunges for me, yanking the gun out of my hands and pulling me hard into his body, wrapping his arms around me as if he can shield me from the effects of what just happened.

I nuzzle my face against his chest, and he furiously kisses the top of my head while combing his fingers through my hair. His body trembles around me, and I bury my hands into his shirt around his midsection, holding him just as close.

"I'm not going to break, Nox."

He holds me at arm's length, as though he's trying to decide for himself.

Ryder says something from behind me, and Lennox nods

once. When I look over my shoulder, Ryder, Cole, and Dagen are walking out of the room.

"We'll give you a minute." Creed approaches us, and Lennox hands him his gun.

When he turns to leave with Ghost and Scout, I stop him.

"We're not done here."

All three of the men stop walking. Ghost and Scout look at Creed and wait for him to turn back to us before they do the same.

He pauses for half a second before slowly asking, "How so?"

His tone is cautious, a warning to tread lightly.

I take a deep breath and give Lennox a squeeze before I let him go and step away.

"You promised my heart for Sebastian's life. You made that deal with Lennox. I was there when you agreed."

Creed sizes me up for a tense minute before crossing his arms. "And?" He draws out the word with a hint of interest in his tone.

"And I want that deal." I don't dare glance at Lennox as I speak, but I sense him tensing up from where I stand.

Ghost sucks in a deep breath and shakes his head as a smirk stretches across Scout's lips.

I lay down my terms. "Sebastian's life for my own. As Elia's heir, I support your bid as his successor. I've ended Sebastian's life; my heart is my own. You'll cut me and Henry loose." When Creed takes a little too long to answer, I stand tall and hold out my hand. "Give me a knife. I'm willing to make it his head for my heart as per the original terms if that's what it takes." My stomach mutinies at the thought. I hope it doesn't come to that.

Ghost whistles under his breath.

"Give us a minute." Creed looks at his men, and they both nod before shooting me a sly glance and leaving.

When the door finally closes the three of us in, Creed looks from Lennox to me before saying, "Done. But it will take time. You know you will never be absolutely free from this, but I can distance you and Henry enough that you will never be obligated to my organization the way you would have been to Elia's, but you will always have our protection."

"I know. Thank you, Creed."

His face breaks into a soft smile when he exhales, and he takes a step away from us and toward the door. "We'll talk soon."

Lennox has been silent since I claimed myself, and I feel his fears as though they are my own.

His voice is weathered with hurt. "You shot him so I couldn't claim you?" His raw emotions make my heart ache.

"No. I shot him so *we* could claim *each other*. I could never be yours like that. You know me. I'm not a possession to be given. I very literally killed so I could claw back my own personhood, because I want you to know, without a shadow of a doubt, that *I* am the one who is giving myself to you, Nox. With my free heart, body, mind, and soul, I choose you."

THE END...FOR NOW

In short, I am not done with the Saints. Or rather, I should say: the Saints are not done with me or any of you. I feel it.

I have a list of projects, and among them, Creed and his men are clamouring to have their own standalone stories heard, so everyone will be back at some point.

If you want to know when my next books are out, you have a variety of options to stay informed. You can follow me on BookBub or Amazon, you can follow any of my social networks that fit you best, or you can sign up for my newsletter and get a free copy of my short novelette titled **Needy** (which is the prequel to one of those projects I mentioned above). All of these options can be found at LunaKayne.com.

Well look at me yammering on when I should be writing.

Here's to the next adventure ;)

ACKNOWLEDGMENTS

A year earlier, I set out to write a complete series, and here we are.

First and foremost, I want to thank my daughters. They have been my cheerleaders—even though they aren't allowed to read my books yet.

Writing an entire series before publishing any of the books has been quite the adventure and I'm grateful to my family for their support and encouragement even though they are never completely sure of what it is that I do (in all fairness, neither am I some days).

Thank you for picking up the first book and sticking with me until the end of this saga. I can't wait for the next adventure.

I want to thank everyone who helped me bring this book to life:

Cover design: Kirsty Still (Pretty Little Design Co.)
Editor: Caroline Knecht
Photographer: Wander Aguiar
Cover Model: Clayton Wells

Until next time...

ABOUT LUNA

Luna Kayne is a multi-genre romance author located in Canada. She writes dark, explicit, romantic suspense with a hint of humor and angst. Her men are dominant and often stubborn, and her women are usually underestimated. As for tropes and sub-genres, nothing is off the table.

In 2021, she won an IPPY (Independent Publisher Book Awards) award with her novel, *Step Darkly* which earned a bronze medal.

Luna Kayne is the pen name of author *Sheri Landry* who writes non-romance action thrillers and has won awards for her writing under both names.

You can learn more at LunaKayne.com.

facebook.com/LunaKayne

twitter.com/LunaKayne

instagram.com/LunaKayne

tiktok.com/@luna.kayne

bookbub.com/profile/luna-kayne